COPYRIGHT

REVIEWS

He Completes Me by Cardeno C.: The author did an outstanding job writing the story through Zach's perspective. Zach is truly a wickedly funny, outrageous and lovable character and I thoroughly enjoyed reading the story through his eyes. He Completes Me has earned a permanent spot on my keeper shelf.

— *Night Owl Reviews (Top Pick)*

Home Again by Cardeno C.: Home Again is a very well-written love story between two amazing heroes that live and breathe off of the written page. It's earned a spot on my keeper shelf where I know I'll re-read it many, many times again... If you are looking for an emotionally driven novel that will leave you with a smile on your face, then Home Again is definitely the book for you. Highly Recommended!

— *Top2Bottom Reviews*

Just What the Truth Is by Cardeno C.: Humorous, heartfelt, sexy romance full of great characters.... This is a sexy and emotional romance between Ben and Micah. Ben's inexperience with gay sex is simultaneously humorous, emotive and hot. These two men make sex fun but have a relationship based on friendship that I could see as a reader. The characters were given time to develop along with the romance.

— *The Book Vixen*

Love at First Sight by Cardeno C.: This was a true pleasure to read... again... for the third time... This is a beautiful, sweet love story that warms your heart and makes you want more. If you want love, romance (with hot sex thrown in) and a happy ever after... then this is for you.

— *MM Good Book Reviews*

The One Who Saves Me by Cardeno C.: The One Who Saves Me is a beautiful story that is wonderfully created and written. A story of unlikely friends that love, adore, and protect one another. It's a journey of two men on a search for the perfect mate, not realizing he was standing by the other's side the entire time. It's a fantastic story of ups and downs, joys and tears. I highly recommend The One Who Saves Me. I adore this series and look forward to reading more in the near future.

— *Joyfully Jay*

Where He Ends and I Begin by Cardeno C.: Wow, these are some amazing men! ... Watching Nate and Jake work through their insecurities to finally find what they never dreamed to have was unreal. The whole story just worked for me and it really reminded me that if there were more loving and tolerant people in the world as portrayed in this story, perhaps so much evil would no longer occur. Thank you, Cardeno, for an unbelievably gorgeous book of the kind of love that lasts from cradle to grave.

— *Rainbow Book Reviews*

DEDICATION

With this book, I say good-bye to the Home series. Just writing that sentence brings tears to my eyes. This is the first series I wrote; it contains the first book I wrote, and I love these characters. But it's time to leave Emile City.

I've had the great honor and pleasure of getting to know wonderful people through my work as a writer, and that started with the Home books.

Mary Calmes, I remember starting the process of writing this book with an air conditioner in front of me and you behind me. Thanks for having my back with this one and with the others.

Kelly Shorten and Jae Ashley, thank you for jumping into this project with me and helping me through it.

And to the generous, kind, loyal readers who are my reason for writing, thank you for loving these characters right along with me. I hope I made you smile.

CHAPTER ONE

Grant us long life.
A life of peace.
A life of goodness.
A life of blessing.
A life of strength and health.
A life of piety.
A life free of shame and reproach.
A life full of love of Torah.
A life in which all our hearts' desires
for goodness are fulfilled.

Judith and Tobias Roberts
and
Lawrence and Natalie Hines
invite you to share in the
union of their children
Lauren and Gregg
Sunday, June 17, 2001 at noon.

Seth Cohen

TWENTY-SEVEN. THAT'S how old I was when we met. Well, it was how old I was when meeting meant something. No. It was how old I was when meeting meant something to *me*. Never mind. That'll all become clear.

The point is that at that time in my life, I thought I was straight. Typically, when you say you thought you were straight until [insert-anything], the first question is, "How old were you when [insert-anything] happened?" with a chaser of "How could you not know you were gay before that?" It's a fair question, because I think most gay people do know before they hit their late twenties. But for me, Eli Block was the first guy to ever hold my attention. Not the first to grab it, mind you, just the first to capture it and hold on. That said, women hadn't ever held my attention for all that long either.

I had hormones just like everyone else, and looking back on it, my head had been turned by some men along the way, but women had caught my eye, too, so I'd just assumed that was typical, that it didn't mean anything. Well, that's what I would have assumed if I had ever stopped to analyze it, which I hadn't. Romantic entanglements weren't high on my priority list, which is to say they weren't on the list at all. My whole focus until that point had been on school and temple life.

I'd had girlfriends—one in high school, one in college, one during the two years I'd spent in Israel as part of my rabbinic training—and though every one of those relationships had lasted for multiple years, none of them had ever been serious. At least not if serious is defined as a feeling that stays front and center in your head and in your chest, even when the subject of that feeling isn't staring you in the face.

So I was a serious guy who had never seriously fallen for anyone. And then Eli ran up.

He was holding a skateboard.

His hair was too long.

His jeans were too fitted.

His shirt was nonexistent.

He was my boss's son.

He was way too young.

And he was a he.

So I ignored the obvious. Well, I tried to ignore it. As it turned out, ignoring anything having to do with Eli Block was impossible. At least for me. But it took me a long time to understand exactly what my feelings for him meant and how rare they were, how important.

"RABBI BLOCK, I want to thank you again for giving me this opportunity," I said as I reached out my hand. "I'm really excited to join the congregation and train under you."

He shook my hand and patted my shoulder before leading me into the living room. "We're colleagues now, Seth. You can call me Avi. And between learning at your father's knee and graduating first in your class from HUC, I doubt you'll need all that much training."

Following in my father's and older brother Jed's footsteps, I had attended Hebrew Union College and become a rabbi. Although they both lived in California, the community was small enough that Avi knew my father pretty well, and he'd met my brother several times too, even though Jed had only been in the rabbinate for five years.

"Don't forget his youth work," the rabbi's wife said as she approached. "The folks at Camp Ahava were miserable when you got too busy with rabbinical school to work for them."

I dipped my head and felt my cheeks warm. "Hi, Mrs. Block. It's good to see you again."

"You can call me Meredith, Seth." She kissed my cheek and then wiped off what I presumed was a smidge of lipstick. "Sit down." She tilted her head toward the sofa.

I lowered myself onto the cushion, and Meredith sat next to me while Avi settled into the armchair across from us.

"How's your mother?" Meredith asked.

"She's doing well. She wanted me to tell you hello."

"I'll call her later," she said with a sharp dip of her chin. "I'll let her know you look good and tell her we'll make sure you get settled in well."

The phone call wasn't necessary. Not because I was a grown man and hadn't lived with my parents since I was eighteen, but because I talked to my mother almost every day. One year during finals, I had been too busy to return her calls for close to a week. When I finally called, she answered the phone with a pointed, "I'm dead." I never went that long without making contact again. It wasn't worth the guilt trip.

"Thanks, Mrs. Bl—" She arched one eyebrow, and I changed course midword. "Meredith."

She patted my shoulder. "What do you have on deck for Seth's first day?" she asked her husband.

"We'll chat a little right now and then tomorrow we'll—"

"Mom!"

Meredith stood and Avi turned toward the door.

"Mom!"

"In here, Eli," Meredith said.

Loud, fast footsteps sounded along with, "What's for dinner? I'm starv—"

The words stopped the instant Eli Block turned the corner. He came to a skidding halt. Literally. His shoes actually made a skidding sound on the wood floor. He was holding a skateboard in his right hand, and he slammed his left one against the wall, presumably to support himself.

His hair hung in his face, and I noticed it was brown, like mine. But where my hair was curly, his was straight. When he moved his left hand up to his forehead and pushed back the curtain of hair, I noticed another difference: his eyes were green, not like my boring brown, and they were huge. My breath caught for a moment, and I had to remind myself to breathe.

"Seth," he panted, his voice surprisingly deep for a person who looked so very young. It wasn't his height—he was maybe a couple of inches shorter than my own five foot ten—but he was trim with a hairless chest (which I could see because he wasn't wearing a shirt) and skinny legs (which I could tell because his jeans were unreasonably tight), but most of all, it was his face: those big eyes, the rosy cheeks, the perfectly smooth ivory skin.

Beautiful. That was the thought that slammed into

my head. It was so sudden and strong I couldn't stop it from taking root. So I squirmed uncomfortably in my seat and darted my gaze around, wondering if Avi and Meredith could sense my inappropriately lustful thoughts about their son.

"Eli," Meredith said, holding her arm out toward him. "You remember Seth Cohen from Camp Ahava, don't you?"

Eli's gaze was glued on me. Without looking up at his mother, he said, "Remember him?" He let go of his board, and it clunked on the ground. "I still dream about him."

My jaw dropped and I felt all the blood drain from my face. I jerked my head toward Avi, expecting to see anger or shock but instead he had his PalmPilot out and he was tapping at the keys.

"Eli," Meredith sighed. "Please don't embarrass Seth. He just got here."

"I'm not embarrassing him," Eli said as he marched over to me. "Embarrassing would be talking about what kinds of dreams they are."

I suddenly felt like I was choking on nothing. An odd sound left my body, and then I gasped for air.

"Eli!" Meredith snapped in warning. It was impressive, actually, how she could say his name and make it sound like so many different things.

"What, Mom?" He looked back over his shoulder at her but didn't deviate from his path toward me. "I didn't say they were dirty dreams." He turned his head back around and locked his gaze with mine. "But they were."

I started coughing. I mean, hack-up-a-lung coughing. My brain was swimming, trying to process everything going on, and I bent over, trying to catch my breath.

"I don't... We didn't..." I couldn't get enough oxygen in my brain to complete a thought or say the words. I had a vague recollection of Eli Block as a kid in the summer camp where I used to work. But I hadn't been there in five years and I didn't recall any meaningful interactions with him, let alone any that could have led to *dreams*.

"Eli!" Avi snapped, finally looking up from his PalmPilot. "You can't upset Seth this way. He's here to work, not to deal with your childhood crush. You're eighteen now. Start acting like an adult." He looked at me. "Ignore him, Seth. He's an only child, so we indulged him too much and now..." He shook his head and sighed. Then he bent his forearms over his knees and focused his attention on me. "Tomorrow we have a wedding where two members of the congregation are getting married. I'll officiate and you can watch and meet some of the members. The bride is..."

It was impossible to concentrate on Avi's words. For starters, I was confused about Eli's shamelessly blunt comments and his parents' nonchalant reaction. Also, he had finally reached me and seated himself right next to me on the couch. And by that I mean I was scooted all the way in the corner, wedged between the arm and him. He had one leg tucked underneath his backside with his thigh pressed to mine, and he was twisted so he was looking right at me.

He was so close I could smell him—a little sweaty, but not in a way I found offensive. I put my hands on my lap to hide exactly how not offensive it was.

"I have pictures of you," Eli said quietly. When I didn't answer, he elaborated. "I took a bunch every chance I got, but they never came out right."

"Eli, come help me in the kitchen," Meredith said.

He ignored her and somehow managed to get even closer to me. "You're even hotter now than you were then," he said wistfully and then sighed loudly.

I must have looked petrified, because Avi frowned, threw his arm out, pointing toward the kitchen, and said, "Go!"

"But—"

"Eli Solomon Block, so help me, if you scare Seth off after the congregation spent the past year courting him and getting him to come here, you will live to regret it. Do I make myself clear?"

Eli muttered something unintelligible.

"Now go help your mother in the kitchen or take a shower or bang your head against the wall, but whatever you do, get away from Seth. You're making him uncomfortable."

"I'll see you at dinner," Eli said in what seemed to be an attempt at a seductive tone. It didn't come across as sexy, but it was cute and sweet and funny that he tried, which in a lot of ways was the ultimate seduction. He put his hand on my knee, squeezed it, ran it up my thigh, and then...

"Eli!" Avi bellowed.

"I'm going to take a shower," Eli said in a rush as he jumped to his feet. He moved his hands to his jeans button, stared at me, and licked his lips as he started to unfasten them.

I looked at Avi in a panic.

"Have you lost your ever-loving mind?" he yelled at his son. "Aside from how ridiculous you look and how uncomfortable you're making Seth, I am sitting right here!"

Eli glared at him, then gave me a saucy grin and a wink before sauntering away, wagging his hips exaggeratedly.

Avi shook his head and let out a long breath when Eli left the room. I was still numb with shock or fear or both, so I couldn't speak.

"I'm sorry about that, Seth," Avi said. "You remember how it was at eighteen. Eli is all hormones right now, and along with decimating his common sense, it's making his mother and me crazy. Apparently he took quite a shine to you at summer camp, which he has made sure to mention on an almost daily basis since I told him you'd be our new associate rabbi."

"I didn't... I don't..." I took a deep breath and wiped my sweaty palms on my chinos. "I only vaguely remember him from back then."

Avi shrugged. "Yes, well, you made an impression without knowing it. He was young and hormonal..." He shook his head. "I'm sensing a common theme here." He rubbed his hands over his eyes. "Oh well, it could be worse. I suppose if my son is going to fixate on someone, I'd rather it be a man like you than some pierced, tattooed biker." He paused and then looked at me appraisingly. "You don't have any tattoos or piercings, do you?"

That was his concern? His son's crush on a man didn't bother him. His teenager's shockingly overt sexual innuendos didn't bother him. But tattoos or piercings got under his skin?

That last thought struck me as funny because those things do actually get under skin, so I laughed. Avi scrunched his eyebrows and looked at me suspiciously. I cleared my throat and wiped the smile from my face.

"No, sir. I don't have any tattoos or piercings. And if I ever got on a motorcycle, my mother would surely appear out of thin air and make me regret the day I was born. After a twenty-two hour labor, with no drugs, during the summer, with the air conditioner at the hospital on the fritz and scratchy linens on the beds."

Avi chuckled. "Good to know."

"Does it—" I licked my lips. "Does it bother you?" I moved my eyes toward the direction where Eli had gone.

Avi squinted dangerously. "Does what bother me?" he asked. Before I could answer he added, "Every human being is made in the image of God and *he* makes no mistakes." He paused. "Isn't that right?"

I bobbed my head up and down. "Yes, of course. That's not what I meant. It's just Eli was really...he was really..."

Avi sighed. "Eli is eighteen. He thinks with the wrong head about ninety-nine percent of the time, but sexuality is part of any human being and I wouldn't want my son to be without it. He'll calm down in a few years." He looked at me and gave me a chance to respond, but I had nothing to add. "Okay, let's talk about tomorrow's wedding before Eli comes back wearing nothing but a towel and then *accidentally* drops it."

I hoped he didn't notice me swallowing my tongue.

I'D HAD jobs since high school—a counselor at summer camp, a youth group leader, a gofer—but being the associate rabbi at Temple Beth Shalom was my first position in the career I hoped to have for the rest of my life, so I was nervous about it. I decided the best way to make a good impression on the congregants and make sure they didn't regret hiring me was to work hard. I'd rented a tiny, furnished one-bedroom apartment within walking distance to work, but I barely spent any time there. I just stumbled in to sleep, then woke up, showered, and went back to work.

I was new to Emile City so other than one guy from my youth group in LA who'd moved there, I didn't know anyone. And Micah Trains, my old friend, was a workaholic who rarely took a break to breathe, let alone socialize. Because I didn't have anything else to do, it was easy to spend all my time at the temple. And besides, I enjoyed my job.

"You're here late."

Startled by the unexpected voice, I jumped out of my seat and jerked my head toward the door, trying to get my bleary eyes to focus.

"Eli," I said nervously. He was wearing yet another pair of slim-fitting jeans, black this time, and the red shirt he'd paired with them clung to his narrow chest and showed the lean muscles on his arms. I was dragging my gaze up and down his body before I realized what I was doing. When I caught myself, I backed up until I was almost pressed against the wall. "What are you doing here?" I looked at the clock on my desk. It was after ten. "Shouldn't you be home in bed?"

"Is that an offer?" he asked as he leaned against the doorframe and cocked his hip.

And once again he had me speechless. I didn't know how to react to him. Or, more to the point, I didn't understand my reaction to him.

"I don't...I uh..."

He strolled over to the empty chair in front of my desk and sat down, his posture relaxed, spread his legs, and rested his hands on his hips with his fingers tilting inward, drawing my attention where it absolutely shouldn't have gone.

"Can I ask you something?" he said.

Nothing good could come out of anything he'd want to ask me, so I ignored his question and said, "It's really late. Do your parents know you're here?"

He furrowed his brow, crossed his arms over his chest, and frowned. "It's not that late. And besides, I don't need to tell my parents where I am every second. I'm an adult."

"Adults almost never have to tell people they're adults," I pointed out.

He pursed his lips in frustration, causing the bottom one to stick out. It was red and full and I wanted to suck on it. I squeezed my eyes shut to eradicate the completely inappropriate thought.

"I'm here because I want to ask you something, but when I try to talk to you during the day, you're always surrounded by a million people or you're running off to a meeting."

Immediately I felt guilty. I'd seen Eli several times over the past couple of weeks, and he'd tried to get my attention every time, but I'd hidden behind whoever was around or my many duties in order to avoid him. If the reason for that had been his inappropriate flirtations, I'd have a good excuse. But deep down, I knew my discomfort was based on my reaction to Eli and not on anything he said or did. That wasn't fair to him.

I took a calming breath, sat back down, and said, "What can I help you with?"

The words were barely out of my mouth when he said, "You're not straight, right? I mean, that's what they said at camp, that you had a girlfriend, but I knew they were wrong. Or even if they weren't, that was a long time ago and you're not, right? I just know you're not. Right?"

My instinct was to say that I was, in fact, straight. But he asked the question with such desperation in his voice and hope in his eyes that a stronger instinct was to hold him in my arms and feel his lean body pressed to mine, inhale his scent, and taste his skin. And there was nothing straight about that. I was confused about my own feelings, no doubt about it. But regardless of anything I felt, nothing could ever happen between me and Eli, and that was what I needed to make clear.

"Eli, my love life is not an appropriate topic of conversation," I said while trying to sound stern.

"Oh come on." He rolled his eyes. "Quit acting like you're some old man. We're practically the same age."

"We are not the same age. I'm nine years older than you." I'd done the math over and over again, hoping I'd get a different answer. "And I work for your father. The, uh, come-ons and the personal questions are inappropriate, and they need to stop."

He slumped in his chair, dropped his arms limply to his sides, and didn't say anything right away, so I thought I'd made my point and he'd give me a reprieve from the enticing looks and poses. But then he raised his gaze, looked right at me, and said, "No."

"No?" I hadn't expected that answer.

"Yes," he said. "I mean, yes, I said no."

At that point I was confused. "You're eighteen. I'm

twenty-seven. That's a nine-year age difference. You can't argue with math."

"I'm not arguing with *your* math," he said, as if I had somehow created the numbers or the way they fit together.

"It's not *my* math," I pointed out. "It's just math!"

"Whatever." He rolled his eyes. "I'm not talking about the numbers."

I'd completely lost control of the conversation. Actually, I wasn't sure I'd ever had control of the conversation. "What *are* you talking about?" I asked.

"What I'm saying is that my feelings aren't inappropriate, or whatever you said." He sat up straight and crossed his arms over his chest again. "My parents taught me that my feelings are natural and healthy and normal and nothing to be ashamed of." He tightened his lips in a thin line, and I could see the frustration mapped on his face. "You can ask my dad if you don't believe me."

And with that comment right there, he vanquished any chance he had of convincing me that being eighteen made him old enough to date—putting all the other roadblocks aside. Anyone who still used his parents as a source of confirmation for basic life truths was more a child than a grown-up. No matter how grown up his body looked.

"I'm not saying there's anything wrong with you or that you should be ashamed," I assured him, trying to keep my voice gentle.

"But you said that it's...it's inappropriate!"

He was chewing his lips, blinking his eyes rapidly, and sniffling. Hurting his feelings was the last thing I meant to do, but there was no way I could give him what he wanted.

"It's inappropriate because of my role here, because I work for your father, because you're too young for me, because your friends at camp were right about me having a girlfriend, but most of all"—I took a deep breath—"it's inappropriate because I told you I'm not interested."

His expression went from sad to angry to determined in the blink of an eye. "If it isn't you, it'll be somebody else."

"What do you mean?"

"I'm going to college in a month. I'm not going to be a virgin forever."

"I don't...I...what?" I was way out of my league with the conversation.

"I'm saying that I'm going to do it anyway, so there's no point in being all noble and pushing me away."

Yet another reason I wouldn't want to pursue anything with him, but I didn't say that. Because even though he wasn't right for me in any way, Eli was right about one thing—he wasn't a child and he had to make his own life decisions.

"I hope you change your mind about that," I said.

"You think I should stay a virgin forever?" he scoffed.

I smiled softly. "I think sex and love should be connected and that we don't find true happiness or satisfaction trying to collect notches on our bedposts."

He raised his eyebrows and looked at me disbelievingly.

"You're not married." He jutted his chin toward my left hand, where I didn't wear a ring. "So based on your theory, you've never had sex. Is that honestly what you're trying to feed me here?"

In high school, I'd made out with my girlfriend, but we'd never gone to the no-clothing stage. I'd gone further with the girl I'd dated in college. Both of us lived in dorms and then in our sorority and fraternity houses, so alone time was rare. But there were a few memorable nights when we shared a bed and our bodies in ways that were very intimate, though short of intercourse. The longest relationship I'd had was during rabbinical school. It had lasted two years, and she was the first and only woman I'd had full-on sex with. We had loved each other, but it wasn't the kind of love meant to be the foundation of a marriage. She had ended up marrying the guy she dated after me, and they were very happy together. Last I'd heard, they were expecting a baby.

"I'm not trying to convince you of anything," I said. "I'm only telling you my opinion. I know you're going off to college and you think that means you have to cross some sort of line, but you don't. Sex and love and emotions all go together. Your body has a brain and a heart." I paused and looked into his eyes. "I hope you don't forget them when you're focusing on that lower organ."

Eli left my office sulking, and we didn't talk much after that. I was busy with work. He was busy getting ready to move away to college. And though I still noticed him staring

at me, and though we shared several dinners at his parents'
house, once I took sex off the table, he stopped the aggressive
flirting.

Neither of us brought up our conversation about his
plans to find someone else to meet his needs. I assumed I had
gotten through to him but didn't have the courage to check. It
didn't take long before I regretted that weakness.

CHAPTER TWO

Dance as if no one were watching
Sing as if no one were listening
And live every day
As if it were your last

Adrienne Wolf and Bruce Linder
ask you to share with us as we broaden our circle of family and friends at our
ceremony of marriage.
Here's hoping everyone remains upright.

December 22, 2001 at 6:30 p.m.

Seth Cohen

"HEY."

I looked up from my view of the dance floor and was surprised to see Eli Block standing next to me. He was still slender, but his body had filled out a little since the last time I'd seen him, and his face had lost some of its roundness, making his jawline look stronger. If I'd thought distance would change the way I reacted to him, the fact I was staring for way too long proved me wrong.

"Eli! Hi." I stood and reached my hand out. "Were you here during the wedding? I didn't see you."

Which meant he wasn't there. Even with two hundred fifty people in attendance and me standing at the front nervously officiating my first solo ceremony, I was sure I would have noticed Eli.

"No, I wasn't here." He took my hand, yanked me close, and whispered conspiratorially, "I wasn't technically invited, so I'm sort of crashing."

"Sort of crashing?" I asked, trying to pretend my heart hadn't started beating a little bit faster as soon as he'd touched me.

"Well." Eli licked his lips. They were so red. "Adrienne's younger sister Sabrina is a friend of mine, and she invited a bunch of us to come over and help finish up the booze and the food."

It was hard to focus on anything with him standing so close and looking right at me. He had the most gorgeous eyes. They reminded me of fresh-cut grass.

"You're too young to drink."

Even as I said the words, I knew they sounded ridiculous. It was a wedding, not a frat party. And besides, he had probably spent the previous six months getting utterly wasted at college parties along with most other freshman. During my college days, I'd been one of the only people in the dorms by nine, even on weekends. My GPA had always mattered to me more than my social life, but with Eli's outgoing personality, I doubted the same was true for him.

"Of course that's what you'd say," he said with a chuckle and a fond shake of his head. I was surprised he didn't snap at me or roll his eyes. It seemed no matter what the circumstance, Eli had a way to catch me off guard and put me off balance. "Don't worry. I don't think there's any liquor left to consume with the way the groomsmen and bridesmaids have been hitting the bar."

I turned toward the dance floor and nodded. "Yeah. Someone should cut them off before they hurt themselves."

The bride and groom were happily dancing and singing and laughing. They were still able to stay upright without swaying. The same couldn't be said for two groomsmen, who were slumped in their seats looking like they were barely able to keep their necks straight. The other two groomsmen were doing what I assumed was meant to resemble dancing with one of the bridesmaids, but it looked more like they were trying to hold each other up. Two bridesmaids were in each other's arms with their eyes closed and their heads resting on each other's shoulders as they swayed gently. It would have been sweet and romantic, but the DJ was playing "YMCA," and every so often one or both of them would try to raise their arms and then they'd flop uselessly back to their sides, giving them the appearance of a toy winding down as it ran out of batteries.

But none of that compared to the fourth bridesmaid.

She was hooting and throwing her arms in the air, causing her strapless dress to dip precariously low, and grinding against whoever and whatever was closest to her. The dance moves were dirty enough to make the other guests nervous, so a wide-open space surrounded her, and as she tried to approach the other dancers, the invisible shield moved with her.

"Are you planning to ask her to dance?" Eli asked, sounding strained. "You can't keep your eyes off her."

"No!" I answered, feeling horrified at the prospect. Then I realized how rude that sounded, so I cleared my throat and slowly lowered myself to my seat. "I'm, uh, not much of a dancer."

Eli dragged his gaze from my face down my body and then back up, flaring his nostrils when he met my eyes again. "I doubt that," he said huskily as he took the chair next to mine and slid it closer. "I bet you know how to move."

Unlike his previous flirtations, he didn't sound cheeky. And I couldn't help noticing that his smile wasn't as free as I remembered and there was some sort of sadness in his eyes.

"Do you want to talk about it?" I asked. It was possible I had just opened the door to more come-ons, but it was worth the risk if there was something I could do to help bring back the lightheartedness I remembered Eli exuding.

He opened his mouth and then quickly snapped it shut and sighed. "Not really." He rested his wrists on the table, worried his fingers, and cracked his knuckles.

I found myself wishing he felt like he could share his burden with me. Then again, why would he? From the moment I'd met him, I'd been ignoring him, pushing him away, lecturing him, or doing a combination of the three. I felt a pang of regret for what I might have lost. Eli's joyful spirit was rare and enticing. The thought that it might have been quashed made my chest ache.

"Well, I'm here if you change your mind." I patted his wrist and immediately noticed how warm and soft his skin felt.

"Thanks." He glanced down at my hand and then closed his eyes and smiled. "So, uh, my mom said all the single women in the congregation have been scrambling to catch your eye."

My cheeks burned and I dipped my chin. "Oh, I don't know about that."

"They have a pool going on which one lands the hot young rabbi."

I shook my head and waved my hand. "Your mother is exaggerating."

"No," Eli said firmly. "It's an actual pool. I've seen the spreadsheet."

My jaw dropped. I slowly raised my head and stared at him.

"Seriously," he said with a chuckle. "Sabrina sent it to me."

I opened my mouth again but no words came out.

Heat rose up the back of my neck. "I don't..." I gulped and forced myself to meet his eyes. "I don't date members of the congregation. That wouldn't be appropriate."

I wasn't lying about not dating congregants. It was a bad idea. First off, people tended to talk to one another, so there was always a risk that a relationship with one person would translate into many people knowing about my personal life. Also, the line between a girlfriend and an ex-girlfriend was very thin, and hurt feelings made people act out. Anger and resentment weren't what I wanted to instill in our temple membership. Besides, it wasn't as if I was making a big sacrifice. Six months into my job, I had yet to meet anyone who interested me for anything outside of my professional duties.

"I know," he agreed. "Not about the appropriate part, that's a bunch of..." He stopped, cleared his throat, and said, "Not about the appropriate part. But I do know about the not-dating-anyone part because that particular column in the spreadsheet is blank." He paused and lowered his voice. "So either that means you're seeing someone who doesn't belong to the temple and you've been able to keep the secret from everyone *or* it means you're still single."

"I just moved here," I said defensively and then wondered why I felt like I had to defend my dating habits—or nondating habits—to Eli.

"You moved here half a year ago. People get married in less time."

"Not without a shotgun pointing at their backs, they don't," I argued, trying to lighten the mood.

"Fine." Eli laughed. "Maybe that'd be a rush to the altar. But it's not a rush to dinner. So what gives?"

Other than my mother, nobody had ever taken such a strong interest in my love life. I would have been annoyed at the invasiveness if it were based in nosiness, but I knew there was more to Eli's questioning. I could see the hope simmering in his eyes. But all the reasons I'd had for refusing him during the summer were still alive and well. So even if I had wanted to date him, he'd have been off-limits. And I didn't want to date him. Of that I was sure. Well, pretty sure.

"Work keeps me really busy. I'm still getting to know all the members, and we've been growing like crazy. Plus, I'm starting a social action committee and trying to build up the havurahs. They've stopped being active, but I really think having people make meaningful connections in small groups helps create a sense of community that bonds them to the temple as a whole."

"That's a nice speech." He nodded solemnly. "And those sure are lots of reasons."

Though he sounded serious, I sensed he was teasing me. "They're good reasons," I pointed out.

He nodded again, his expression unchanged. "Those sure are lots of *good* reasons."

I looked at him warily. It was clear from his tone that he had more to say.

Sure enough, after a few moments of silence, he turned up one corner of his mouth and said, "I mean, with all that going on, it's not like you have time to eat or watch a movie or make out on a couch while you're watching a movie after you're done eating."

"Ha ha," I said dryly and then snorted in amusement even though I was the butt of the joke. I couldn't help it. I liked his sarcastic way of talking. I liked how he made his already huge eyes look even bigger when he was trying to act innocent. I liked seeing him smile. It was hard to force myself to focus on the conversation, but I muddled through. "I tried to explain this to you before, remember? For me to pursue a relationship, I need to feel a connection and to believe there's a potential for a future."

"And in half a year you haven't met a single wom... person who fits that description?" he asked disbelievingly.

I shrugged. "No, I haven't. And I'm not interested in dating someone just to be dating someone. I can watch movies and eat dinner by myself or with friends."

He arched one eyebrow. "What about the making out? Are you doing that with your friends too?"

"Eli," I said, making sure to put a warning edge in my voice.

"What?" he asked, doing that wide-eyed innocent thing again. "We're two buddies hanging out. Buddies talk about sports and chicks and shit, right?" He thumped his fist against his chest and forced out a burp, then grabbed his crotch.

The whole thing looked and sounded so put-on and unnatural that I barked out a laugh. "Does this mean you're going to tell me about your fantasy basketball team and all the people you've been dating?" I asked.

"My fantasies have nothing to do with basketball," he scoffed. Then he looked down, bit his bottom lip, and mumbled, "And I'd have to actually be dating someone to tell you about him."

"Why aren't you dating anyone?"

He opened his mouth, then closed it and shook his head. "I don't want to talk about it."

Suddenly, I wanted nothing more than to talk with Eli about whatever was bothering him, and about school, and his friends, and his classes, and whether he'd decided on a major—I just wanted to talk with him.

"Are you sure?" I said. "I'm a really good listener."

He gazed into my eyes, and I could see that he was trying to make a decision. A wave of disappointment hit me when he said, "No thanks."

"Okay, well, uh, if you change your mi—"

"Oh crap!" Eli gasped.

"What?"

He pointed over my shoulder. "Should she be doing that?"

I twisted my head and looked behind me. The bridesmaid who had been dancing solo had given up on finding a partner and was now clinging to a post holding up the tent we were under.

"I don't know how sturdy those posts are," I said as I got up.

Eli looked at the post and then at the woman who was holding on to it and leaning back with all her weight, moving around and around in circles. "Well, it's holding up the tent, so it's got to be pretty strong."

"Yes, but it's a temporary structure, so it's set in grass, not concrete." Right at that moment, the woman grasped the post tightly and swung herself in the air, starting to do a stripper twirl. "If she yanks too hard on it, the post might come down. I better go over there and—"

The post tilted, the woman hung on, and both of them went toppling down to the grass. The rest of my sentence was drowned out by screams as the tent collapsed, knocking everyone under it to the ground, including the bride and groom. Then the heavy fabric fell on us, along with the dangling lights and surrounding furniture, and everything went black.

"Is everyone okay?" I asked, the words muffled in the confined space.

"Seth?" Eli sounded strained. "Seth?" Strained and panicked.

"I'm right here," I said, trying to scoot toward him. "Are you okay?"

"My ankle hurts. It hurts a lot."

"Can you see it?" I asked, trying to sound calm for him

even though my stomach rolled over when he said he was in pain.

"I can't move," he said, and then he grunted. "Something's on me and I can't move."

"I'm coming." I pulled myself forward over remarkably sturdy melamine plates and glasses and toppled chairs. "I'm almost there."

"Okay," he panted.

Something tall and hard stopped my progress toward Eli. I blinked and squinted and then realized I was looking at the top of the table. It was on its side.

"Eli?"

"Yeah."

He sounded so close. I ran my hands over the table and moved to the side. When I was almost at the edge, I saw him. He was pinned under the table. Two of the table legs were lying across his chest, and one of the metal support beams for the tent was lying on his ankle.

I took a deep breath, reminded myself that being emotional wouldn't help anyone, and then got as close to the beam as I could. "If it's not one thing with you, it's another," I joked.

"Yeah," he said with what almost passed for a laugh. "This is my new way to pick up guys—get crushed under heavy objects so they feel sorry for me."

I didn't feel sorry for him. I was terrified he was seriously injured. The pain and panic in his voice devastated me. If we weren't stuck under the fallen tent pieces, I would have pulled him into my lap and held him close. But I didn't tell him that.

"I'm sure you don't have any trouble getting people's attention," I said instead. "Even without being crushed under temporary outdoor rooms."

"The wrong people," he grumbled, sounding frustrated. At least the almost crying tone was gone. "Or maybe the wrong kind of attention."

I managed to climb over the beam, plant my feet on either side of it, and hook my hands underneath it. "What do you mean?" I asked, more because I was trying to distract him by talking than because I was paying close attention to what he was saying. The blood on his pants leg had done an effective job of distracting me.

"You were right," he answered.

I had no idea what he meant. "I usually am," I said, trying to make him laugh again.

It worked. He chuckled and said, "I'm sure you think so."

"On the count of three, Eli."

"What?"

"On the count of three, pull your leg toward you."

"What do you—"

"One." I arched my back. "Two." I tightened my grip on the beam. "Three." I yanked up and he pulled his leg out from under the heavy metal. "You out?" I asked through gritted teeth.

"Yeah."

I released the beam and gasped for air.

"I'll move the table next," I said.

"It's okay," he said. "The table doesn't hurt. I'm just wedged in here."

"You sure?"

He paused. "Yeah. But I wouldn't mind some company."

"Company?"

"Uh-huh."

I crawled over to him and collapsed onto my back as soon as I could see his face.

He gazed into my eyes, raised his eyebrows, and said, "So, uh, fancy meeting you here."

"Is that another of the new lines you're testing out?" I asked.

"Why? Would it work?"

I smiled. "I'm sure it would, but not on me."

"Figures." He looked up at the ceiling, which was only a few inches above him at that moment.

With his ankle freed from the weight of the post, my brain could focus on other things, like what he'd said about the wrong guys and the wrong attention.

"Eli?"

"Yeah."

"Do you want to tell me what happened?"

"No."

But I knew he did. He wouldn't have brought it up otherwise. And he had been talking about not dating anyone before the tent collapsed. The way he had said it made it clear that he wasn't happy about it. Nobody brought something up twice unless he wanted to get it off his chest.

"Come on," I said. "We've got nothing else to do."

"You're bored so you want me to bare my soul?"

"Why not?" I shrugged and arched my eyebrows.

He scoffed, but when I didn't say anything else, he sighed and said, "Dating sucks."

I refused to think about the sharp pain in my chest. "Oh?"

"Yeah. It seems like all people want to do is drink and fuck."

"Oh?" I knew I should say something else, but my mouth was too dry.

"Yeah. I mean, not that there's anything wrong with drinking. But the fucking isn't what I thought it'd be like."

"Oh?" Thankfully, Eli was too immersed in his story or his memories to notice my less than eloquent contribution to our discussion.

"Yeah. I always thought I'd want to bottom, because when I'm jerking off, I like to—" He coughed. "Anyway, it turns out that it hurts and it's over so fast there's no way it could get me off." He paused. "Which sounds weird, because on the one hand, I'm glad it's over fast so he pulls out but on the other hand, if I'm going to bring myself off, why bother having him there to begin with, you know?"

My heart hurt. "Eli," I sighed and reached for his hand, tangling my fingers with his.

"I didn't think it'd be like that," he said sadly.

"It won't."

"It was," he argued. "You weren't there. You don't know. I tried. Lots of times. It hurt and it sucked and—"

"I know. But maybe if you try it while you're sober and not in such a rush and—"

"And with the right guy?"

"Yes." I let out a relieved breath and nodded. "Exactly."

He squeezed my hand. "I knew you'd say that."

"You did?" I was unaccountably pleased that he knew me well enough to predict my reaction.

"Yeah. It's a total old man thing to say."

And *poof* my ego deflated. I smiled anyway. "Whatever. If you can learn to be patient, I'm sure you'll meet a great guy soon. Then it'll all fall into place."

"I already did," Eli whispered.

"Oh?" I was back to my one-word answers.

"Yup." He lolled his head to the side and looked at me. "I'm just waiting for him to figure out he's my right guy."

I swallowed hard. "Oh."

He turned away and looked up again. "Yup. Oh."

"Are you guys okay?" A voice interrupted our conversation and then light shone in our eyes.

After a second to remember where we were and what

happened, I answered, "Yes, we're okay, but one of us is stuck under a table. We'll need help moving it off him. And I think his ankle might be broken."

It was a mad rush after that, people and noise and lifting, and then we were out from under the tent and in the middle of a big crowd of people, talking about what happened. Nobody was seriously injured, but it looked like some of the guests had abrasions and sprained or broken bones. People were climbing into cars to go to the hospital, and they offered Eli a ride.

"Seth?" he said.

I looked at him. His skin was pale and he was trembling. I wanted to scoop him up in my arms and stay by his side until he was all patched up. But the bride was crying, the groom was pacing, and the dancing, pole-swinging bridesmaid was vomiting in the bushes.

"You need to go to the hospital, Eli." Though his eyes had remained dry up to that point, they suddenly looked shiny. I walked over to him, helped him stand, and draped his arm over my shoulder so I could support his weight. "You're hurt and you need to see a doctor."

"What about you?" he asked as I walked us over to one of the cars heading to the hospital.

"I'm a little bumped and bruised, but nothing serious." I settled him into the backseat and brushed his hair off his forehead, exposing pretty green eyes filled with longing. "Let me make sure everyone here is okay, and then I'll come over to be with you."

"Yeah?" he said, the worry leaving his face just like that.

"She ruined my wedding!" The devastated scream drew my attention. "Your cousin ruined my wedding!"

I swallowed down the emotion in my throat, nodded to Eli, and closed the car door.

"She didn't mean to, Adrienne. It was an accident." That was the groom's voice.

"Oh yes, she did! She hates me. Your whole family hates me!"

Wonderful. Now on top of mayhem and bodily harm, we were adding marital discord and family strife to the evening's already full agenda. I took a deep breath and went to help calm everyone down.

CHAPTER THREE

Mawage. Mawage is wot bwings us togeder tooday.
Mawage, that bwessed awangment, that dweam wifin a
dweam. And wuv, tru wuv, will fowow you foweva. So
tweasure your wuv. – *The Princess Bride*

Julia Owens and Bart Thornton
invite you to celebrate
the end of the year and the beginning of our marriage.
Sunday, December 30, 2001 at
One thirty in the afternoon.

Eli Block

MY FRESHMAN year in college, I came home for winter
break planning to seduce my childhood crush. It all started
out well enough. I found him at a wedding—romantic setting
with flowers and music and love in the air. I sat close to him
and started making small talk. Things were right on track.
And then the wedding fiasco of the century unfolded when a

drunk bridesmaid took down the wedding tent. It would have earned a win on that *America's Funniest Home Videos* show but it wasn't captured on film because everyone, including the photographer, had been keeping a safe distance from the scene of the crime-of-absurdity.

Unfortunately, my ankle was a casualty of the chaos, and I was rushed to the hospital while Seth stayed behind and tried to keep the bride and groom from setting a world record for shortest marriage ever. When I left the postwedding festivities that night, I still planned to make him mine. It wasn't a new desire. If anything, it was the status quo. I had a lot of years under my belt during which I thought Seth was the one and he didn't know I was alive.

I first met him at summer camp when I was eleven. Yup, eleven. For as long as I could remember, when people made comments about my future girlfriends or wives, they struck me as wrong. Something inside me always knew the right fit for me would be a boyfriend. But it wasn't until that summer that it all solidified in my mind as a clear picture of what I wanted and therefore who I was.

The bus pulled up to Camp Ahava, and I shuffled out alongside dozens of other campers. We huddled next to the bus and waited for the counselors to get our bags out from the underneath storage area and line them up so we could haul them to our cabins. The camp director came over to welcome us, and we mostly didn't listen to what she said. We were way too busy looking around at the place that would be our home for the next week or more.

For me, it was only a week, because my mother said she was worried I'd get homesick. If you ask me, the real reason I wasn't signed up for a longer session was because she wasn't ready for her only child to be away from the nest for that long. Meredith Block was a helicopter parent before the phrase was coined.

Anyway, I was standing outside, enjoying the scent of pine and the warm sun, when I heard him. I say *heard* because I remember hearing Seth before I saw him. He was singing "Little Plastic Castle." It was the first time I'd heard the song and I instantly became an Ani DiFranco fan.

I'd always been musically inclined. I started taking piano lessons at four, and by the time I was ten, I was damn good at piano, guitar, and harmonica, and I could stumble through a half dozen other instruments. When I was in a boys' choir, I'd been awarded a solo at every one of our recitals.

Seth adored music, listened to it all the time, and appreciated it more than anyone I knew. But as far as creating music? Well, that wasn't one of his strengths.

I wasn't saying he had a bad voice. I loved his voice, actually. It was deep and warm and soothing. I could listen to him read from a dictionary and feel safe and relaxed. But he didn't hold a tune all that well. Despite that, when I heard him singing that day, I stopped chatting with my buddies and looked for the source of the sound. By then he was next to the bus, bent at the waist, yanking out duffle bags and suitcases.

I caught glimpses of his smile as he spoke to the other counselors. I saw his chocolate-brown eyes twinkle as he tried to get them to join him in song. His brown hair was long enough for the curls to fall over his ears, and I wondered if they felt as soft as they looked. At the time, all I could think was that he was gorgeous. I'd never had that thought before, not about anyone, but the word fit Seth.

And then there was his trim but toned body. He was wearing sneakers without socks, cut-off jean shorts, and a white T-shirt that clung to his chest because he was wet. I later realized he must have come straight from the ropes course he taught. Part of it ran over the lake, and on hot days, people liked to leap into the water to cool off. Seth was attractive in any setting, but with his wet body glistening in the sun, he was enough to be the basis for my first ever feeling of a new kind of desire. Over the years, I learned what that desire meant, I realized that Seth's beauty wasn't only skin-deep, and I came to yearn for him inside as well as out.

When I hear people talk about puppy love like it's a cute little crush that doesn't mean anything, I wonder if they somehow managed to get through their teen years without ever experiencing the heart-stopping joy and heart-shattering pain of falling in love at that age. Everything felt so huge back then, so unique.

I went to Camp Ahava every summer, and Seth was there. I remember looking at him and being certain, absolutely certain, that nobody in the history of the world had ever wanted anyone as much as I wanted him. And when I came to camp the summer before my sophomore year in high school and found out he wouldn't be there, that he was done with his camp counselor stint, the pain was so severe I was sure my heart was bleeding inside my chest. I cried in my bunk night after night with the certainty that I'd never love anyone as much as I loved Seth. Never mind that he had never been my counselor, so I hadn't had a whole lot of contact with him; I still loved him with all my heart and soul, and the loss of his presence in my life, however brief and distant, was one of my most painful childhood experiences. Anyone who says that pain was silly and childish might be right, but it was also intense and real, so very real.

So when Seth became the associate rabbi at our temple, I was certain fate had sent him especially for me. Then I was injured in the Great Wedding Dance Debacle of 2001, and Seth came over regularly to check on me. We ended up spending more real time together in a week than we had in the entirety of our lives to that point, which made me realize I had to stop with the silly seduction plan and leave the man be.

It wasn't because I no longer wanted him. If anything, I wanted him more than ever, and I knew that would never change. It was because I was becoming doubtful he would ever want me back and starting to feel a little foolish and a lot selfish about constantly throwing myself at him despite his obvious discomfort. But mostly it was because I realized how much I enjoyed being Seth's friend, and I didn't want to annoy him to the point where he pushed me away.

"ELI?" THERE was a light knock on my door. "Your mom said you're awake. Can I come in?"

I had been slumped against my headboard, playing video games on my TV, but at the sound of Seth's voice, I paused my game and tossed the controller aside. "It's barely six o'clock," I shouted as I peeled my shirt off and flung it in the corner. "Of course I'm awake." I adjusted my jeans, hoping to make myself look sexy even though I was sitting on one of my best attributes.

My bedroom door creaked open, and Seth peeked inside. "How're you doing?" he asked.

He checked me out, his gaze roaming over my body, but there was no lust in his expression, only concern.

I sighed in disappointment. "Come on in." I waved my hand at him.

He walked in, sat on the edge of the bed, and ghosted his hand over my ankle brace. "How're you doing today?"

I wished he would touch me. Of course, even if he did, it wouldn't mean anything. Or at least it wouldn't mean what I wanted it to mean.

"Bored out of my gourd," I answered with a pout only partially due to that boredom.

He smiled and nudged his chin toward the TV that had

The Legend of Zelda paused midframe. "Getting sick of video games?"

"Yeah. This sucks!" I huffed dramatically. "The doctor said I'm not supposed to put any weight on my ankle for two weeks, so I'm trapped in here. I can't see my friends or go out or anything." I crossed my arms over my chest.

He nodded in understanding. "That's not a fun way to spend winter break."

For some reason his calm response made me feel a little silly for being so worked up. So I was lying around my parents' house playing video games. It wasn't like it was the end of the world.

I averted my eyes, relaxed my arms, and picked at my blanket. Acting like the kid he accused me of being was no way to win him over. I forced myself to look up and smile.

"It's fine," I said, hoping I sounded sincere. "I like video games." As soon as the words left my mouth, I winced. That sentence was doing nothing to make me seem more mature.

"Good." Seth grinned. "How do you feel about *The Princess Bride*?"

"What is that?" I asked.

His eyes widened. "Don't tell me you've never heard of *The Princess Bride*?"

I shrugged.

"It's a movie," he said incredulously.

"I've never been into, uh, princess movies," I said in confusion.

"It's not a princess movie."

I arched one eyebrow. "It's called *The Princess Bride* and it's not a princess movie?"

He smiled and shook his head. "Well, I guess it sort of is, but not like how you think. It's not a kid's movie." My expression must have made my disbelief apparent, because Seth chuckled and said, "Seriously. The wedding I officiated this afternoon? They had a line from *The Princess Bride* in their invitation. That's what made me think of it when I was trying to pick a movie to bring over."

"You brought over a movie?" I asked, practically shaking with excitement. I was thrilled that he wanted to spend time with me. The type of movie he chose was irrelevant.

"Yup." He raised his hand and showed me a video tape. "I thought we could have a movie night."

A movie night meant at least two hours with Seth. And because I wasn't exactly mobile, it meant two hours in my room with Seth. I doubted he'd want to sit in my uncomfortable desk chair, so it probably meant two hours on my bed with Seth.

"I'm sure it's great," I said.

"It is!" He patted my knee. "Just wait. You're going to love it." He climbed off the bed, stepped over to my TV/VCR combo, and said, "You'll see."

Right at that moment, what I was seeing was his butt. He was wearing what looked to be suit pants, and when he bent over to fiddle with my VCR, the fabric hugged his firm backside, which was at my eye level. I groaned.

He looked back at me over his shoulder and said, "Are you okay?"

"Oh, uh—" I coughed. "Just a little something in my throat." I rubbed my neck and cleared my throat. "I'm good."

"Is there something on my pants?" He twisted around and tried to look at the back of his pants.

Admitting I had been shamelessly ogling his butt would have risked an end to the shared-bed movie night, so I pressed my lips together, shook my head, and mumbled, "Uh-uh."

"Are you sure?"

He shook his right leg, which made his butt wiggle. Oh damn. It looked even better in motion. I managed to hold back another groan but then he repeated the action with his left leg and all bets were off. I moaned and then coughed again to cover it up.

Seth jerked his head up and stared at me. "Now you're laughing." He turned around. "I have horse dung on my pants, don't I?"

"No, your pants are fi—" His words registered, making me stop midword and furrow my brow. "Did you say horse dung?"

"Yes." He kept twisting this way and that while he tugged on his pants looking for, apparently, horse shit. Actual, literal horse shit.

I wasn't sure how I managed to keep a straight face.

"Why would there be horse shi—uh, dung on your suit pants?"

Without looking up from his task, he said, "They were trying to keep to the movie theme, so the bridal party rode in on horses."

"There are horses in the movie?" I asked.

"Uh-huh," he said distractedly, still focusing on his pants. "Horses and giants and rodents of unusual size."

"They had rodents at their wedding?" I screeched.

"No," he said in a tone that made it seem as if my question was ridiculous. "Just horses."

Which was weird all on its own, but I decided not to press that issue because I knew from my dad that people did all sorts of crazy things at weddings. That still didn't explain the pants problem.

"So, uh, what do the horses for the bridal party have to do with horse shit on your pants?"

"Horses aren't exactly trainable," he said as he toed off his shoes. "At least not when it comes to bodily functions. It turned out they chose an, uh, unfortunate time to relieve themselves."

I swallowed down my laughter. Again. "Unfortunate time?"

Seth shook his head and pursed his lips. "Yes. They were trotting down the aisle."

"Wait." I held my hand out and tried to keep my breathing even. "Are you saying a horse took a dump on the wedding aisle?"

"Not *a* horse. *All* the horses." He paused and furrowed his brow in thought. "That's weird, right? That their schedules are lined up like that?"

"Yeah." No amount of slow breathing and swallowing could keep me in complete check, but I managed to limit myself to a snort and a chuckle. "That's weird. Maybe they had a long, uh, drive or something, so they'd been holding it."

He tilted his head to the side. "Do horses do that? Hold it, I mean?"

I had no idea. "I have no idea. So, anyway. You were saying?"

"I was saying?" He moved his hand to his pants button, which distracted me. Thankfully, he didn't really need an answer. "Oh, yeah, so the horses relieved themselves in the aisle and with the volume of their, uh"—he glanced up at me and his cheeks colored slightly—"excrement and the number of horses, their stuff was everywhere."

I would have laughed at that point because, come on, really? But he had pushed the button through the hole and was lowering his zipper, which made me stop breathing. As it turned out, without air in your lungs, you couldn't laugh, so all I could do was bob my head in what I hoped passed for an "I'm listening" nod.

"Anyway." He finished unzipping his pants. "The wedding was on this huge lawn, and it rained last night, so the grass was wet to the point of being almost muddy. There was a temporary floor thing put out to hold the chairs with the aisle in between them, but there was no extra space. So to get out, we had to step off the plywood floor thing and walk on the grass, climb over the chairs, or walk down the aisle."

Dear God, he was taking off his pants. It was a dream come true and I didn't want it to stop. Of course that meant keeping myself together and not screaming or fainting or ejaculating in my pants.

Act cool. Act cool. Act cool, I chanted internally.

"So, uh, what'd you do?" I asked, hoping my voice didn't sound as oddly high-pitched to him as it did to me.

"I walked through the grass and got my shoes muddy, but it wasn't terrible. A couple of bridesmaids tried it but, unfortunately, stepping on grass in high heels was impossible because the shoes poked right into it, so they got stuck. Eventually they gave up on the grass and tried to cross over the floor instead."

He dropped his pants and I whimpered. Before he could notice, I covered it by asking, "So they walked through the shit?"

"At first they tried to climb over the chairs." He scooped up his pants, shook them out, and started eyeing them, presumably inspecting them for horse shit. "A bunch of the guys did that too. But there were three hundred people there, so it didn't take long before the chairs were falling and people were tripping and *things* were smearing around. Ugh, it was a mess."

I shifted so I could look around the pants and check out his groin. Unfortunately, with the distance, the pants obstruction, and his loose boxers, it was impossible for me to see what he was packing. One thing I knew for sure, though—he didn't have a hard-on.

That moment right there, with Seth partially undressed and me trying to scope out his dick, was when I realized I had to make a change. After what sounded like a shitty day—pun intended—he had chosen to come spend time with me. That had to mean he enjoyed my company. And he had no qualms about dropping trou in front of me, which was normal for guys to do in front of their buddies. So even though my seduction plan had failed, I had managed to attain friend status with a guy who previously hadn't known I was alive.

But if I kept coming on to Seth, I risked ruining our budding friendship. Even if that didn't happen, even if he was willing to continue putting up with my little comments and looks, there was no way he'd be comfortable enough to take off his pants in front of me, no way he would consider me a trusted friend, someone he could let loose with, someone who he could turn to after a stressful day.

Seth didn't seem to want me the same way I wanted him. If his words weren't enough to make that clear, his physical reaction—or lack of physical reaction—to me was. But he wanted to be my friend, which was better than nothing. And maybe if I was a good friend, he'd want to spend even more time with me. Telling myself to be thankful for what I could get and not blow it (pun intended), I forced myself to stop staring at his dick and start focusing on the conversation. Even if it was shitty. Pun still intended.

"So did everyone make it out all right?" I asked.

He dragged in a deep breath. "For the most part."

I was almost afraid to ask but I couldn't help myself. It was like a train wreck and I couldn't seem to look away. "For the most part?"

"Well, most of the guests got out clean. Some had a little, uh, smudging on their shoes or pants, but the bride and groom—" He grimaced.

"Oh no." I gulped, actually focused on his story now instead of his body. "What happened?"

"The bride's dress was really big and poufy with this long train, so there was no way she could climb over the chairs."

"She walked on the grass?" I asked, already knowing the answer.

"Afraid not. She had on high heels and the groom had this great idea that he could carry her down the aisle like an early threshold thing."

I raised my eyebrows and said, "He wanted to carry her over a threshold of shit?"

"I was helping some of the older guests cross over the grass by then, so I didn't hear them talking, but, yes, that's what people said happened. He lifted her up, started walking, slipped, and then—"

I gasped. "He slipped?"

"Yes. He slipped on the horse dung and fell down. He managed to hold on to the bride, but honestly, there was so much of it on the ground and her dress was so big, there was no avoiding it."

"So you're telling me you spent your afternoon at a wedding where the bride and groom got covered in shit?"

"I wouldn't say 'covered.' More like it was liberally applied. We all got at least a little poop shrapnel. That's why I don't have my jacket anymore, but I thought my pants were fine." He held his pants out. "Speaking of which, I think they're clean other than a little mud around the ankles, but I don't want to take a chance and get your bed dirty. Do you have some sweats or something I can borrow?"

Without so much as a leer, I nodded and pointed to my dresser. "Yup. I have a bunch of stuff in there. Help yourself."

Seth pulled on a pair of pants, started the movie, and hopped onto the bed. "I haven't seen this movie in forever." He sat down so close our shoulders were almost touching. I tensed up at first, not sure how to react, but then I forced myself to relax and enjoy his closeness, even if it was platonic. "You're going to love it," he said.

"It's a movie that inspired the shittiest wedding of all time," I said. "I have no doubt it'll slide right up to the top of my rewatch list."

CHAPTER FOUR

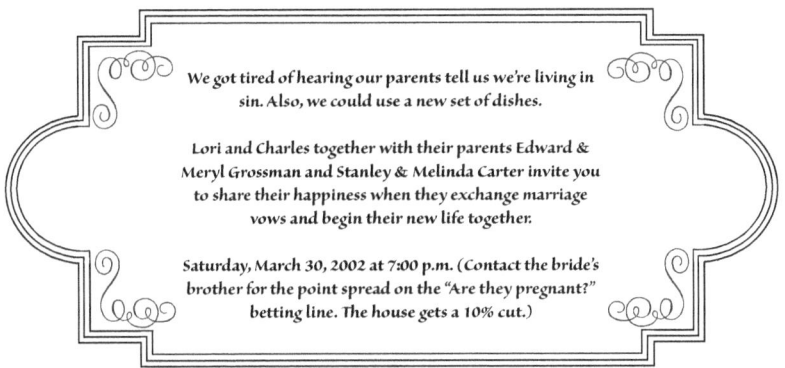

We got tired of hearing our parents tell us we're living in sin. Also, we could use a new set of dishes.

Lori and Charles together with their parents Edward & Meryl Grossman and Stanley & Melinda Carter invite you to share their happiness when they exchange marriage vows and begin their new life together.

Saturday, March 30, 2002 at 7:00 p.m. (Contact the bride's brother for the point spread on the "Are they pregnant?" betting line. The house gets a 10% cut.)

Eli Block

WHEN PEOPLE hear "Spring Break" certain images come to mind. Often they involve a beach, copious alcohol, bad decision-making, and hopefully nudity. The start to my spring break involved taking in the Temple Beth Shalom preschool Passover play. Wild times.

All right, so to go over the reason I spent my spring break at home and at temple. It wasn't because I was lacking in friends. It wasn't because my friends were all going home too. It wasn't because I couldn't chip in for my share of the gas and the motel room with two beds shared by ten people. It wasn't because I had ever attended the play since I had finished preschool, which was saying something because my father was the rabbi who started the congregation.

It was because—drum roll, please—I wanted to see Seth Cohen. Shocking, I know.

My second semester of college differed from my first semester. I still focused more on my music classes than I did on the academic ones. I still watched a lot of porn. I still hung out with my friends and partied. I still flirted shamelessly with just about anybody with two balls and a dick, but I no longer meant the flirting to result in any version of the horizontal mambo. That hadn't gone well when I'd arrived on campus and jumped into the "It's college. Sex! I can have sex!" pool with both feet and a raging hard-on.

I wasn't sure if it was because I chose the worst lays of all time or if it was because of what Seth had told me— that sex and love and emotions are connected. Either way, celibacy wasn't a realistic long-term lifestyle choice for me, I knew that. But my heart was stuck on Seth. So for a while at least, I figured if my body couldn't have him, I'd lay off the mission to get laid by any willing comer.

Over winter break, I'd intellectually slotted Seth in the "friend" category, which meant I'd chilled out on the come-ons. But no amount of internal reminders could change the feelings I'd been harboring for years. And those feelings weren't relegated to a desire to see him naked and lick every inch of his skin. I genuinely liked the guy, and I wanted to hang out with him. Which was why I sat through Friday night services on my first night back in town and then stuck around to watch a bunch of three- and four-year-olds put on their rendition of the Passover story.

"Eli!" Seth said excitedly as he stepped down from the bimah after services ended. "Welcome home."

I walked forward to give him a hug, but a bunch of other congregants were closer and they closed in on him like a wave. Apparently everyone wanted to wish him a chag sameach—happy holiday. My father was making the rounds too, but I'd seen him when I'd arrived that afternoon, so it wasn't him I was anxious to greet. My mother gave me an amused smile, kissed my cheek, and then wandered off to help the kids get ready for the play.

"I'm glad you're here," Seth said when he finally managed to quell his rabid fans enough to make his way to me.

"Are you a rock star or a rabbi?" I asked him, feeling a little grumpy about all the people he smiled at and hugged and basically anything else he did that resulted in him paying attention to anybody but me. Reasonable? No. But it was how I felt.

Seth chuckled and pulled me into a loose hug. "See? That's why I missed having you around. You're the only one who not so subtly gives me a hard time."

I could have made a lewd comment about the type of

hard time I wanted to give him, but I leaned into him instead. When he gave me a little squeeze, I clutched his shirt, closed my eyes, and inhaled deeply, shuddering as his scent flowed through me. "I missed you too," I whispered.

He let me hold on to him until I stopped trembling. I forced my eyes open and gazed at him.

"Are you okay?" he asked.

I nodded and swallowed hard.

"How's your ankle?"

I tilted the corner of my mouth up. "Like I told you in half a dozen e-mails and just as many phone calls, I'm all healed up."

He shrugged sheepishly. "I worry."

"Yeah, old man, I know."

He rolled his eyes, shook his head, and huffed. "Are you staying for the play?"

"I wouldn't miss it for the world," I said. "It's been getting rave reviews."

He ignored my sarcasm. "The kids are adorable in their costumes. They're a little nervous, but mostly excited." His eyes sparkled. "You'll love it."

What I loved was his hand on my lower back as he steered us out of the sanctuary and into the social hall. There was a little stage on one end, and folding chairs arranged in rows took up the rest of the room.

"Do you have lots of fun plans while you're here?"

My plan was to follow him around like a lost puppy

hoping to get a pat on the head.

"I'm going to catch up with some friends, spend time with my parents." I shrugged, trying to look nonchalant. "And anything else that comes up. You know. Whatever."

Seth arched an eyebrow and looked at me like I was amusing. "Wow. Well, with all those cool guy plans, do you have time to grab a late dinner?"

"Yes!" I said eagerly. "When? Tonight? Yes!"

"If your parents don't mind me hijacking you on your first night home, tonight would be great. I was too busy to eat before services, and by the time the play ends, it'll be past my dinnertime."

"You have a dinnertime?" I snorted. "What am I saying? Of course you have a dinnertime. Do you normally hit the cafeteria buffets at five thirty with the other senior citizens?"

He punched my shoulder.

"Ow!" I rubbed the not actually injured area. "You hit hard for an old man."

"I'll see you after the play, Eli," he said. Then he ruffled my hair and joined my father next to the stage.

I found a seat and hoped the play would start soon so that it could end soon and I could be alone with Seth. It didn't take long before my dad and Seth climbed onstage, talked a little about the preschool, thanked the teachers, and then introduced the kids. After that, they stepped away and I prepared myself to be bored.

I totally wasn't.

Seth was right about my loving the play. It was hilarious. Seriously. It was like the *Saturday Night Live* writers had scripted the production. Okay, so, to summarize the high points:

The pharaoh's daughter tripped over her robe and dropped baby Moses.

The pharaoh and grown-up Moses inexplicably got into a sword fight using their staffs. I had watched *The Princess Bride* a time or ten since Seth had introduced me to it, and I kept waiting for one of them to say, "My name is Inigo Montoya. You killed my father. Prepare to die."

The parting of the Red Sea was like a wave gone bad, with dozens of children throwing their arms up in the air and then collapsing to the ground.

And the crowning jewel on what had to be the best play ever was when a group of kids came up to the front, each of them holding a letter. They lined up intending, I assumed, to spell "chag sameach." But at that age, they'd have been lucky to spell "happy holiday" in English, let alone Hebrew, so instead the order of their letters spelled "shag cam ache."

I had to blink a few times to confirm it didn't say "cum" because that would have made total sense: you shag, there's cum, you ache. Thankfully the kids cleared it up when each of them screamed out their own pronunciation of the Hebrew words for happy holiday. By the time they got offstage, I was wiping away tears of laughter.

It was close to eight o'clock by then, which was late for all the young families, so they pretty much gathered up their kids and bolted. I was in full support of the fast evacuation because I figured with fewer people around to bombard Seth, we'd be able to leave sooner and I'd have him all to myself.

"Eli, are you ready to go?"

I had been so busy shifting from foot to foot impatiently and staring at Seth that I hadn't noticed my mother walking up. "Huh?" I said without moving my attention from soft brown eyes, a warm smile, and perfectly formed hands. Really, Seth had the best hands. Even from across the room, they made me tingle in fun places.

"Didn't you tell me you were done with this?" she asked.

"Huh?"

She sighed. "Eli Block. I'm your mother. That means you can at least have the courtesy to look at me when I'm speaking to you."

It was hard to tear my gaze away from Seth but I managed to do it. With great reluctance. "What?" I asked, stretching out the word to express my frustration.

She gave me the look. You know the one. The mom look that means, *"Oh, no, you didn't."*

"Sorry, Mom." I looked down and rubbed the toe of my shoe over the floor. "What were you saying?"

"It's okay. I know you were preoccupied." She threaded her arm with mine. "Are you ready to go home or are you going to keep watching Seth?"

"I wasn't..." Yeah, I stopped midsentence. That lie was so obvious it would have been ridiculous and insulting to try to sell it.

"Last time you were home, you told me you were moving on from this crush," she reminded me.

"We're friends, Mom." I let out a deep breath, slumped my shoulders, and chewed on my bottom lip. "That's all."

"Uh-huh," she said disbelievingly.

"I didn't say that's what I want. I'm just saying that's all there can ever be and I'm okay with it." I smiled and hoped it looked genuine. "We're having dinner tonight. As friends."

"Eli, honey." She looked so worried. "Pining away for someone who doesn't return your feelings isn't healthy. You're nineteen. There are lots of fish in the sea. I wish you'd do a little fishing."

It was a terrible analogy because I wasn't outdoorsy and because the smell of fresh fish had always made me queasy. I went with it anyway.

"At some point I'll go find a guy to hook," I assured her. "But for right now, I'm happy hanging out with Seth."

"I've chatted with several people who've known him for a long time," my mother said. I automatically translated the words to their literal meaning—she had been nosing around about Seth's past. "He's had long-term girlfriends, Eli. Not boyfriends. *Girlfriends.*" Translation—Seth Cohen is a breeder. Stay away.

"I know," I said.

"He isn't gay," she clarified her earlier statement. Not that I needed the clarification. The meaning had come through loud and clear.

"I know, Mom. I get it." I crossed my arms over my chest. "Is there some reason I can't have straight friends?"

"Don't be ridiculous. You know that's not what I'm saying."

No, it wasn't. I knew her concern wasn't about the friendship. She knew me inside and out, so I had no hope of hiding anything from her, least of all something as profound as my feelings for Seth. And that was what worried her.

"Good. Then we don't have an issue. Seth is my friend. Nothing more. And I have no problem with that."

She didn't believe me. I didn't believe me. But I think both of us hoped it'd be true eventually.

FOR THE next week, I spent more nights with Seth than I did away from him. Two of the nights—Wednesday and Thursday—were the first and second Passover seders, so they included my family and a few dozen other people. But the rest of the time we hung out, just the two of us, and I loved it. I was leaving early Sunday to go back to school, so spending Saturday night with Seth was imperative. He seemed truly disappointed when he told me he couldn't make it.

"I'm sorry. I wish I could, but I'm working on Saturday."

"Working doing what?" I asked. "Is it something I can do too?"

"I'm officiating a wedding, so no, I don't think so. Not unless you know another family member who's going to extend a secret invitation."

The reference to the last wedding we'd experienced together made my ankle throb with remembered pain. I wedged my phone between my ear and shoulder and rubbed the spot that used to hurt.

"I think I'm throwing in the towel on my wedding-crasher career," I said. "It's too dangerous."

He snickered. "I don't blame you."

I tossed myself across my bed and asked, "So what are you doing after?"

"After the wedding?" He sounded confused.

"Yeah."

"Nothing. Just going home."

"Cool." I sat up excitedly. "I'll come over and we can hang out."

He paused for a second and I expected him to turn me away, but instead he said, "Are you sure? It might be pretty late."

I punched my hand in the air in a silent gesture of success. "I'm a night owl," I said. "What time's the wedding start?"

"It's supposed to start at seven, which means seven

thirty at the earliest. But I'm not staying for the reception, so I should be able to get out of there by nine."

I scoffed. "Only in old man land is nine o'clock on a Saturday night considered late."

"Hey, don't knock old man land," he said playfully. "We have great benefits."

"Oh yeah?" I asked, loving the easy banter that had become common between us. "Like what?"

"Dental," he answered, deadpan.

"Ooooh, dental. That does sound exciting. But how's your prescription drug plan? Does it cover the basics?"

Without missing a beat, he said, "You mean Bengay? Yeah, it's covered. Denture cream too."

"Aaaand now we're back to the dental. I think I'm starting to detect a trend slash obsession."

"Oral health is very important," he justified.

I had to bite my tongue to keep from responding with a sexual innuendo. "All right, so your place around nine o'clock. I'll bring a pizza."

THE PIZZA place was crazy busy, so they were behind in their orders. That meant I got to Seth's apartment at quarter after nine. Not exactly something that would be categorized as late, but had things gone according to my schedule, I would have been sitting on his front mat, panting when he got home.

Taking a chance that the ceremony ended on time, I knocked on his door.

"Come in," he said.

At least I thought that was what he said. Mostly, I just heard a muffled sound, but the knowledge that he was behind the door was all I needed to forge ahead. I grasped the doorknob, turned it, and barged inside with a pizza and a smile.

The smile quickly turned into a furrowed brow when I saw Seth lying facedown on the couch.

"Seth?"

"Umph."

"Uh, is everything okay?"

"Mmm-hmm."

Okay, that sounded like a verbal yes to everything being okay, but his nonverbal communication indicated a different answer.

"Umm, shouldn't you take your suit off before you get wrinkled?" There. That was practical.

He said something that sounded like a yes, but I had a hard time understanding him because he was mumbling into the couch cushion.

I set the pizza box on the counter and turned back to the couch. That was when I noticed something on the floor next to it. I walked over, picked it up, and asked, "Uh, what is this?"

A muffled sound was his response.

"Did you say party hat? Why would they have—"

He said, "No," and then something else, but I had no idea what.

"I can't understand you when you talk into the furniture," I said. "Plus you probably can't breathe that way. Flip over."

Seth turned his head to the side and sighed loudly. "Safari hat."

I looked at the hat, and sure enough it was one of those tan mesh round hats with black straps over the sides. Of course the answer didn't really cover all aspects of my question.

"Why is there a safari hat here?"

"Theme wedding," he said tiredly.

"Again? You're kidding."

"No, I'm afraid I'm not. They're going on an African safari for their honeymoon, and at the last minute, they decided it'd be fun to get started early, so they brought that hat and asked me to wear it instead of a kippah."

"They asked you to wear this hat while you officiated their wedding?"

"Uh-huh."

"And you did it?" I asked in disbelief.

"Well, technically my head was covered and the hat is round, showing that God is above us and all around us and...." He sighed again, sounding defeated. "Yes, I wore the hat."

"You're way too nice." I sat on the edge of the couch.

"My dad would have told them to pound sand."

"No, he wouldn't."

"Uh, yeah, he totally would."

Seth sat up and dropped his head against the back of the couch. "Well, maybe if your dad had been there, they wouldn't have lost the rings."

I scooted closer to him. "They lost their wedding rings?"

He nodded.

"Do I want to know?" I asked hesitantly.

"No."

He was probably right, but I was too curious for my own good. "Tell me anyway."

"The happy couple owns a ridgeback."

"What's a ridgeback?"

"Rhodesian ridgeback. It's a big African hunting dog. Their dog matched their honeymoon, so, of course, they decided he was perfect for the wedding theme."

"Oh no."

"Oh yes." Seth looked at me and shook his head. "They had to put the dog in the wedding. Had to."

"Did it poop on the aisle like the horses?" I asked.

"Don't I wish," Seth said.

I was afraid to ask, but I did anyway. "What's worse than a shitty aisle?"

"They decided to make the dog the ring bearer."

That didn't sound so bad. I folded my leg underneath

me and twisted sideways so my torso was facing him. There was something on his dark suit, discoloration or dirt or something. I peered at it as I asked my next question. "Uh, okay, so they attached the rings to his collar or something?"

Seth nodded. "Yup. They put the rings in a bag, tied the bag to the collar, and had a friend hold the dog at the end of the aisle. Then, at just the right moment, they called for the dog. It would have worked fine but—" He grimaced and bit his lip. I wanted to lick it to soothe the sting. "Did I mention the wedding was outside?"

"No."

He drew in a deep breath and mirrored my pose. "It was at the preserve."

We were close enough to each other that if I leaned forward just a couple of inches, I could have kissed him. Instead, I reached for one of the marks on his suit to see if I could brush it off.

"You don't want to touch that," he said, grabbing my wrist firmly but gently. "There were squirrels."

"Oh God," I said. Outdoor wedding plus dog plus squirrels equaled a disaster in the making. I looked at his suit and then back up at his face. "What happened?"

"Randy was running—"

"Randy?"

"The ridgeback. Randy the Rhodesian ridgeback was running toward the bride and groom, and then he saw a squirrel."

"Oh no. Did he go after the squirrel?"

"Yes, but remember, we were in a preserve. There were *lots* of squirrels, and they're used to being fed not hunted, so their reflexes were slow." Seth looked a little green. "At least they seemed slow when the dog..." He shook his head and squeezed his eyes shut. "There was so much blood."

"That's what's smeared on your suit?"

He nodded.

I officially lost my appetite. "And the rings?" I asked once I got my gag reflex under control.

"We don't know. The bag must have fallen off the dog's collar at some point. But between the shrubs and all the carnage, nobody was able to find it."

After several minutes of silence, I patted his shoulder. "Well, I think you've learned a valuable lesson."

"Wear rubber boots to weddings?" he asked.

"I was thinking more along the line of no more animals in weddings."

He furrowed his brow in thought. "That's a good idea."

With the wedding carnage discussion coming to a close, I refocused on where I was—in Seth's apartment, on his couch, just the two of us. I had fantasized about all sorts of situations that started out just like that and ended with both of us naked and covered in jizz. Before those memories left me with an obvious hard-on, I made myself think about something else.

"So, uh." I darted my head around his apartment and

my gaze landed on the pizza box. "Are you hungry? I brought pizza."

Seth groaned and closed his eyes. "I don't think I'll be able to eat anything with red sauce for a long time."

I couldn't blame him, but without food to keep us occupied, I wasn't sure what to do. I knew what I *wanted* to do, but that wasn't an option either. I twisted my fingers together nervously and hoped Seth wouldn't tell me he was too tired to hang out. It was our last night together before I had to go back to school, and I wouldn't see him again until summer break. I was nowhere near ready to say goodbye.

"Do you want to play cards?" I said out of nowhere.

"Cards?" He looked at me in confusion.

"Yeah, cards." I smirked and waggled my eyebrows. "Isn't that what old men like to do on Saturday nights?"

"Very funny. I don't play cards."

"Are you saying you don't own a deck of cards?"

"Of course I do."

"Well, then, bring 'em out. Unless you're worried I'll embarrass you," I challenged.

Seth squinted at me. "What're we playing?"

Relieved that my idea of an alternative plan worked, I said, "Whatever you want. Your house, your choice."

"Okay." He jumped up and hustled toward his bedroom. "I'll get out of this suit, take a super quick shower, and then we can play gin rummy."

When I realized he wasn't joking, I started laughing

hysterically.

"What?" he shouted from his bedroom. "Why're you laughing?"

"No reason," I said breathlessly. Then I paused for a few beats and quietly added, "Old man."

"I heard that!"

I cracked up all over again.

CHAPTER FIVE

WITH A BIT OF A MIND FLIP YOU'RE INTO A TIME SLIP AND NOTHING CAN EVER BE THE SAME. JOIN ANITHA LANCASTER AND ROBIN WESTER AS WE GET MARRIED. THEN COME TO THE RECEPTION WHERE WE'LL DO THE TIME WARP AGAIN. — INSPIRED BY THE ROCKY HORROR PICTURE SHOW

SATURDAY, JUNE 8, 2002. SEATING (ARRIVE) AT 11P.M., PRESHOW (COCKTAILS) AT 11:30P.M., SHOW (CEREMONY) AT MIDNIGHT.

Eli Block

"ELI BLOCK. How the hell are you, man?" my friend Noah's deep voice boomed across the coffee shop. "Welcome back."

I stood and let Noah pull me into a hug. The man was huge—his shoulders had to be twice as wide as mine and he was half a foot taller, even though I'd grown over the past year and now measured in at five foot ten inches. Add to that his rough face, day-old beard, and the tattoo on the back of his neck, and he made an imposing impression.

"I'm good, Noah. Glad to be home." I patted his back and gave him a squeeze before we released each other and sat down. "Is Clark joining us?"

Clark was Noah's boyfriend. He was a really nice, slender strawberry blond covered in freckles. I'd known Noah since we were kids, but I'd only met Clark a couple of times because the two of them hadn't gotten together until a year prior, when Noah graduated from boarding school and came home to Emile City. But even without being around him much, I felt like I knew Clark because he was Noah's favorite topic of conversation whenever we e-mailed or talked on the phone.

"Nah. He had to work but he said to tell you hi. You're here all summer, right?" he asked, and when I nodded, he said, "We'll have you over for dinner or something so the three of us can hang out."

"Sounds good." I looked down and fiddled with my coffee cup, thinking about being the third wheel and how nice it'd be if I had my own plus one, a guy who was just mine. Noah was lucky.

"I'm going to get a drink and then you're going to tell me why you're mopey all of a sudden."

Before I could say everything was fine or that I didn't want to talk, or anything at all, for that matter, Noah was out of his seat and at the counter. That gave me a few minutes to think about whether I wanted to deflect the conversation from what had actually been on my mind or try to get advice from a guy whose vocabulary had been dominated by four-letter words when he was an often-inebriated kid. My deciding factor was Noah's relationship with Clark.

At nineteen, I didn't have a lot of friends in committed relationships. The girls and guys I went to school with tended to date someone for a few months and then move on. Sometimes they moved on while they were still with their current boyfriend or girlfriend. Advice on sex was a dime a dozen, and I didn't need any help landing a guy for a night in the sack. What I wanted to know was how to get the attention of someone who would be interested in more than a little fun. And if that someone happened to be an allegedly straight, overly serious, super-sexy rabbi, all the better.

"So what's up, man?" Noah set his glass on the table, plopped down in the chair across from mine, and stretched his long legs out, bumping my ankles in the process. "Spill."

"When did you become a talker?" I asked.

He took a sip of his drink and kept his gaze on me.

"I just got back," I said, trying a different approach. "Don't you want to tell me about your classes or how things are going with your family or Clark or something?"

"My classes are fine. I'm not into them, but Clark thinks it's important for me to get my degree and he's always right about shit like that, so I'm doing it. My family sucks, but I don't give a fuck about them anyway, so, whatever. Clark is"—Noah's eyes softened and he smiled tenderly—"amazing and brilliant and finally living with him is like heaven on earth."

"Who knew you were so poetic?" I said tightly, trying not to sound envious. I was happy for him. I was. But I couldn't help selfishly thinking about myself and how much I wanted someone in my life the way Noah was describing.

"Only about Clark," Noah said without any hesitation or shame.

I'd always admired that about him. We'd met in middle school outside of my piano teacher's studio. Noah did kickboxing at the dojo next door. After we chatted a few times, he spouted off some comment, making me realize he was gay. I remember being amazed at how free he was about it, how secure. No matter how many mistakes Noah had made in his misspent youth, his inner strength had been unlike anyone else's, so I'd held on to his example when I came out to my parents. Maybe it was time to learn from him again.

"Quit trying to goad me into changing the topic, Eli. It won't work. What's up with you?"

I breathed in deeply. "Did you, uh, play around with a lot of guys before you got together with Clark?" I bit my lip. "I know you were in boarding school with a lot of—"

"No." He shook his head. "I screwed around before I met him, but everything changed after that."

"But you were just a kid," I reminded him.

"I was thirteen," he confirmed.

"Do you think you'll regret it?"

He furrowed his brow. "What do you mean?"

"I don't know." I shrugged. "We're nineteen. Aren't we supposed to play the field for a while before we settle down with one guy? Some people even say we should never be with just one person. This guy I go to school with says monogamy is a heterosexual construct and we should make our own mold instead of fitting into theirs."

Noah rested his forearms on the table and leaned toward me. "I don't know what mold that guy from your school wants to fit into, and, honestly, I don't give a fuck. For me, what's right is being with Clark. I have no interest in other guys, haven't for a lot of years. Why would I want anyone else when I have him?"

"Yeah." I slumped down in my chair and traced the pattern on the table with my fingertip.

"I can't figure out if you're asking me these questions because you're, like, some total player now and you think I'll judge you, or if you met someone and you want to know what it's like to settle down." He covered my hand with his and stayed quiet until I looked up and met his gaze. "Eli, man, you remember the shit I was into when we were kids. I'd probably be dead now if Clark hadn't come into my life and saved me. Whatever you've got going on, you can talk to me. I might not have all the answers, but I won't think anything bad about you."

"It's nothing serious," I assured him, realizing my reaction may have been a little dramatic. "You're right. I did meet someone, but he's not interested in me. I tried playing the field, but that wasn't right either. I guess I'm just trying to figure out what I should do."

"What do you want to do?"

I furrowed my brow. "What do you mean?"

"What do you mean, what do I mean? You said you're trying to figure out what to do. I'm asking what you want. Once you have that answer, you'll have the answer to your question too."

I might or might not have understood him. I wasn't sure. My response would have been the same either way, though, so I said, "What I want is Seth, but he doesn't want me."

"And if he did?"

It was one of the most confusing conversations I'd had. "If he did what?"

"The guy you want, if he wanted you, then what would you want?"

That was an easy question to answer. "If Seth wanted me, I'd want what you and Clark have."

"But you only want it with him?"

I nodded. "So far, yeah."

"Hmm." Noah leaned back in his chair, crossed his muscular arms over his broad chest, pursed his lips, and narrowed his eyes, his expression thoughtful. "It seems to me," he said after a minute, "that you have two choices." He held up a finger. "One: you go after this Seth guy and convince him to give you a chance." He held up another finger. "Or two:

you can see if there's someone else out there who wants the same thing you want and see if you can get something going with him."

That sounded about right. I sighed sadly and dragged my fingers through my hair. "I wish there was a way to do number one."

"Are you sure there isn't?"

I nodded sadly.

Noah squinted and crossed his arms over his chest. "Tell me the deal with him."

"With Seth?" I asked. He nodded. "He's a rabbi at my synagogue. He works for my dad, and he's older than me, and supposedly he's straight, but I've always gotten a different vibe. Doesn't matter, anyway, because he's told me over and over that he isn't interested, and I'm worried if I push too hard, he won't want to hang out with me anymore, which would suck hard."

"So you guys hang out a lot?"

I thought about it. "When I'm home, yeah."

"Why would he want to hang out with you if he isn't interested?"

"I don't know." I fiddled with my cup again. "Maybe he feels sorry for me or maybe he wants to be friends. But I'm telling you, Noah, I've thrown myself at the guy, and nothing. Zippo. Nada. He isn't interested."

"Yeah, that doesn't sound good. You should probably move on and try to find someone else."

The answer surprised me, and his tone didn't ring as genuine. "Is that what you'd do?" I asked.

"No." He shook his head. "If I really wanted the guy and I was getting that kind of vibe, I'd be relentless. I mean, no way would I ever give up on Clark, no matter what." He took a swig of his drink and then wiped the back of his hand across his mouth. "But I've been kickboxed in the head a few times too many, Eli. I'm not sure you should be taking advice from me."

I chuckled and finished my coffee. I still didn't know what to do, but I'd definitely think about what Noah said. For the moment, though, I wanted to talk about something less serious.

"Hey, do you know of any jobs? I'm here until August and I want to earn a little extra cash."

"I can talk to the owner of the dojo where I work, see if he needs anyone else part-time."

"Thanks. Just make sure it isn't anything where I'd get kicked in the head."

I HAD been home for three days and I hadn't run into Seth yet. At first blush, that shouldn't sound like a big deal. I mean, it's not like people go around running into each other all the time. But if you considered the fact that I'd been stalking his office daily, then it became more worrisome. I finally gave up on stealth and interrogated my dad when he got home from work.

"Dad?"

He had just walked in the door. I mean that literally. Like, his hand was on the doorknob, one foot was in the house, and the other was still in the air.

"Eli," he said warily.

I decided against beating around the bush. "Where's Seth?"

"Oh, for crying out loud." He rolled his eyes and dropped his keys into the bowl my mom kept by the door. "He's not feeling well, Eli. Give him some space before you start harassing him."

"What do you mean not feeling well? Is he sick? I can bring him soup." I stopped, thought about it, and nodded to myself. "Yeah, that's what I'll do. Mom!" I turned away from my dad and jogged into the kitchen. "Mom! Can you make me soup?"

"Oh." She looked surprised when I rushed in asking her to cook something. I usually ate whatever they put in front of me. "You're in the mood for soup? Sure, I can—"

"It's for Seth," my father said as he walked in. He kissed my mom's cheek and shook his head. I knew that particular gesture was aimed at me.

"Eli," my mom sighed disapprovingly and turned around to keep chopping whatever it was she had on the cutting board.

"Dad said he's sick!" I shouted. She didn't react, so I brought out the big guns. "His mother is all the way in LA, and he's alone in that apartment. Who's there to make sure he eats right?"

My mom's posture stiffened, her arm froze in midair, and I knew I'd won.

"Fine," she said. "But you're going to help me."

"I am?" I asked in surprise. I did dishes and put away groceries, but cooking? She'd never asked for help, and she usually seemed annoyed when people were in her way while she was in the kitchen.

"Yes, you are. That way if you end up with a man as hopeless as you, someone will be able to keep the both of you fed even after I'm dead."

At least half of her reasons for things involved her eventual death.

"You're not going to die, Mom," I said for what had to be the millionth time in my life.

"We're all going to die, Eli. Now wash your hands and then get the carrots and celery out of the fridge. We're going to make your bubby's chicken noodle soup."

Two hours later, I was in front of Seth's door with a pot of soup, a salad, a loaf of bread, and a package my dad asked me to give him. I rang the bell with my elbow.

"Who is it?"

"It's me. Eli. It's Eli. Block. It's Eli Block."

I heard him laughing before the deadbolt clicked and

the door swung open.

"Hello, Eli Block," he said.

"Oh my God!" I shouted and almost dropped the food when I saw him. He had a bandage across his swollen nose and bruises under both eyes.

"Well, I guess it's official. I'm Frankenstein's monster." He reached for the pot, leaving me with only the bags draped over my arms. "Come on in and set that stuff down. By the way, what is all this?"

I was incapable of concentrating on anything other than his injuries. "What happened to you?" I dropped the bags on the counter next to where he'd placed the soup, and then I stepped over to him. I reached for his face but stopped before I made contact, leaving my palm hovering close to his skin.

"It'd be great if I could say something really exciting, but sadly, it was just another wedding." He turned away and started unloading the bags.

"A wedding?" I asked incredulously.

"Yup. It was nice of your mom to cook for me. I'll call her later to thank her."

"I cooked too."

He snapped his head toward me. "You did?"

"'Course." I stepped closer. "I would have done it sooner, but I only found out today that you weren't feeling well."

"Thanks, Eli." He opened his arms, and I moved

quickly, pressing myself against his chest and clinging to him tightly. "That was really nice of you."

"Does it hurt?" I asked when he ended the hug.

"Not so much anymore, but it still looks scary, so I'm taking another couple of days off work." He picked up the yellow envelope and said, "What's this?"

"I don't know. My dad said to give it to you." He started opening the envelope. "Tell me what happened. Was there a fight at the wedding?"

"No, nothing like that. The glass the groom tried to break at the end of the ceremony was this heavy-duty catering glass, so instead of smashing into a bunch of pieces, it flew up in the air and broke my nose." He pulled an album out of the envelope and then grinned at me. "Want to see the latest wedding fiasco captured on film?"

"You have pictures?"

He waved the album in the air. "Looks that way. Apparently this is my get-well gift—photographic evidence of the Wedding of Horror."

"Okay, yeah, I want to see, but you need to eat, so you go sit on the couch. I'll get a bowl of soup for you, and then we can look at the album."

He gave me a look that made my stomach flip over. "Thanks, Eli. Nobody's ever taken care of me like that."

I blushed and dipped my chin. "I'm sure your mom did it all the time."

"Yes," he admitted. "But that's different. She's my

mom and you're..."

He walked over to the couch and didn't finish the sentence. I was too busy basking in his praise to give it much thought. Once I had a bowl of soup sitting on a plate with a buttered piece of bread on the lip, I threw a towel over my shoulder and joined him on the sofa.

"Here you go." I set the food on the coffee table, covered his lap with the towel, and then handed him the spoon. "So tell me about this wedding."

He handed me the album. I flipped open the first page of the album and saw the invitation.

"It started at midnight?" I asked in surprise. He nodded and spooned the soup into his mouth. "Who starts a wedding at midnight?"

"It was a Rocky-Horror-themed wedding, and they thought it'd be fun," he answered. His tone was even, but his arched eyebrow told me he thought it was a weird starting time.

"What's *Rocky Horror*?"

Seth choked on his soup. "First *Princess Bride* and now *Rocky Horror*. You have a complete void when it comes to the classics."

"Okay, old man, point taken. I take it this is another movie?"

"Technically, yes, but *Rocky Horror* is more like an experience. The movie came out forever ago, but they still show it in theaters at midnight. People dress up and bring props and act it out. It's a whole thing."

I saw what he meant about the costumes. Some of the pictures of the guests were pretty out there. Seth was in his regular suit, though, so he looked normal. Well, sort of normal. He never looked quite right in pictures. It was like how the ones I had from camp as a kid never did him justice.

"This is a wedding?" I asked after I saw a picture of a man in a gold-lamé bikini.

He nodded and kept eating the soup. Though I'd been trying to goad my mom into cooking, it turned out I'd been right about nobody taking care of him. I kicked myself internally for not having asked my dad where he was sooner.

Trying not to stare at Seth, I looked back down, flipped the page, and tilted my head, trying to understand what I was seeing. "Am I looking at dead birds?" I asked.

"Yes. Dead doves."

I gaped at him. "Actual dead doves?"

He nodded.

"Is that from the movie? Do they bite their heads off like that rocker?"

"Ozzy Osbourne bit the head off a bat, not a dove and, no, they're not from the movie. They released the doves before the ceremony, thinking it'd be peaceful and pretty."

"Then why are they dead?"

"Because in the movie they throw rice at the screen."

I wasn't getting the connection. "Okay?"

Seth took a bite of bread, chewed, and swallowed.

"You know how people don't throw rice at weddings anymore because the birds eat it and then it swells in their stomachs and they die?"

"Uh, no, I didn't."

Seth gestured toward the album with his chin, spooned more soup into his mouth, and said, "Well, now you know."

"Huh."

"Yup."

I turned the page.

"Are these butterflies?"

He nodded.

"Did they release butterflies too?"

"Well, they tried."

"What do you—" I flipped the page. "Oh, I see." I looked at him and flinched. "Looks like the surviving birds liked the butterflies."

"Uh-huh."

"This is horrible. Why would they give you these pictures?"

"For the same reason they thought it'd be a good idea to have a Rocky-Horror-themed wedding."

I looked at the pictures again and rubbed my hand over my chest. "This is really gross."

"In that case you might want to stop, because in *Rocky Horror* they throw the rice at the *beginning* of the movie."

I jerked my head up. "You're saying there's more?"

He grimaced and said, "Yes. Lots more. They haven't

even walked down the aisle yet." He took the album from me and tossed it on the coffee table. "Trust me. You don't want to see what happened when they brought out the water pistols and hot dogs."

Normally my curiosity would have driven me to ask for details and look at the rest of the pictures, but catching up with Seth was more interesting, and less likely to result in my vomiting, so I went along with his advice.

"Does my dad know what happened?"

"He was the first person I called when I left the hospital."

"Why were you at the hospital?"

He pointed at his nose.

"Oh, yeah, right, uh, what'd my dad say?"

"He laughed," Seth answered.

Yeah, I could see that. "You should ask him for hazard pay."

He shrugged. "Hey, at least I didn't get poop on me at this one like I did at the horse wedding."

I chuckled. "Or blood and guts, like at the squirrel wedding."

"Actually there was blood."

"From the birds?"

"From my nose. It was gushing at first." He paused. "I wonder if the dry cleaner was able to get it out of my suit. I should call there tomorrow." He shook off the thought and then set the empty bowl on the coffee table. "No more wedding talk. Tell me how you did on your finals."

I liked that he cared enough to ask. "I think I did okay. Oh," I crowed. "I chose a major."

"Music?" he asked.

"How'd you know?"

"Because I pay attention. Now tell me what you mean by you did *okay*."

I tried to ignore the way my heart tightened in response to how well he knew me. It made me feel like I was special to him. That had to mean something. It had to.

And if I kept holding on to that hope, how would I be able to get past him enough to notice another guy, let alone get into a serious relationship with one?

CHAPTER SIX

You've played an important role in our lives, now play an important role in our wedding.

It's a murder mystery!

Please see the enclosed description of your character and join Elizabeth Rogers and Darrell Silver to solve a murder and watch them get married.

Thursday, June 5, 2003, 6:00 p.m. sharp — the time, not the weapon. Okay, maybe the weapon too, but you'll need to attend to know for certain.

Seth Cohen

"YOU HAVE got to be kidding."

"Nope."

I looked down at the invitation in my hand and then at Avi Block. "A theme wedding is one thing, but a murder mystery?"

"The bride and groom met in drama school," he explained as he rested his wrists on his desk and threaded his fingers together.

"Drama school?" I looked at him quizzically. "She's a Realtor and he's a lawyer."

He shrugged and nonchalantly said, "Turned out it was hard to find jobs in their chosen field, so they had to take a different approach."

Officiating weddings was quickly turning into the least favorite part of my job. I didn't want to be a whiner, but desperate times called for desperate measures, and my pride would have to take a backseat.

"We had a deal, Avi. Remember? Plus, I think it's your turn. I did the last wedding."

He got up from his desk. "The deal was that you'd get a break from weddings with animals, not all theme weddings. But, hey, on the plus side, the actual ceremony is going to be long before midnight this time. After that, you can claim a medical condition or something and leave."

"That's supposed to make me feel better?"

"No, not really. I was just stating a fact." He patted my shoulder as he made his way to his office door. "Either way, I'm not jumping in on this one. It's all you."

"Oh." I slumped my shoulders in defeat. "You have other plans?"

"No." He shook his head and walked out of his office into the administrative section of the synagogue. "But shit flows downhill, and I'm king of this particular mountain. When you're my age, you can give all the crappy weddings to the associate rabbi. Until then, they're yours."

After working with Avi for close to two years, I had gotten used to his laid-back attitude and casual-bordering-on-crass demeanor. More than that, I'd learned from it by seeing firsthand how comfortable people felt in his presence. He wasn't a man who put on airs, which made everyone around him feel like they could talk openly about their own fears and shortcomings without being judged.

"I've already done a crappy wedding, Avi!" I shouted after him, my frustration lowering my inhibitions. I jumped out of the chair and followed him. "And a bloody one! And a horror one!"

My little outburst had no impact on him whatsoever. He opened the exterior door, said, "Well, then, you should be well-prepared for the murder wedding, so have fun," and then he waved goodbye, all without turning around or changing his tone.

"Damn it!" As soon as the words left my mouth I realized where I was. Thankfully a quick glance around the office confirmed that I was alone, everyone already having gone home for the day. I was still stuck officiating yet another ridiculous wedding, but, hey, at least nobody had heard me cuss and shout about it. Great.

I shuffled over to my office, collapsed onto my chair, and reached for my phone. There was only one person who'd be able to find something good or funny about a murder-mystery wedding. *A murder-mystery wedding.* Just thinking it made me grimace.

"Hello."

"Hi, Eli."

"Seth!" Like he did every time we spoke—which was becoming more and more frequent—Eli sounded happy to hear from me. It felt good. "Hi! How are you? What're you doing? How's work?"

His exuberance and high energy level reminded me of a bouncy puppy. It was cute.

"I'm good. Work is busy. Are you ready for finals?"

"I will be by next week, when I have my first exam." He paused. "What's going on? You sound tired."

Not for the first time, I noticed how attentive Eli was, how in tune with something as minor as a tone of voice. It was a great quality—having the ability to make people feel like they were truly being heard.

"You're really good at that," I told him.

"Good at what?"

"Listening."

"Listening?" he repeated, sounding confused.

"Yes. You always pay close attention to people."

"Some people, yeah, now quit changing the subject. What's wrong?"

I smiled. "Nothing's wrong. I'm just being whiney about a wedding next month."

He groaned. "You and weddings. What's it gonna be this time? No, wait, don't tell me. Let me guess." He paused for a moment and then said, "I know. Ritual sacrifice. Am I right?"

"Actually, you might be."

"Uh, what?"

I sighed. "Well, it's a murder mystery, so I suppose it's possible the underlying crime is a ritual sacrifice."

"Shut the fuck up! You're joking, right?"

"I wish I was joking, but sadly, no. It's an actual murder-mystery wedding."

"That is so cool!"

I hadn't expected that reaction, so I was struck speechless. Not that it mattered because Eli was chatty enough for both of us. Yet another reason I enjoyed talking with him—there were no dull moments or long silences.

"Are you Colonel Mustard? No! Professor Plum. I bet you're Professor Plum."

"I don't, uh, think I have a role in the mystery game because I'm not a guest." At least I hoped that was true. Avi hadn't said anything about me playing any part other than rabbi.

"Oh," Eli said sadly. "Don't worry about it. You'll still have fun."

He was trying to make me feel better about the one aspect of the wedding I was already happy about—my nonparticipation in the role-playing game. That alone was funny enough to make me smile. Leave it to Eli to take an unexpected approach to a situation. I knew talking to him would cheer me up.

"Do you think they'll still let you guess?"

I had become distracted with my thoughts about him, so he lost me with that question. "What?"

"I bet they will. I mean, if you're going to be there, you should get a chance to figure out the killer and the weapon. It'd really suck for them to make you attend and not let you play." He paused. "You don't think they'll do that, right?"

He sounded so genuinely disappointed at the prospect that I found myself trying to make him feel better. "No, I'm sure they won't," I said. When he didn't respond, I added, "But even if they do, I can still try to figure it out on my own and then I'll know if I got it right."

"Yeah, I guess."

I could see the pout over the phone lines.

"I had no idea you were such a big Clue fan, Eli."

"Uh." He hesitated. "I don't know if I'd say I was a *big* fan. I mean, my family used to play a lot when I was a kid but—"

Eli wasn't the only person with observational skills. I'd learned a good bit about him during the time we'd spent together when he came home to Emile City and on phone calls in the intervening periods. And that knowledge told me that my comment had made him feel embarrassed or ashamed.

Wanting to remedy that mistake, I said, "That sounds really nice."

"It does?" he asked hesitantly.

"Yes. I love board games. My family played them too, but we didn't have Clue. Maybe we can play when you're here this summer."

"Seriously?" Excitement made Eli's usually warm, rich voice sound high-pitched. He cleared his throat. "I mean, yeah, that'd be cool."

I was grinning from ear to ear in response to his reactions.

"Good. Now go study."

"You're not my dad, Seth," he reminded me for what felt like the hundredth time.

"I know, Eli," I responded with my usual line. "But I am your friend, and I want you to do well in school."

"Yeah, yeah, fine. But I'm done studying for the night. My brain is fried. I'm going to watch some porn and hit the sack. But don't worry, old man, I'll go to the library first thing in the morning and hit the books again."

"You study in the library?" I asked, hoping to sway the conversation away from Eli watching porn, and my brain away from what Eli would be doing while he watched said porn.

"Yeah. Where did you study when you were in school?"

"Uh, I went to the library if I needed to look something up, but usually I studied in my room."

"Oh." He sounded surprised. "That totally wouldn't work for me."

"Why not?" I asked, mostly just to keep the conversation

going. I really enjoyed talking to him.

"'Cause if I were by myself in my room, I'd end up beating off all day instead of studying. Seriously. I'd probably fail all my classes and get carpal tunnel or something."

At that point, I mentally declared Operation Topic Change a complete and utter failure.

AFTER A thorough interrogation ("Avi, please tell me I don't have to be a character in this wedding"), Avi assured me all I had to do was give my usual spiel, declare the happy couple husband and wife, and then I could leave ("Suck it up, Seth, you'll be fine"). So off I went in my best suit, which had at one time been my least favorite suit but had moved up in the rankings after I got horse dung on one suit, squirrel entrails on another, and my own blood on a third.

The wedding was being held in an old mansion in EC South. It wasn't a part of town I frequented often, so I made sure to leave extra time in case I had trouble finding the place. As it turned out, I needn't have worried. Once I got off the freeway and made the first two turns, there was nothing visible except empty fields and a lone house. It was creepy to the point where I wondered whether they used the place as a haunted house for Halloween. I couldn't imagine there was a lot of call for murder-mystery wedding venues.

A long, winding path took me from the road to a large

brick parking lot already filling with cars. I parked my Honda and considered whether I needed to wear the suit coat. Summer was just getting started but it was unseasonably hot, so even at six, it was sweltering outside. Deciding that being professional at work took precedence over my own comfort, I got out of the car and shrugged into the jacket.

I took a deep breath, readied myself for handshakes and smiles and Mrs. White with a candlestick, and then headed over to the group gathered by the tall doors at the front of the mansion. I recognized several congregants from the temple, so I said hello and caught up with them. It wasn't long before the bride and groom pulled me aside to go over the schedule—introductions, murder, ceremony, then dinner and investigation with the killer unveiled after the cake cutting.

"So the typical wedding itinerary, then?" I said to them. They didn't laugh. I assumed the problem was my delivery. Whatever the reason, I was grateful when I saw my old friend Micah Trains walking over. "Micah, hi. I didn't know you'd be here."

"Hey, Seth." He held his hand out and I shook it. "Elizabeth works for one of my clients, and she threatened me with bodily harm and loss of future income if I didn't come to her wedding. I said no, but then she put Darrell on the job and said she'd cut him off if he didn't come through. I didn't want to be slapped with a loss of consortium claim, so here I am."

The bride and groom were right behind me, so I

widened my eyes in horror and tried to think of what I could say to soothe over what I was sure would be ruffled feathers. But then Micah winked at me, looked over my shoulder, and said, "Oh, Elizabeth. I didn't see you there. You look lovely."

"Fuck you, Micah," she said, but she was smiling, which was more than she'd done in response to my attempt at humor, so I knew she wasn't mad. She stepped over to Micah and gave him a tight hug. "It's not like you had anything else going on, and spending one night away from your office isn't going to kill you."

"Don't knock my work ethic, Lizzy—it helps keep your company in the black. In fact, I doubt your boss would appreciate knowing I'm here instead of toiling away on his case."

She arched her eyebrows. "My boss is over there"—she tilted her chin in the direction of the front steps—"wearing a cape and a fedora. I don't think he's going to complain about anything having to do with this party."

I followed her gaze, and sure enough, there was a tall, thin man wearing a red cape, houndstooth fedora, and, though Elizabeth had left it out of her description, black knee-high boots.

"Their whole firm is a little off balance," Micah mock whispered to me.

I secretly agreed, but I kept my opinion to myself.

"How are you, Micah?" the groom asked.

Micah shook his hand and slapped his back. "Better

than you right now, man. It's not too late, you know. I can hide you away in my trunk, and we can make a mad dash for the border. She'll never find you."

Darrell laughed.

The bride rolled her eyes, and said, "Quit monopolizing our time with your unique brand of flattery and charm. We need to go say hello to our other guests before the doors open and the mystery begins."

"Better make it snappy," Micah said. "It's hotter than hell out here, and your boss is wearing layers. If he passes out, I'm going to get a new case across my desk."

She flipped him off and then tugged the groom away. A few minutes later, the doors opened and we made our way inside. A man playing the part of the butler welcomed us to the Heritage House and showed us to the drawing room, where cocktails and appetizers were being served by candlelight.

"What do you think this is?" Micah asked as he held out a tiny puff pastry covered in something white and purple, which was overlaid with a gelatinous yellow substance.

I squinted and tried to identify it. "I have no idea. It's hard to see in here."

He shrugged, put it in his mouth, and promptly spit it into his napkin. "That's disgusting," he coughed.

I handed him my water and he chugged it down. "What was it?"

"I don't know," he said, and then he coughed again. "But I think it moved."

"Maybe you should try something else," I suggested.

"I can't see anything else."

He had a point. My stomach growled, but I decided to ignore it. I could eat when I got home. It seemed safer.

"Hopefully they'll turn on the lights later."

"I doubt it. Lizzy never got over her goth phase." Micah smiled fondly as he looked across the room at the bride. "I'd bet you anything her toenails are painted black."

"So you two are pretty good friends?" I asked.

He nodded. "Uh-huh. Darrell too. I represent his father's firm. That's how they met, actually."

"You set them up?" I asked in surprise. "I had no idea my workaholic friend had a romantic bone in his body, and here you are responsible for a successful shidduch."

"Oh please." He snorted. "My firm had a holiday luncheon for clients, and both of them came. I'm no matchmaker. Hell, I can't even find a guy for myself."

I knew Micah was gay, and because we'd gone to the same youth group growing up, I must have known him when he'd come out. But we hadn't been close enough for me to hear the details or even remember them. It wasn't something I had wondered about back then, but with my own thoughts and feelings leaving me confused, I suddenly wanted to talk to him about how he knew he was gay.

"Hey, Micah, can I ask you something?"

He arched his eyebrows. "You just did."

"Elizabeth is right," I said sarcastically. "You are quite

"All right, all right." Micah smiled broadly. "Ask away."

I looked around, leaned a little closer, and steeled my nerves. "How did you figure out that you're gay?"

His expression hardened. "How did you figure out that you're straight?"

"That's just it," I admitted quietly. "I'm not sure I am."

Catching Micah Trains off guard wasn't easy. He was the type of guy who always seemed prepared for anything, but I was pretty sure he hadn't seen that answer coming.

"You're gay?" he whispered.

I shook my head. "No, I'm not gay. I've had girlfriends," I said. He opened his mouth, probably to point out that the same could be said for many gay men, but I kept talking. "And I was attracted to them. It wasn't an act."

"Huh," he said, looking thoughtful.

"You don't feel that way?" I asked.

"About women?"

I nodded.

"No. I mean, I'm not blind. I can see a woman and think she's pretty or beautiful, but as far as being attracted to women emotionally or physically, no. Not even once."

It wasn't the answer I had been hoping to hear. Not that I knew exactly what I wanted him to say, but something to make me feel like I wasn't alone would have been nice.

I sighed.

"Do you think maybe you're bi?" he asked.

I shrugged. "I don't know. Maybe." I lowered my gaze. "I, uh, looked around online, and it seems like a lot of people think that's not real. They say bisexuals are just scared to admit they're gay, or they're people looking for reasons to sleep around."

"Yeah, that's stupid," Micah said bluntly. I raised my gaze and met his. "Seriously, people are idiots, and I don't need to tell you that you can't believe everything you read on the Internet. Besides, how can they know how you feel? They're not you. Hell, they don't even know you."

"I know. But how else am I supposed to figure out what I am?"

We were both quiet for a few seconds, and then Micah said, "Why does it matter?"

"What do you mean?"

"Gay, straight, bi. They're all just labels we use to make things easier, put us into neat little categories everyone can understand. But what really matters is understanding yourself, right?"

"Right," I agreed.

"There you go. Stop focusing on the labels and start focusing on your feelings. If you—"

A piercing scream cut off whatever he was saying. It was chaos after that, with every person in the room trying to get a good look at the source of the noise—a buxom blonde collapsed on a settee in a corner. Her arms were splayed to the sides, her legs were situated so her dress showed a good bit of thigh, and her eyes were closed. It looked like her head had some blood on it, but it was too dark to see much of anything. Plus, the twinkling candlelight was casting weird shadows.

None of that stopped the guests from furiously scribbling notes on little pads that had been handed out at the entrance. I wondered what they could be writing: possible blood on forehead; incredibly fake scream; nice rack.

Eventually the butler appeared and led us into an adjoining room set up in traditional wedding fashion—aisle in the middle with chairs on either side. I walked up the front and took my spot in the center. A round table draped with golden fabric and holding an assortment of flowers and a tall unlit candle was behind me and a little to the left. Unlike the short white candles in the candelabras attached to the walls, this candle was a vivid purple.

Darrell walked down the aisle first. He carried a lit blue candle.

Elizabeth followed him, carrying a lit red candle.

When they both reached the table, they lifted their candles and, in unison, lit the purple candle.

"The flames of our love join together today," Elizabeth said.

"The light we shine together is much brighter than those we had apart," Darrell added.

Then they both blew out their candles. Even though the purple candle was huge, with no natural light and the candelabras on the walls being our only other sources of illumination, it was really hard to see. Not wanting to tell the happy couple that the light of their love wasn't literally bright enough to shine on much of anything, and thinking that the visual impediment was probably a good idea because it prevented us from seeing people rolling their eyes or silently laughing, I started the ceremony.

Everything was fine at first. But then, during the moments when nobody was talking, I heard a strange noise. I couldn't identify it right away, but eventually I realized it was a steady dripping sound. I was trying to focus on the bride and groom, so I didn't give much thought to the source of the sound, chalking it up to a leaky pipe in an old house.

Then, sometime between "I now pronounce" and "husband and wife" the guests started shouting. I don't mean the high-pitched clearly fake scream from the faux murder-mystery victim. I mean people were leaping out of their chairs, and there were so many voices at once it was impossible to understand what they were saying. At first I thought maybe they were cheering, but then I noticed the panic on their faces. When I felt something hotter than the summer temperature beating against my back, I turned around and realized what they were screaming—"Fire!"

As in, the purple candle had dripped wax hot enough to catch the flowers and the tablecloth on fire. As in, sparks were flying and the drapes behind us were starting to go up. As in, the train on the bride's dress was about half the length it had been at the beginning of the ceremony and that ratio was getting smaller by the second.

After a moment to assimilate what I was seeing into something that made sense in my brain, I stripped off my suit jacket and got to work beating the flames out of the bride's dress. Once that was handled, I attacked the drapes alongside the groom. The red aisle was next.

I don't remember how long we stayed there, containing and then putting out the flames, but at some point, the people who worked at the mansion came in with fire extinguishers. By the time the fire truck got to our remote location, everything was under control and it didn't look like there was all that much damage to the building. My best (meaning *last*) suit on the other hand, was toast. And I mean that literally.

Somehow I doubted that would be enough to convince Avi to take on the next theme wedding.

CHAPTER SEVEN

Entreat me not to leave you or return from following you. Where you go I will go. Where you live I will live. Your people shall be my people. And your God shall be my God. ~ Ruth 1:16

Rabbi Amber Miller and Dr. Patrick Cantos
ask that you join them to witness their marriage.
The Central Park Boathouse,
Manhattan, New York.
Sunday, the seventh of September, 2003.
Ceremony at 4:00 p.m. Reception to follow.

Seth Cohen

BY THE time I finally left the Flaming Murder-Mystery Wedding, my clothes were burnt, charred, wet, and coated in a white film from the fire-extinguisher spray. Seemed all those things shouldn't be possible in unison, but I had the permanent stains on my car seat to prove it. Anyway, it wasn't the discomfort or odor that bothered me most, it was that I hadn't eaten since breakfast, and the exertion of playing amateur firefighter had drained all my stored fuel resources.

There was no way I could be seen in public in my

condition, so restaurants were off the menu. I headed home and used the unreasonably long drive time to take a mental inventory of my refrigerator contents. No matter how many times I went over it, the answer was lacking. As I pulled into my apartment complex, I was trying to remember whether or not I'd finished the container of fresh mozzarella. The thought had me so distracted I didn't notice a familiar car in the parking lot.

I was stepping out of my car when I heard his voice.

"Seth!"

I snapped my head around, looking for Eli.

"Hey!" he shouted as he jogged over to me. "I caught an earlier flight home, so I thought I'd…" When he stopped talking, I figured he had gotten close enough to notice my appearance or get a whiff of my delightful wet-charred-guy fragrance. His jaw dropped and his eyes widened in horror. "What happened?"

In some ways the answer was long and complicated, but in other ways it was pretty simple.

"Wedding," I said tiredly, summarizing everything with that one word. I started shuffling toward my apartment. "I thought you weren't getting in until Tuesday."

Eli stayed by my side. "I talked my prof into letting me take my last exam this morning and caught an earlier flight." He leaned toward me. "Is that… Are you—" He inhaled deeply and then wrinkled his nose and blinked rapidly. The expression made him look even more adorable than usual, and his usual was already heart-melting. "Do I smell smoke?" he asked.

I nodded tiredly. "Yes. Sorry. I know it's gross. I'll hop right into the shower."

"Hey." He bumped my shoulder with his. "Don't apologize. I wasn't complaining."

We'd reached my apartment, so I raised my shaky arm and after three tries managed to get the key into the lock.

"You're trembling." Eli put his arm around me and opened the door. "Are you okay? You're not hurt, are you?"

I wanted to lean against him and let the feeling of his body pressed to mine comfort me. *Too young,* I reminded myself. *Even if I knew what I wanted, which I don't, he's too young to know what he wants. I'd be taking advantage.*

I sighed. "I'm a little sore and my back and arms feel like I was out at the beach too long without sunscreen, but it's not too bad. I'm just tired and hungry and I can't stand smelling myself."

"I'll make you a deal," Eli said once we got inside. "You go bathe and I'll make you something to eat. How's that sound?"

It sounded amazing, actually. "Thanks, Eli. I'll only be a...wait, do you know how to cook?"

He rolled his eyes.

"No, seriously. Because if you're going to burn my kitchen down, I'd rather take my chances with starvation. I don't think I can handle another fire right now."

"I made you that soup last summer, remember?" He gave me a gentle shove. "Get in the shower, old man. I'll figure out how to have sustenance ready for you without having to call in emergency personnel."

I was too tired to put up a fight, so I turned around and stepped toward my bedroom.

"On the other hand," Eli said, his tone devious. "I do like a man in uniform. It might be nice to have a bunch of firefighters fighting over who gets to give me mouth-to-mouth."

I shook my head and kept walking. "Don't let your fantasies distract you if you're using the stove. I meant what I said about being done with fires for the day."

"Don't be jealous!" he shouted after me. "It isn't becoming."

Though I wouldn't have thought it possible with how drained I was, I laughed. Eli definitely had a way of creating humor in any situation. Not that I'd be laughing if I saw somebody actually put his mouth on Eli's. I sighed and shook my head.

I didn't want to be with him. Or, more accurately, I wasn't sure what I wanted, but I knew it would be wrong for me to be with him. So I refused to give in to his advances. And, okay, fine, I refused to give in to my (possible) feelings. And yet, I didn't want him to be with anybody else either. Man, was I ever a jerk. I really had to get myself together.

After stripping off my clothes, I looked them over and

decided they were a lost cause. *Another suit bites the dust.* I stuffed them into a plastic bag and tied it shut to hold in the stench until I could take it outside. I was going to need a clothing allowance if I had to keep officiating weddings of doom. I dragged myself into the shower, closed my eyes, and moaned in pleasure when the water flowed over me, massaging aching muscles and washing away grime.

"You didn't drown in there, did you?"

The sound of Eli's voice jerked me out of my relaxed-to-the-point-of-being-semiconscious state. I had no idea how long I had been in under the water.

"Are you in my bathroom?" I asked. Okay, it was a silly question. His voice was too close for him to be anywhere else.

"Yes, but don't worry, I won't peek." He paused. "Unless you let me, and then I'll totally ogle you." Another pause. "Forget I said that. I brought you apples. They're sliced."

My head was spinning. Between my exhaustion and the skipped meals, I wasn't lucid enough to follow Eli's frenetic conversation pace.

"You brought me sliced apples? In the shower?"

"Well, yeah. You were really hungry, and the sandwich I made would get soggy because bread totally isn't waterproof, and I'm not sure about cheese but I figured apples would be fine, and then I thought it'd be easier if I cut them up and you could just nibble on them while you wash and, uh, do whatever else you do when you're in the shower." He paused. "Naked." Another pause. "Using conditioner."

He groaned and the sound had my tired member starting to get interested.

"I use conditioner on my hair," I told him, which was true. It wasn't the only place I used it, but that was neither here nor there.

"Right. Right. I know. Sorry. Forget I said that. Do you want your apples?" The edge of the curtain rustled, and then Eli's hand shot into the shower.

I darted forward and snatched the plate. "I don't think you should be in the shower with me."

He groaned again, and I realized my word choice could have been better.

Before I could tell him to leave, I heard the toilet lid slam shut and he said, "I'm all the way over here. I'll be good. I promise. I just want to talk." He paused, and when he spoke again, his voice was lower. "I missed hanging out with you."

It felt weird to be naked with him just a few feet away, but it wasn't like he could see me. Plus, he sounded so eager I didn't want to turn him away.

"When did you get in?" I asked.

He sighed in relief. "My flight landed at seven. My parents picked me up at the airport and we went to dinner, and then they went home and I took the car and came over here."

That meant he had been waiting for me for a while, because it had been close to midnight by the time I'd gotten home.

"Sorry to keep you waiting. The wedding ran longer than I anticipated."

"That's okay. It's not like you knew I was coming. You were at the murder-mystery wedding, right? What happened?"

I stuffed a few slices of apple in my mouth, set the small plate down on the ledge, and grabbed the shampoo. "Fire."

"Fire?"

"Mmm-hmm." I chewed, swallowed, and then elaborated. "They had this huge unity candle thing, and hot wax was pouring off it. I think the tablecloth or the flowers caught on fire, and then it spread."

"Holy shit!"

"Yeah." I rinsed off my hair. "Nobody got seriously hurt, but it was a little scary and really messy."

"Wow. I remember my dad telling me some crazy wedding stories over the years, but nothing like that. You have some seriously bad wedding mojo."

I grabbed the soap and lathered up. "Bad mojo and a shortage of suits. Maybe now your dad will give me a break and let me do baby namings or bar mitzvahs or something."

"I don't think that's a good idea," Eli said.

"Why not?" I asked before I tossed the last of the apple in my mouth and stepped under the spray.

"With the way things are going for you, I'm afraid children will get hurt if you're responsible for their life events."

"Hardy har har."

"I think you're better off with funerals," he said, sounding very serious. "Those people are already dead."

"You're a real comedian, Eli. Are you sure you want to major in music? I think you're missing your calling."

It was fun bantering with him, and for a brief moment, my worn-out brain let me imagine something I'd normally shut down before it could take root: coming home from a long day and chatting with Eli, but instead of me in the shower and him sitting on the other side of the curtain, we'd be together, maybe lying in the tub, holding each other. That image had me breathless, erect, and feeling a dull ache in my chest, like my heart knew what it was missing.

I was too exhausted to berate myself for my thoughts, but I'd need to be careful once I stepped out of the shower. My defenses were low, and I couldn't let myself do something Eli and I would both regret. With him home for the summer, there would be plenty of other tempting moments. I'd never forgive myself if my confusion and anxiety somehow ended up causing Eli pain. Right then and there I promised myself that after a good night's sleep, I'd do some self-analysis and figure out what was going on with me.

THE NEXT few weeks were blissfully wedding-free, which was

great. And Eli regularly showed up at my office right around dinnertime, which was even better. I knew we weren't just coincidentally running into each other. I knew he planned those interactions. But I didn't call him on it, both because I didn't want to shame him and also because I liked it. One thing my self-reflection had taught me was that whatever else happened, I had to be honest with myself about my feelings if I wanted any chance of figuring out what they were. So I internally admitted that I always enjoyed spending time with Eli.

Thursday night wasn't one of my, "Oh, hi, Seth. You're still here? So, uh, you wanna go grab dinner or hang out or something?" nights. Eli actually all but told me in advance that he wouldn't *happen* to be at Temple Beth Shalom that evening, something about plans with friends. I had just gotten home when my phone rang.

"Seth, hey, it's Micah."

"Hi, Micah." I flopped down on my couch and rubbed my hand over my face. "How are you?"

"Good. Sorry I didn't call sooner. I meant to but then things got busy with work. You know how it is."

I knew he was a workaholic but I had no idea why he was apologizing for not calling me. Before I could ask, he kept talking.

"So, listen, I know it's last minute, but it turns out I'm going to get out of here early tonight. Want to grab dinner and catch up?"

I looked at the clock. It was after seven. Only in Micah's world did that constitute a light day at the office.

"Sounds good. I haven't eaten yet and I'm overdue for a grocery run."

"Cool. Figure out where you want to go. I'm leaving the office now. I'll come pick you up."

Twenty minutes later I heard a knock on my door. I grabbed my wallet and keys and opened it.

"Hi, Micah."

"Hey." He waited until I locked up, and then he wrapped his arm around my back and squeezed my shoulder. "How've you been?"

He was being more affectionate than usual, and he sounded genuinely concerned. I was a little lost.

"I'm good. Now that I finally have a grip on everything at work, things are slowing down, which is good."

"How're you liking it there?" he asked as we walked over to his car. "I've been meaning to join a temple since I moved to Emile City, but I've been really—"

"Busy," I said with a wink.

He snickered, opened his door, and climbed in. "Where're we going?"

"There's a place called the Dubliner down the street. I've been wanting to try it. But if you're in the mood for something else, that's fine too."

"Nope." Micah turned out of the parking lot. "The Dubliner sounds good. I haven't been there either, and I drive by it all the time."

"How's your mom?" I asked, making small talk.

"She's good. My dad is too. And my sister. But I didn't ask you to dinner to talk about them." Leave it to Micah to cut right to the chase. "We were interrupted by a pretend murder and a real fire right in the middle of our conversation the other night. I've been thinking about you and how you're doing."

The last part of that sentence wasn't what I would have expected from him. Micah wasn't someone I considered warm and fuzzy. Plus, as invested as he was in his job, I was surprised anything else made it onto his radar.

I stretched my neck from side to side. "I'm doing okay, actually," I said. "What you said about ignoring what other people think and focusing on my feelings helped. But I guess I'm still trying to figure myself out."

He was quiet for a moment, his thoughtful expression telling me he was processing what I said.

"Tell me what you mean."

What did I mean? "Well, like I told you the other night, I've only ever dated women. I was attracted to them. It was easy. It just made sense, you know?"

"Sure." Micah nodded. "So what's changed?"

"I'm not sure anything has *changed* exactly." I furrowed my brow as I reflected on my past. "All those feelings are still the same. It's just that when I think about it, I realize I have the same reactions to men. It wasn't ever something I gave much thought to before. I guess I figured it was normal, that everybody was like that. And it wasn't like I wanted to be in a relationship with a man, more like I've thought some were, uh—"

"Hot?"

I felt my cheeks warming. "Yes."

"But now?"

Knowing I had to be honest with myself was one thing. Actually being honest with myself was something harder. Being honest about my feelings with someone else? I felt shaky.

"Seth?" Micah pulled into the restaurant parking lot. "You met a guy who's more than hot. Is that it?"

He parked the car and then twisted around to look at me.

I took a deep breath and nodded.

"What's the problem? Is it that you're scared to be with a man? Is he straight? What?"

"No." I shook my head. "It's neither of those things." I paused. "Okay, maybe I'm a little anxious about being with a man, but I think I could deal with it if I knew it was going to work out. But—" I gulped and barged ahead with my confession. "This guy? He's barely out of his teens." I paused and examined Micah's expression, expecting to find shock or disgust, but he didn't react at all to what I considered a big announcement. I cleared my throat and continued listing my concerns. "What if I jump in and he realizes I'm too old for him, or he decides he needs to sow some more wild oats, or—"

"So you're looking for an up-front guarantee, is that it?" Micah asked.

"When you say it like that, it sounds silly, but—"

"If it sounds that way, it's only because it *is* silly," he said firmly. "Let me ask you a question." He looked me straight in the face. "Did you have the same expectation with the women you dated?"

I blinked in surprise. "Well, no, but that's different."

"Because they're women?"

"No!"

"Then what? How is it different?"

It was a fair question. "Fine," I admitted. "One part is because he's a guy. Dating him means everyone knows I'm with a guy, which isn't a problem if it works out. But if it doesn't—"

"You're marked for life with the scarlet G letter?" Micah asked sarcastically.

"Yes." I nodded. He opened his mouth, but I kept talking. "And before you lay into me, let me remind you of something. I'm not gay, Micah." His mouth slammed shut. "I've never been a player. I only ask someone out if I think there could be something real there. The biggest problem I've had is finding someone I can be really serious about, you know? But that's what I want. I want the forever person. It's hard enough to find a woman...a person who fits that. But if women know I was with a guy, then they'll all assume I'm gay and ashamed, or that I'll go back to guys eventually, or that I'll cheat." I paused and peered at him. "Tell me how I'll find a wife with all that on the table. You might not think labels matter, but in some ways they *do* matter."

His nostrils flared and he nodded. "Okay, I hear you. I haven't been in your position, so I hadn't thought of it that way. First off, I know I'm not ready for anything serious. But when that time comes—if that time comes—it'll be with a man." Micah rubbed his hand across his nose and sighed. "All right, let me ask you this. You said dating this man will create problems if you want to date women after, but you also said none of the women you dated were people you could get serious about. So how do you know you wouldn't want to date men if it doesn't work out with him? Maybe the reason you couldn't get serious about women is because—"

I dragged my fingers through my hair in frustration. "Do you see what I mean? Even you're doing it. I told you I'm into one guy and you're assuming that means I couldn't ever really be into women. Micah." I looked into his eyes. "I'm not gay."

"Right." He nodded. "I'm sorry. Okay, so let's go over the facts." He was such a lawyer. "One: you're attracted to women. You've dated them and it was good but not great." He paused and looked at me, presumably waiting for agreement. I nodded. "Two: you're attracted to men but you haven't dated them." He paused again, waiting for my nod before continuing. "Which brings me to three: you're worried about this now for the first time." He squinted at me. "Why is that?"

"Uh, because this is the first time it's come up," I answered.

"But you said you've always found men attractive in the same way you find women attractive, right?"

How had I landed in the middle of a cross-examination? Oh, yeah, I went to a lawyer for advice. "Yes, but I also told you what I want is a serious relationship—a wife or a, uh, life partner. I'm not going to feel that way about every person who happens to be attractive."

He smirked. "That's my point. You're thinking about the issues surrounding being with a man for the first time in your life, and yet you say the feelings you have for men have always been there. That tells me there's something different about the way you feel about *this* man, the twenty-year-old. Whatever's going on with him must be different." He arched his eyebrows. "Am I right?"

"Yes," I said without hesitation. That much I knew. "Nobody has ever made me feel the way I do when I'm with him."

"But you're worried he's too young to be serious, and if you take a chance and things don't work out, you'll be screwed for life."

I wouldn't have phrased it quite like that, but the bottom line was the same. "Yes, that's one of the things I'm worried about."

"What're the other things?"

I chewed on my bottom lip. "What if *I* decide it's not right?" I let out a deep breath and looked out the window. "Thinking a guy on TV is cute is one thing. How do I know I can actually, uh, date a man?"

He furrowed his brow. "What do you mean? Like you're worried if you can get it up with him?"

Micah's frankness caught me off guard and I reflexively squeezed my eyes shut. "Not exactly," I said, thinking about my physical reactions to Eli and knowing erections weren't going to be a problem.

"Well, then, what?"

"I don't know." I really didn't. "I guess it's just that I've never done this before, and he's so young and—" I sighed and whispered, "I don't want to hurt him, Micah. I care about this guy. I care about him a lot. He's made it clear that he wants us to be together. If I say yes and then I change my mind..." I shook my head. "I can't do that to him."

"All right, so to summarize, you want to be with him but you're worried he'll change his mind and render you undateable, and you're worried you'll try it and decide you can't actually be with a man."

"Yes. You've managed to narrow my biggest life crisis into two sentences."

"It was one sentence."

I snorted. "That's helpful, Micah."

"Look, nobody can guarantee anything in life, least of

all that a relationship is going to work out. So as far as the first problem, you're just going to have to decide if the possibility of being with this guy for the long haul is worth the fallout if you give it a chance and it goes south."

I nodded in agreement with his assessment.

"As far as the second problem, I say you try to find another man you might want to date. I don't mean someone you're serious about, like this guy, but someone you can spend a little time with and see if those attractions of yours can coalesce into something more tangible."

"Is that a fancy way of telling me I should hook up with someone?"

"I didn't realize I was being fancy."

I chuckled and punched his shoulder. "Thanks, Micah. I'll think about it."

"So you're good?"

I nodded.

"Great. Let's go eat."

I THOUGHT a lot about Micah's advice over the next few months, but I couldn't date anybody in Emile City without risking people at work finding out about it, so that was off the table. Then in September, I went to a wedding in New York. One of my classmates from rabbinical school was marrying a doctor who worked with a really bright, really cute blond guy.

We met at the rehearsal dinner on Saturday, sat next to each other at the wedding on Sunday, spent most of the reception talking, and then went out to the bars Sunday night. I'm not sure making out with someone at the edge of a dance floor counted as a hookup, but by the time my flight left LaGuardia, I felt confident being with Eli wouldn't be a problem on my end. It turned out I enjoyed touching hard planes and muscles just as much as soft curves and breasts.

But even with that concern lifted, I remained worried that Eli's age, and the fact that he was still in college and living out of state, meant a relationship with him would be too risky. So I kept talking to him on the phone, writing him, and spending time with him whenever he came home, but I made sure not to give him any indication that I could be interested in anything other than his friendship.

CHAPTER EIGHT

You be words and I'll be music. Ain't you heard, that's how they do it? – Words and Music

We rejoice in the celebration uniting our families at the marriage of Brooke Jayden and Bradley Barton. June 27, 2004 at 4:30 p.m. Your presence is requested and your support will enrich us throughout our marital journey.

Seth Cohen

"RABBI!" A panicked voice sounded outside my office along with rapid footsteps. I was a few hours away from officiating a wedding. This one was at Temple Beth Shalom, and the guests wouldn't be arriving for another hour, so I was getting some work done. "Rabbi, are you in there?"

"I'm right here." I stood and stepped toward the door. "What's going—"

"Oh, thank goodness!" the bride said as she rushed

into my office. She bent at the waist, rested her hands on her knees, and gasped for air. "I need your help. Brad is freaking out and you're our only hope of calming him down."

Inside my head I heard, "Help me, Obi-Wan Kenobi; you're my only hope." Brooke even looked a little like Princess Leia right then because her hair was up in curlers and she was wearing a white bath robe.

I grabbed my new suit jacket and slipped it on. "What's going on?"

She straightened, grasped my elbow, and tugged me out of my office. "Brad's family, that's what's going on. They're nuts, the lot of them." She paused and looked up at me, wide-eyed. "Don't tell anyone I said that. I don't want them to hate me."

"I won't," I assured her.

The bride had grown up in the congregation, but the groom had moved to Emile City with her after college, so I knew nothing about his family.

"What happened?" I asked as we walked toward the preschool rooms. We used them as dressing areas when we held weddings in the sanctuary.

"Well, you know his sister Marilyn is this aspiring singer, right?" No, I didn't, but I kept that information to myself. "So when we told his parents we were going to have someone sing during the cocktail hour, they said he should ask her to do it. Brad was against it from the start. He said her voice isn't very good and that she's a flake, but then his parents got mad and I didn't want to have wedding drama, so I told him to let it go. Well, he let it go and now—"

"Because there's nowhere to put up a stripper pole, Marilyn! We're in a synagogue."

I came to a halt outside of the groom's room and slowly turned my head toward the bride.

"Do you see?" she asked. Her eyes filled with tears and her bottom lip trembled. "I told my parents I couldn't find my favorite lipstick and I had to have it just so they'd go to the mall to buy me another one. Brad will be so embarrassed if they see his family acting like this."

"Okay." I patted her arm. "It'll be fine."

We walked into the room and saw Brad standing in front of a woman I gathered was his sister. She was next to a long metal pole leaning against the wall. A man and woman in their early fifties were beside them. I assumed they were Brad's parents.

"It's not a stripper pole!" Marilyn shouted as she pointed to what sure looked to be a stripper pole. "It's a prop."

"You're supposed to be singing," Brad's mother said. "Why do you need a prop?"

"And what in the hell are you wearing?" Brad added.

"Brad!" his father snapped. "Don't talk to your sister that way."

"Why not?" he yelled. "She's wearing clear five-inch heels, for fuck's sake. You know what they say about girls in clear heels?"

Marilyn squinted her eyes dangerously. "If you have a problem with the way I look, blame your girlfriend. She made me wear this horrible color!"

"It's purple, Marilyn," Brad's mother said. "She asked us to wear purple because the wedding colors are purple and gold. She let us pick our own dresses. Anything we wanted." She raised her hand in her daughter's direction and moved it up and down. "And this is what you chose?"

"What're you saying, Mom?" Marilyn asked.

"She's saying you look like a whore!" Brad yelled.

Whoa. That snapped me out of my shock. "Hi," I said as I stepped forward, making the Barton family aware of the fact they weren't alone. "I'm Rabbi Cohen. I don't think we've met yet."

"Now isn't a great time, Rabbi," Brad said. "We're working out some issues."

"Uh, Brad," Brooke said hesitantly as she approached her fiancé. "I thought maybe Rabbi Cohen could help us, um, figure things out."

"Oh look, Sandy's here," Marilyn sneered.

"It's, um, Brooke," Brooke said quietly, her eyes lowered.

"It was a theatrical reference," Marilyn snapped. "I guess people who aren't in the business wouldn't get it."

"Screw you, Mare. I got your reference just fine!" Brad curled his arm protectively around Brooke. "And taking your clothes off for money doesn't mean you're in the theater business!" he yelled.

"What did you say to me?" Marilyn flared her nostrils and tightened her fists.

"I'm sure he didn't mean anything by it," I said, stepping between them and trying to de-escalate the situation.

"Don't stick up for him, Rabbi. He knows what he said." She flipped her hair over her shoulder, darted her gaze around the room until it landed on a purse in the corner, and then stomped over to it. "You know what? I don't need this. You have your perfect wedding with your perfect girlfriend. I'm out of here."

"Marilyn!" her mother said in horror. "You can't leave. It's your brother's wedding."

"Oh please." She rolled her eyes. "Like you care." She shoved her way past us and stomped out of the room.

"Bruce," Brad's mother said as she turned to her husband. "Talk to her. She'll listen to you."

He grunted and followed his daughter.

"Just great!" Brad shouted, throwing his arms in the air. "Now we're stuck without a singer."

"Um, honey," his mother said. "Maybe if you go after her and apologize, she'll—"

"No." He shook his head. "Absolutely not."

"Honestly, Brad, what did you expect her to do with the way you were talking to her?" his mother asked reasonably.

"How was I supposed to talk to her, Mom? She's been insulting Brooke from the minute she stepped off the plane, and there's no reason for it! Brooke's been nothing but nice to her. She even put together a basket with all of Marilyn's favorite things and had it waiting in her hotel room." He looked down at his bride and his eyes softened. "I couldn't take another minute of her giving Brooke dirty looks and making snide remarks."

"Brad," his mother sighed. "You know your sister's just jealous."

Brooke licked her lips nervously. "Look, I, uh, need to finish getting ready, and my parents will be back soon and then the guests are coming, so I guess"—her eyes looked wet—"it's not a big deal if we don't have a singer."

"Oh, honey, I'm sorry." Brad looked truly contrite. "I know how much it meant to you. You even wrote the invitation around it."

Brooke sniffled. Brad hugged her.

"I might know someone who can fill in," I volunteered.

Brooke jerked her gaze toward me, her expression suddenly filled with hope. "You do?"

I nodded. "Do you know Eli Block?"

"Rabbi Block's son?" she asked. Her eyes widened. "Oh my gosh. He has the most amazing voice. I heard him sing all the time when we were growing up. Do you really think he'd help us?"

I had no doubt. "You go get ready, and I'll call him and see what I can do."

"And I'll go talk to my sister," Brad said. "I'm sorry I

lost my temper, Brooke. I get a little crazy when people run you down."

"I know." She circled her arms around his waist, and he gathered her in his arms, holding her close. "I love you."

Despite the family drama and the cussing and the fiasco unfolding in front of my face, my spirits lifted at their display of love and affection. The wedding was one day; the marriage was supposed to last a lifetime. Seeing Brad and Brooke together told me that even if their big day didn't work out quite like they'd been expecting, they were going to be happy for the long haul.

I went to my office, called Eli, and explained the situation. Thirty minutes later, he was standing at my door, wearing his best suit and a purple tie and holding his guitar. And he looked so gorgeous I stopped breathing when I saw him. Actually stopped breathing.

At twenty-one, Eli still looked young enough that he'd raise eyebrows if someone saw him in a bar, but dressed up in a dark suit with his hair neatly brushed, he no longer looked like a kid. Seeing him standing there, I got a glimpse into the man he'd grow into, and I ached to be by his side, watching it happen.

"Hi," he said breathlessly. "I rushed right over. I'm not late, am I?"

I opened my mouth to answer but the sight of him had stolen my voice along with my every ounce of air in my lungs, so I gulped and nodded instead.

"Do I look okay?" he asked, combing his hand along the sides and back of his hair. "You're looking at me funny."

You're beautiful. That's why I'm staring. You're so beautiful I never want to stop looking at you.

"You look nice," I said.

He blushed, dropped his gaze, and smiled shyly. "Thanks, Seth. So do you." He looked up at me from underneath his lashes, a move seemingly designed to melt my heart. "Is that a new suit?"

"Yes." I coughed and cleared the thickness from my throat. "All my other suits met wedding-related demises, so I did some shopping."

He dragged his gaze from my face, down my body, to my feet, and trembled. With the way he looked and the way he was gazing at me, I knew I needed to change the topic before I tossed out my good judgment, ignored all my concerns, and jumped him right there in my office.

"So, uh, did you decide about that master's program?"

Eli had one more year to go before he graduated with a dual major—music and education. He'd been trying to decide whether to pursue a master's or come home to Emile City and try to get a teaching job.

"Uh-huh. I think you talked me into it. Like you said, that way I have more options because I can teach at a college too."

Over the years, my relationship with Eli had gotten more complex. He no longer came on to me in his overt, campy ways, but the expressions on his face when I noticed him staring at me, the way he clung tightly when I gave him a hug, the way his entire body seemed to shake if I accidently brushed against him, all those things told me Eli's desire to be with me hadn't waned. And though I still gave him advice in a way that reminded me of our age difference, Eli always listened to what I had to say and took it to heart, something he didn't do with his parents, or, from what I'd heard Avi say when he was complaining to Meredith, other authority figures in his life. So I knew that in Eli's mind, I occupied a different space from those people, which made me wonder if he finally saw me as someone other than the camp counselor who was the subject of his childhood crush.

"Eli?" I said, stepping closer to him.

"Yeah?" He must have heard something in my tone, because his expression morphed into one of hopeful trepidation.

What was I doing? Did I actually think I could ask him if his feelings for me were grown-up enough to be trusted? Could he even know the answer to that question?

Getting my emotions under control, I changed tracks and said, "What're you planning to sing?"

"Oh, uh, I hadn't thought about it." He sat down in the chair across from my desk, propped the guitar across his chest, and started strumming and humming to himself. "I know," he said eventually. "How about 'I Swear'? Have you heard it? John Michael Montgomery?"

I shook my head.

He moved his hand elegantly over his guitar, filling my office with beautiful music, and then he started to sing about knowing someone has questions but promising you'll stand by them and never break their heart.

The song wasn't familiar, but hearing it in Eli's voice made me wonder if he had read my mind. I'd been drawn to him from the start. I'd known I wanted him for months, years even. But standing in my office, seeing him all dressed up and listening to his beautiful voice croon while he gazed at me like I was the only person in the world that mattered, I ached for him. Bone deep.

By the time he was done singing, every hair on my body was standing on end and I was shivering. "Eli," I said breathlessly.

"Wow." I had been so focused on him that the new voice made me jump. I jerked my head toward the door and saw Brooke looking very much the part of the bride in her sparkling white gown. "That was so beautiful, Eli," she said.

"Thank you." He smiled at her. "You look great."

"Brooke." I shook my head to clear my thoughts and put my head back on work. "Are you ready for us?"

"We have a little time. The guests aren't here yet," she said. "I came to tell you that Brad somehow made up with his sister and she agreed to sing after all, but—" She bit her lip. "Eli, your voice is so amazing. If she agrees, would you be willing to sing with her?"

"Sure," he said happily. "Whatever you want." He got up, stepped over to her, and kissed her cheek. "It's your big day."

She beamed. "Thank you!" She grasped his elbow. "Come on. I'll introduce you to Marilyn and see what she thinks."

"See you in a bit, Seth." He winked at me as she pulled him out of the office.

It was no surprise to me that the groom's sister hit it off with Eli; he was such an incredibly likeable guy. So after all the angst and consternation, Brooke got not one but two singers and a musical accompaniment to boot—Eli on his acoustic guitar. The duet Eli and Marilyn pulled off was moving and romantic and brought more than one guest to tears. The bride was thrilled, the groom was grateful, and I finally officiated a romantic, heart-warming wedding.

CHAPTER NINE

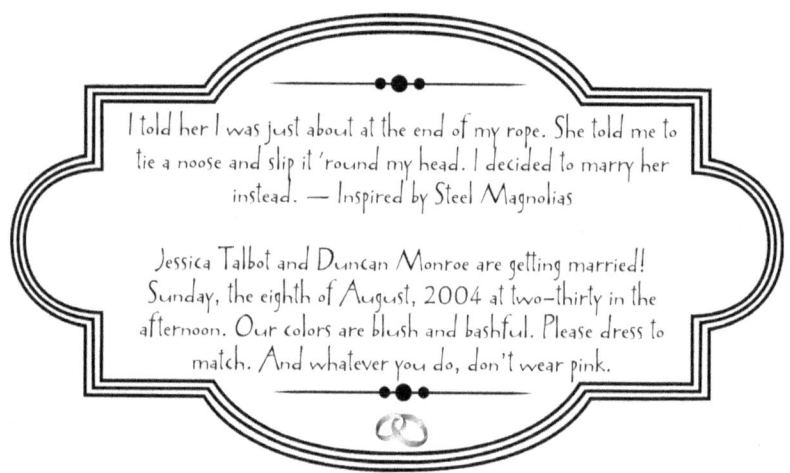

I told her I was just about at the end of my rope. She told me to tie a noose and slip it 'round my head. I decided to marry her instead. — Inspired by Steel Magnolias

Jessica Talbot and Duncan Monroe are getting married! Sunday, the eighth of August, 2004 at two-thirty in the afternoon. Our colors are blush and bashful. Please dress to match. And whatever you do, don't wear pink.

Eli Block

"HELLO."

"Hi, it's me. I didn't wake you up, did I?"

I heard Seth's voice, and my heart rate immediately sped up. No matter how many times I lectured myself about hopeless crushes, my stupid reactions to him stayed the same. I was pathetic.

"Hey, Seth," I said, praying I sounded breathless only to my own ears. "It's ten o'clock in the morning. I've already been up for at least, uh, ten or fifteen minutes."

Awake and up, actually. And I was still in bed thinking of getting myself worked into round two.

He chuckled. "You're back in classes next week. Better get your body used to a more normal starting hour."

There was a time when I'd resented his constant stream of advice, because it frustrated me to feel like Seth thought of me as a kid. But over the years, I'd come to realize it meant he cared about me. I watched Seth whenever I had the chance, not just when he was talking to me. So I saw how he was with other people. He listened well, nodded a lot, and made the occasional suggestion, but I never saw him truly insinuate himself into anybody else's life. When I realized he was different with me, his advice made me feel special and any resentment melted away.

I slid down on my mattress, cupped my balls, and said, "Don't worry, old man. It's my senior year. I won't fall apart at the last minute."

He grunted.

"So, what's up? Is there a change of plans? Or am I still coming to your place at around five."

"No change." He paused. "Make sure you bring your key, though, in case I'm late. You know how these weddings can get."

I had a key to his apartment because he'd asked me to house-sit when he'd gone to LA to visit his family for a week earlier in the summer. I'd jumped at the chance to have some space from my parents (success quotient: minimal—my mother showed up almost every evening with food). Plus, I'd relished the opportunity to snoop through Seth's things when he wasn't around to catch me (success quotient: goal accomplished but results disappointing—his place was bare except for a few photo albums with no nudity).

There was so little there that I wondered if he'd had issues with whoever watched his place before me and had gotten in the habit of hiding anything worth seeing in his office when he traveled. But when I asked what happened to his previous house sitter, he said he'd never had one.

"I don't have any plants or pets, and I'm never gone very long, so there's no reason to have someone in my space, sleeping in my bed." He shuddered. "Kind of gives me the creeps."

I hadn't wanted him to change his mind about my staying there, so I didn't point out that I'd been doing that very thing. Hell, he'd told me not to bother stripping the sheets before he came home because he'd be washing all his clothes from the trip anyway and he could combine the laundry.

"The key's on my keychain. I won't forget it." I rolled my eyes and snorted when I realized I was responding to yet another piece of advice.

"Good." He sounded happy. I heard him sigh, clear his throat, and then he said, "So the reason I'm calling is I want to borrow the tie you wore to services the first night of Rosh Hashanah."

"The tie I wore to…" I furrowed my brow. "Seth, that was in September. It's been almost a year. How am I supposed to remem—"

"The bride's mom called and asked me to coordinate my tie with the rest of the color theme, which is blush and bashful, but not pink. I have no idea what that means, but your tie is a really light peachy-pink color with silver stripes. You wore it with your navy suit and mine's black, but I have a light-gray shirt almost the same color as the pewter one you were wearing, so I think it'll work."

It took me a moment to remember the tie he was talking about. I let go of my nuts and climbed out of bed. "I think it's here. Give me a sec." I stepped over to my closet and rustled through the clothes until I got to the hanger holding my ties. "Found it. Do you need me to bring it over?"

"No, you don't have to do that. I'll come by on my way to the ceremony. I know you're busy and—"

"Yeah, I'm super busy." I laughed. "I just finished beating off and I'm trying to decide if I should shower or get in another *hallelujah* before I clean up."

Seth made a strange sound, almost like he was choking. "Are you okay?"

"Yes." He coughed and cleared his throat. "I'm fine."

"Okay." I tossed the tie on my bed. "Give me ten minutes to get showered and dressed, then I'll pick up some bagels from that place you like and head your way."

"Are you sure?" he asked, but I could tell from his tone

that he was pleased. Nobody ever fed the man. It was sad. If he were mine… I shook off the thoughts. No hopeless crushes.

"Yeah, I'm sure. You're officiating a wedding, that's like a major workout for you. There might be animals or fires or fistfights. The possibilities are endless. We need to make sure you march into battle with a full stomach."

"NOAH," I frantically said the second my friend answered his phone. "Do you have a big bowl? I mean a giant one?"

"Eli?"

"Yeah, it's me." I wiped the back of my hand across my forehead and then sneezed when a cloud of flour drifted down. "A big bowl. Do you have one?"

"Uh, Eli, man, I haven't been into that shit for a long time." He lowered his voice. "I might be able to find someone who can help you out, but are you sure you wanna do that? I mean, whatever you're into, but—"

I paused in midstir. "What are you talking about? I'm making challah and I measured wrong, put in too much flour. So now I need a bigger bowl so I can increase the rest of the ingredients. I'd call my mom, but then she'd come over here and complain about how I didn't listen when she gave me her recipe." I rubbed my hand over my eye and then started blinking furiously when it started to burn. "I can't deal with that right now."

"Ooooh," he said, drawing the word out. "That kind of bowl."

"What did you think I meant?" I asked, furrowing my brow.

"Never mind. What size bowl?"

I considered the large metal bowl I'd brought over to Seth's from my mother's house. It was close to overflowing by that point, and I still needed to add more water and yeast. "Uh, one that's, like, three times the size of one of those big bowls that comes in the nesting set."

"I have no idea what you're talking about. Hold on. Let me ask Clark."

I heard him set the phone down, so I took the opportunity to click the speaker button on my phone, put it on the counter, and start searching Seth's cabinets on the off chance he was stashing a sink-sized bowl somewhere.

"Oh!" I said to myself. "That's it." I hopped up, forgetting I was looking inside a cabinet, and slammed my head. "Fuck!"

"Clark says he's never seen a bowl that big," Noah chirped from the phone. I rubbed my head and crawled backward until I was sure I was clear. "Eli? You there?"

"I'm here!" I called out and rushed over to the phone. "Never mind. I figured it out. I'll use the sink."

There was a pause and then, "You're going to use the sink as a bowl?"

I nodded even though he couldn't see me. Then I reached for the ingredients I had lining the counter and moved them closer to the sink.

"Yeah, that's what he said," Noah mumbled, presumably to Clark. "Eli, Clark says to make sure you scrub it down first so you don't get bacteria in the food and then rinse it out really well so you don't get cleaner in there."

"Good point. Thanks."

"No problem. So what're you making?"

"Challah for Seth."

"What's challah?"

"Bread. It's a Jewish thing. Braided egg bread. My mom has a great recipe, and he loved it when he went to my parents' house for Shabbat so I'm making some for him."

"You're at his place?"

"Uh-huh."

"Is he there?"

"No. He's working." I squatted down and shuffled the stuff under the sink, looking for something I could use to clean it. "Is Simple Green a cleaner?"

"Yeah."

"Cool. Listen, I gotta go. I have to do math so I can figure out how much of everything else I need to add to make up for the flour issue."

"Okay. Good luck. Call me later and tell me how it went."

"The bread?" I asked distractedly.

"No. Not the bread." Noah chuckled. "The man."

"We're just friends," I insisted as soon as I realized

what he meant. "I'm not trying to—"

"Sure you're not. Go bake bread for your *friend* and call me later."

He hung up before I could say anything else, which was fine by me. I was being truthful when I said Seth and I were friends. Then again, Noah was right too. Whatever. I didn't have time to think about my pathetic mental state right then. I was busy calculating how much water, yeast, sugar, salt, and eggs I needed to add to make up for the fact that I'd put in eight cups of flour instead of three. It was the first time in my life I wished I'd paid closer attention in math class.

BETWEEN THE impromptu math exam, the sink scrubbing, and the extra trip to the grocery store, making the bread took much longer than I anticipated. Thankfully, Seth didn't get home by five like he'd projected. It was a little after six when I heard the door open. A fresh loaf of challah was cooling on the counter, and I had just finished washing the last dish. I dried off my hands and hurried out of the kitchen.

"Hey! You're late. Is everything okay?" I stopped short at the sight of him. "What happened to your neck?" I rushed toward him. "Is that a burn or a cut or..." I furrowed my brow when I got closer. "Is that lipstick?" I jerked my gaze up.

"Probably." He sounded tired and it seemed like the "I've had a long day at work" kind of tired but, really, what did

I know? Maybe his "I just got lucky" tired looked the same.

"Why is there lipstick on your neck?"

"Do I have any beer?" he mumbled to himself.

"Seth?" I licked my lips. "The lipstick?"

"Or wine. Maybe I have wine."

I took in a calming breath, got a whiff of him, and started coughing.

"Are you drunk?" My stomach plummeted as I thought of him partying with some woman, letting her touch him, kiss him. I thought I might throw up.

"I wish," he said.

It took me a few seconds to realize he was answering my question about being drunk and not responding to my thought about him making out with someone.

"Why do you smell like a frat house?"

He dragged his fingers through his already disheveled hair. "There were kegs at the wedding."

"Kegs?" I repeated. "As in, more than one?"

He nodded. "And a champagne fountain too." He loosened his tie—my tie—peeled it off, and then carefully draped it over the back of the couch. "I think it's clean, but if it smells funny, I'll have it dry cleaned."

"Don't worry about the tie. Tell me why you were at an afternoon wedding that sounds like the training ground for an AA meeting." I squinted at him. "And why you're covered in lipstick."

"I need a drink and then a shower." He walked toward

the kitchen and shrugged out of his jacket. "In that order." He dropped the jacket on the ground, which was completely out of character given his freakish need for neatness and order.

I picked up the jacket and then crouched down when I saw something fall out of one of the pockets. "Seth, maybe you've had enough to dri—" I stopped midword when I realized what I'd just picked up off the floor. "Is this a rubber?"

"Probably," he said.

I heard a cabinet open and marched into the kitchen, digging through his jacket with one hand and holding the condom in the other. "Why do you have a rubber?" I felt something crinkly in his pocket and grasped it. "Correction: two, no, three rubbers. Why do you have three rubbers?"

"You don't want to know." He shook his head.

"Uh, yeah, I do."

"Where's the corkscrew?" he mumbled.

Apparently he'd located a bottle of wine.

"Is this how you prepare for weddings? You stuff your pockets full of prophylactics and hope you get lucky?" I snagged the bottle I saw sitting on the counter. "And I think you've had enough to drink."

"Eli," he sighed tiredly and turned around, a corkscrew in his hand. "I'm completely sober. I haven't had a sip to drink. I promise. And there's no way you think I carry around condoms and try to get wedding guests into bed."

"Fine. I believe the last part, but"—I got closer and sniffed him—"you don't smell sober."

"The keg exploded."

I blinked in surprise. "The keg exploded?"

"Yes."

"How does that happen?"

He held his hand out and I handed him the bottle.

"I have no idea."

"So that's why you smell like a bar?"

"Probably." He put the bottle under his arm and angled the corkscrew into it. "Or it might be from when the champagne fountain got backed up. It sprayed really far."

"The champagne fountain exploded too?"

He shook his head. "It didn't explode. It just sprayed because somebody thought it'd be funny to drop a bunch of strawberries in there."

"Somebody dropped strawberries into the champagne fountain?"

"I think it was one of the bridesmaids. She was pretty drunk."

Drunk women made me think of women around Seth, which made me think of the lipstick. "Is she the one who, uh, gave you those marks?" I asked as I pointed to his neck.

"Maybe." He pulled the cork out, tossed it on the counter, and said, "Are you going to want some of this?"

I shook my head.

"You sure?"

I nodded.

He shrugged and then tipped the bottle against his

lips and started gulping down the wine.

"How is it you don't know who did it?"

Once he lowered the bottle, he said, "Well, it could have been the ushers. They were the groom's frat brothers and they kept talking about all the practical jokes they used to play in college."

"Why would the groom's frat brothers leave lipstick on your neck?"

"Oh, you're asking about the lipstick? I thought you meant who put the fruit in the fountain." He leaned against the counter and raised the bottle again.

I was dangerously close to shaking him.

"Seth!" I shouted. He looked at me and arched his eyebrows but didn't stop drinking. "You're covered in lipstick and you have bone blankets coming out of your pockets. What the hell?" I hoped I didn't sound jealous. I had no right to interrogate him about his personal life. But I was his friend, so I was allowed to be worried, right? I hoped so.

"Bone blankets?"

I rolled my eyes. "Pecker ponchos, dingdong covers, raincoats." I stomped my foot and stopped caring about how I sounded. "Why do you have rubbers in your pocket?"

"I think maybe one of the women put them there."

"One of the women?"

He nodded.

"Just how many women were you with?" I seethed.

"None." He tipped the bottle back all the way, gulped,

and when it was empty, he set it on the counter.

"None?"

"Not in the way you mean, no."

"You're not making any sense. You're covered in lipstick, and you said one of who knows how many women filled your pockets with rubbers, but now you're saying you weren't with any women and—"

"Eli?"

He sounded remarkably calm for a man who'd just downed a full bottle of wine. Or maybe that was the reason he was calm.

"Yeah."

"You know I wouldn't go to a wedding, where I'm working, and pick someone up." He stepped toward me. "You know that." I nodded. "Good." He reached up and cupped my cheek, and I realized for the first time that I was trembling. "I'm sorry I was late," he whispered.

"It's okay," I said hoarsely.

"And I think maybe I'm too drunk to go out to dinner. Or at least I will be once all that wine kicks in." He gave me a crooked grin and my knees buckled. I grabbed on to his waist so I could remain upright. Instead of pushing me away, Seth stepped closer and wrapped his arm around my back. "Right now, I feel pretty good."

I shuddered. He was so close, and damn him, even drunk he was gorgeous. It was all I could do to stop myself from jumping all over him.

"Eli, I've been wanting to tell you that—"

Given how close he was standing, I could smell perfume underneath the liquor and see lip shapes in the red marks on his neck. It was killing me. "You need a shower."

He blinked in surprise. "Oh, right. The beer and the champagne." He stepped away and I started breathing again. "Sorry. I know I stink. I'll go clean up and then we can figure out dinner and talk."

"I baked."

A smile took over his face. "You did?"

I pointed to the challah on the counter. "My mom's challah recipe. It should be good for soaking up all that wine you just poured into your belly."

He beamed at me. "I love your mom's challah!"

"I know." I looked down at my feet. "And I sort of made too much, so you have about a dozen more loaves in your freezer. When this one's gone, you can take out another one, let it rise for about three hours and then pop it in the oven."

"When did you have time to do all this?"

"I came over early." I blushed and looked at the ground. "Guess it's a good thing you haven't made me give the key back."

"No." He shook his head. "I want you to keep it. I had it made for you."

I grinned at him. "Yeah. It helps if I'm meeting you here and you're running late."

He came closer. "It's nice coming home and finding

you here." He glanced at the challah. "Thanks, Eli."

The way he was looking at me, all happy and smiley and loose-limbed, made me think of what he might look like after satisfying sex. I hated my brain. It wouldn't stop torturing me.

"Go disinfect yourself and get all that shit off your neck. I'll slice up the bread and put butter and honey on it."

"Okay." He made it as far as the doorway and then looked back at me. "Then we can talk, right?"

I started slicing bread. "Yup. I'll feed you and we'll catch up on the wedding fun." I waved my arm—and the knife—at him. "Go get clean. Turn the water to boiling if you have to."

He laughed. "Okay. One *Silkwood* shower coming right up."

"What's Silkwood?" I shouted after him.

"You better be kidding, Eli!" he said, stopping dead in his tracks. "And if you're not, we have another addition to our movie list."

"So it's a movie?"

"It's Meryl Streep and Cher and a million Oscars and Golden Globes and—"

"Is this one a musical too?"

His jaw dropped. "Never mind. I'll tell you about it later."

As soon as I knew he was gone, I dropped the knife, braced both hands against the counter, and squeezed my eyes shut. *What am I doing?* I'd asked myself that question a million times when it came to my obsession with Seth Cohen, but I still didn't have any answers. And, yes, it was an obsession. I could own that.

Going on three years and I hadn't so much as made out with a guy. Some of that was because I agreed with Seth about the whole heart-head-dick thing being connected, or should be connected, or whatever. But there was no way I couldn't have found someone who met that requirement if I'd really tried. Or at least that would have been true if I hadn't been pining after Seth.

It was ridiculous. Almost three years of self-imposed celibacy, and for what? It wasn't like Seth was interested in me like that. It wasn't like it would make him want me.

I stumbled over to the couch and collapsed, suddenly feeling exhausted. My last year of college was about to start. Was I going to spend it thinking about a guy I couldn't have? Seth would always be my friend, maybe even my best friend, but I was going to lose my mind if I didn't force myself to move past my hopeless childhood crush.

The best way to get over a guy is to get under another one. I'd heard that joke a time or three and I figured there was a lot of truth to it. I dropped my head against the back of the couch and thought about people I knew from school. There were several guys who'd asked me out a few times and kept hanging around even after I repeatedly turned them down. They were cute and fun, and I decided when I got back, I'd call one of them and ask him out. Didn't matter which one.

"Okay, I'm all clean. Can we talk now?" The couch dipped at the same time I heard Seth's voice.

I blinked my eyes open and looked at him. He was wearing a T-shirt from some fun-run fundraiser and pajama pants. His hair was wet and disheveled and his cheeks were rosy from the alcohol or the warm shower or both. I wanted him. God, but did I want him. I closed my eyes to hide the wetness I could feel forming there.

"Eli?" He scooted closer to me. "Is everything okay?"

I needed to get up. I had to get away from him. But I couldn't.

"Eli?" He moved again. His hip was pressed against mine, and he wrapped his arm around my shoulder. "Talk to me. What're you thinking about that has you so upset?"

He had to be a touchy drunk. The torture wouldn't be complete otherwise. "Nothing." I gulped. "You said you wanted to talk about something. Go ahead. What's up?"

"No." He shook his head. "You first. I can tell you've got things on your mind."

I forced myself to smile and then I lied to Seth. It was one of the hardest things I'd ever done. "It's no biggie, really. I was just thinking about this guy at school."

He dropped his arm from my shoulder in a flash. "What guy?"

"He's a"—I licked my lips and furrowed my brow in thought—"business major. Or maybe accounting." I shrugged.

"Either way, he wants to get his MBA and he's cute."

"Cute?"

I nodded.

"Are you…" He made a squeaking noise and then drew in a deep breath. "Are you seeing this guy?"

"Yes." It hurt to keep lying to him, and there was no reason for it. "Well, not yet, but that's about to change."

"It is?"

I got up, wiped my clammy hands on my jeans, and nodded. "Yes. I'm going to try dipping my foot—and my dick—back in the dating pool. Going this long without is stupid."

Seth jumped off the couch. "But—"

"I know what you're going to say," I told him as I raised my hand up in a stop motion. "But it's been three years since I tried last time. People have to have grown up by now, right? I'm sure I'll find someone who can stimulate all my organs. Like Gregg. I mean, Gary."

"That's not what I…"

"He's smart. You'd like him." I'd go out with Gary, we'd hit it off, and I'd be back on that horse. I paused, thought about it, and felt my shoulders relax. It was a good plan. "Maybe I can bring him home over winter break. That'd be good, right?"

When I looked at Seth for a response, I noticed he seemed really pale and his hands were shaking.

"Shit! I forgot to feed you." I turned toward the kitchen.

"You sit down and I'll get you some challah and soup. Then we can talk about whatever it was you wanted to talk about." I looked back at him over my shoulder. "Thanks for listening, Seth. You're a great friend."

And if I had to write those words a hundred times on a chalkboard so I could remember that was all he'd ever be, I'd do it. Because operation Get Over Childhood Crush was officially underway.

CHAPTER TEN

> **RORY WILDE AND WILLIAM "BILLY" ROWE**
> **INVITE YOU TO JOIN US**
> **AS WE COMMIT TO SURVIVE THE ZOMBIE**
> **APOCALYPSE TOGETHER.**
> **EIGHT P.M.,**
> **SATURDAY, JULY 14, 2007.**

Eli Block

I STUCK with my plan and asked Gary out when I got back to school. And I was right about him being a nice guy. Fun, too, so I kept dating him, kept waiting for the flame to turn on in my chest when I was with him the way it did when I was with Seth.

Speaking of Seth, we stayed friends, but I could sense a distance growing between us. I figured it was my fault. I was trying so hard to get over my crush on him that I probably pushed him away without meaning to. The weakening of our friendship wore on me until I snapped and decided it didn't have to be all or nothing. I'd go out with other guys, find a boyfriend, and with any luck, have some assisted orgasms, but I wouldn't step back from the friendship I'd built with Seth.

I told him as much when I was in Emile City for Yom Kippur my senior year and, to my relief, he promised that nothing I did and nobody I dated would ever change how he felt about me. True to his word, he spent almost every minute I was home with me, and I felt the chasm that had formed between us close. With that concern resolved, I went back to school and followed through on things with Gary. It wasn't serious enough for me to bring him home, but we dated until spring break and ended things amicably. After Gary came my master's program and Roger, a medical student who lived in the apartment next to mine. Then there was Justin, a guy who worked in a store where I bought my cell phone.

One night when I was driving home from a date with Roger—or maybe it was Justin—it hit me that I was looking forward to calling Seth to say good night way more than I'd looked forward to the date I'd just been on. The realization that what I felt for him was no longer something that could be categorized as a childhood crush, that I was actually in love with him, came easily. It wasn't like getting hit by a wave, more like floating in a warm bath and feeling comfortable because the water had been rising slowly.

At first blush, that might make it seem like Operation Get Over Childhood Crush had been a total failure, but that wasn't true. Three years of putting myself out in the dating pool had taught me that I could be attracted to other men, that I could enjoy their company and respect them, and even be in a relationship with them. It also taught me that all those things added together didn't equate to being in love. But the way I saw it, that was okay, because at least I knew I was capable of that emotion, which was more than I could say for lots of people I knew.

Once I'd come to terms with my feelings for Seth, I no longer found them debilitating. I could be with him, notice my heart racing, and revel in that instead of fixating on what I couldn't have. Which was why I'd only been in Emile City long enough to put my bags in my room and catch up with my parents before I was driving to Seth's apartment.

My phone rang right as I'd pulled into his parking lot. "Hey," I said when I saw his number on the screen.

"Are you back?"

"Yeah." I parked the car. "I got in a couple of hours ago."

"You were supposed to call when you landed." I heard rustling. "I want to see you. Is it okay if I come over or are you doing family stuff?"

I chuckled as I climbed out of the car. "I already beat you to it."

"What do you mean?" he asked. I ran up the stairs.

"Eli? What's that—"

I had my key in the lock before he could finish his sentence.

"Seth!"

He came out of the bedroom with his belt unbuckled, one shoe untied, and the other in his hand. "Eli!" He dropped the shoe, rushed over, and pulled me into a hug. "Welcome home!"

"Thanks." I patted his back, gave him a squeeze, and pulled away, cognizant of not holding on too long. "It's good to be back."

He gazed at me and smiled broadly. "And you're here to stay this time. No more school."

"Well, I wouldn't say no more school. I have three years of a doctorate program starting next month."

"But that's different. You're staying in Emile City." He yanked me back into a hug. "I can't believe it."

The first hug had used up all my restraint, so with the second one, I let myself melt against him. I rested my head on his shoulder, wrapped my arms around his waist, and whispered, "I missed you."

"God." Seth ran his hand over the back of my head and sighed. "Me too. So much." After what was probably a long time for a hug but didn't feel long enough, he stepped back and said, "Did your dad tell you about the job?"

I'd been trying to find a job in my field, but with my PhD program, I'd only be able to work part-time, and music-related jobs weren't exactly easy to come by, so I hadn't had any luck.

"No. What job?"

He beamed. "How would you like to be a cantorial soloist at Temple Beth Shalom?"

"Seriously?" I asked excitedly. Being the song and prayer leader at the congregation my father founded and where Seth worked would be a dream come true. "What happened to Cantor Bell?"

"She's going on maternity leave."

"I didn't know she was pregnant again."

"Yup."

"So it's temporary, just until she gets back?"

"We'll see. She's having twin boys this time, and with the two girls at home, she isn't sure if she wants to come back to work. She asked for six months to figure it out, and we agreed to leave her position open until then. If you're interested, you can sub for her until she decides what she wants to do."

"I'd love that!" I hugged him again. It was getting kind of ridiculous. "Thanks, Seth!"

"You're welcome."

"Hey, I just thought of something." I clasped his shoulders and stepped back so I could look at his face.

"What?"

"That means you'll be my boss."

Seth frowned. "No, I wouldn't. We'd both be working

for your dad."

"Uh-huh. But when my dad retires—"

"He isn't retiring yet."

"He's talking about retiring next year." I was surprised Seth didn't know.

"Really? Did he say that?"

"Yeah. I mean, he'll still be rabbi emeritus, so it's not like he'll disappear, but my mom wants to travel more, and he thinks you're ready to lead on your own."

Seth blushed. "He told you that?"

I nodded. "You know my dad loves you, right? He talks about you almost as much as..." I stopped myself before I confessed to how much I talked about Seth. Being comfortable with my feelings for him didn't mean shoving them in his face. "He said he couldn't think of a better person to take care of his congregation. Those were his exact words."

Seth coughed. "His exact words, huh?"

"Yup."

"I'll make sure to thank him for his, uh, confidence in me."

I shrugged. "Yeah, okay. So what do I need to do to get the cantorial soloist job?"

"Not a thing." He paused. "Wait. I guess there is one thing." There was a wicked glint in his eyes, which was weird because Seth almost never looked wicked.

"What?" I asked suspiciously.

"How would you feel about joining me at a wedding?"

That was it? "Yeah, sure." I shrugged.

"I hope you like zombies."

"YOU'RE SHITTING me, right?" I said.

"Nope."

I looked at the building we'd pulled up to and then back at Seth. "This is a club."

"I know." He climbed out of the car.

"No, seriously." I followed him. "I've been here. It's dingy and cramped, and there's no way anyone would hold a wedding here."

"I have two words for you," he said.

"What?"

"Horse wedding."

I rolled my eyes. "That was different, Seth, they were trying to do the *Princess Bride* theme. This is—"

"Okay fine. How about the *Rocky Horror* wedding? Or the murder-mystery wedding?"

I laughed and bumped his shoulder with mine. "You left out the dead squirrels."

He flinched. "I'm still trying to block that one out."

Fair enough.

"So you're actually officiating a wedding at a run-down club?"

"Yes."

"How're you being so nonchalant about this? You know it's weird, right?"

"Nothing fazes me anymore when it comes to weddings." He started walking toward the door and I followed him. "At this point, I just hope to get out with my suit intact and no lasting injuries."

As soon as we walked into the club, Seth turned to me and asked, "Does it look like this in here all the time? Or did they decorate this way for the wedding?"

I squinted at my surroundings in the dim light. "The walls are black all the time. It goes with the goth vibe or something, but I think the dripping faux blood is new and, might I add, classy."

He snorted. "I'm already glad I brought you with me."

"Oh holy shit!" I yelled when I caught sight of what was being displayed in the corner.

"Eli!" Seth hissed. "We're at a wedding. Watch your language."

My jaw dropped. "You're kidding, right?" I raised my hand, jerked it in a circle around us, and pointed at what had grabbed my attention. "You're going to harp on my language when there's a brain cake?"

"What?"

"Look." I cupped his chin and moved his face in the right direction. "That, I believe, is the wedding cake, and in addition to being drizzled in red slime, it's topped by a brain." I paused and then said it again. "A brain."

A loud noise sounded, like a motor, and then fog started rising from along the edges of the room.

"Is that...?" Seth peered toward the corner.

"A brain?" I decided it was fun to keep repeating it. "Yeah. It's a brain. On a cake."

"No. Behind the brain." Seth stepped closer to the cake. The fog was making it hard to see. "Is that a real bird or is it..."

"Billy!" a panicked voice said from what sounded like a nearby location, but with our vision impaired it was hard to know for sure. "There's a pigeon shitting on the cake!"

I couldn't help it; I cracked up. Totally and completely cracked up.

"Eli," Seth whispered. "Stop it." He coughed. "You can't laugh." He swallowed hard, no doubt trying to stop himself from doing exactly the same thing. "It's not professional."

"There's"—I gasped—"a pigeon"—I gasped again—"shitting on the cake." I bent over and held on to my stomach. "Hurts," I wheezed.

Seth had turned around to face the wall so I couldn't see his face, but his shoulders were shaking, which gave me a good idea exactly what Mr. Professional was doing.

A guy—Billy, I assumed—had run over to the cake. He was waving his hands around and yelling, "Shoo, bird! Shoo!"

"Oh my God. This is the best thing I've ever seen."

Seth finally turned around, and, to my surprise, he looked composed. "We need to help the pigeon."

"Help the pigeon? How do you suggest we do that?

Are we supposed to go shit on the cake too?"

He flipped right back around, shook, coughed, and then turned to look at me. "I meant help *with* the pigeon."

I opened my mouth, but he put his hand over it. "Not another word," he warned. "Ehm." He cleared his throat and tugged on his sleeves, straightening them underneath his suit. "I'll be right—"

"Hey, why are we wearing suits when everyone else is dressed like zombies?"

Seth stopped midstep and turned his attention away from what had turned into a major panic situation in the cake zone. "We're working."

"I know, but it's a theme. Couldn't we—"

"No."

"Wouldn't it be more fun if we—"

"No."

"But—"

"No themes!"

I barked out a laugh and inadvertently spit in his face.

He wiped the back of his hand across his mouth. "Very nice."

"Sorry."

He rolled his head from one side to another, took a deep breath, and then stepped toward the cake.

"Billy," he said. "Is everything okay?"

A guy wearing a shredded tuxedo and white face makeup with black around his eyes and red on his jaw and neck, turned around and yelled, "Rabbi! Oh, thank God! This is a disaster."

How Seth kept a straight face in response to that, I'll never know. I, for one, would have asked him if he was referring to the entire wedding. Instead, I dipped my face and hoped it was too dark and too loud for them to notice I was laughing. Still.

"What happened?" Seth asked.

"A pigeon shit on the cake!" someone said.

"A pigeon! Can you believe it?" another person I didn't recognize shouted. "They're, like, the cockroaches of the aviary world. Gross!"

Right. Because the *type* of bird shit was the real issue, not the shitty food. Shitty food. Oh Lord. I was going to sprain a rib.

"Next time they should find lovebirds to shit on the wedding cake," I whispered to Seth. "It'd be festive."

He tripped. Thankfully I was right behind him so I was able to grab his arm and keep him upright.

"Let me see," Seth said when we got to the cake.

I looked over his shoulder and evaluated the damage. Yup, sure enough, a corner of the cake had gray drizzle coated over the red drizzle.

"Looks like the bird ate some of the cake," I pointed out helpfully. "Must be a good multitasker."

"Where?" Billy, who I'd realized was the groom, asked.

"There." I indicated a section of the top tier that had a

hole in it.

"Shit!" yelled Billy.

"See," I quietly said to Seth. "Saying shit at this wedding is fine. Expected, even."

He threw his elbow back and hit my rib, but not hard enough to hurt.

"What are we going to do? If Rory sees this, she'll freak!"

"Where is Rory?" Seth asked.

"She's getting her hair and makeup done."

Based on the groom's appearance, I figured the bride was being done up to look like, well, a freak. It was kind of ironic considering what he'd just said, but I didn't point it out to him. That would have been unprofessional.

"Don't worry," Seth soothed. "I think we can fix this."

"How?" Bill asked.

"Yeah, how?" I chimed in as I looked over his shoulder again. "It looks really bad."

He twisted his head around and glared at me.

"What? It does."

"We can cut off the portion the bird, uh, contaminated. Do you have any more icing?"

"I do!" said a woman who might have been crying. It was hard to tell because, given the setting, the black mascara running down her face could have been intentional. "I brought it with me to do touch-ups." She rushed over and shoved a bag at Seth. "I made the cake. It's red velvet." All of a sudden she burst into tears. "A flying rat ate my cake! It's ruined! I was up all night and it's ruined!"

"Which is it, a rat or a cockroach?" I asked quietly enough that only Seth could hear. Maybe.

"It's not ruined," Seth said calmly. He patted her shoulder and she threw herself at him. There went his goal for a clean suit. Hopefully the white zombie makeup and black mascara would wash off. "It'll be okay," he said. She wrapped her arms around his waist instead of moving away. "I'll take care of it," he added as he tried subtly to extricate himself from her grasp.

I saw her slowly lower her arms, and I knew what was coming. I considered jumping in to help for about two seconds, but then I decided the entertainment was too much fun for me to stop her.

"I'll fix the cake," Seth assured her. "If you just give me space." Her hands reached their destination and she squeezed Seth's ass. He jumped. "You should go look for the pigeon." He managed to shove the bag between them, which gave him the leverage he needed to wiggle away. "So it doesn't do more damage."

"I don't mind staying and helping you, Rabbi." She ran her hand down his arm and fluttered her eyelashes.

Enough was enough and two could play at that game. "No need," I said. "He's got me if he needs any"—I tilted my head, arched my eyebrows, and pitched my voice lower— "help."

Seth took in a sharp breath and stared at me.

The woman looked surprised. Maybe. I couldn't be sure because her eyebrows were painted on in a pronounced arch. Either way, she scurried off.

"You're welcome," I told Seth.

"Eli—"

"Rabbi," Billy interrupted him. "You need to fix the cake before Rory comes out and the shit hits the fan."

"That'd be a lot harder to clean up than the cake." I raised my hand and twirled my finger in a spinning motion. "I'm thinking splatter."

"That's not helping," Seth mumbled as he riffled through the bag. "All we need is a knife and then we can take care of this." He looked at Billy. "Do you have a knife?"

No fewer than five people thrust knives at him.

"Do you have any, uh, *clean* knives?" he clarified. "Without fake blood on them."

"I hope it's fake," I muttered.

Someone handed Seth a knife. I highly doubted it was clean by any definition of the word. Didn't matter—there was no way I was putting that cake anywhere near my mouth.

Seth leaned toward the cake and started blinking. "Can you cut the fog for just a minute? It's a little hard to see."

"Cut the fog!" Billy yelled at Lord knows who. "We need to turn off the fog so Rabbi Cohen can cut out the shit!"

Seth immediately jerked his gaze toward me. "Not a word," he mouthed.

I moved my hand across my lips in a zipper pantomime.

Once some of the fog cleared, Seth carefully sliced the offending piece off the cake, coated the exposed area in frosting, and then turned the whole thing around so the damaged portion was in the corner and no longer visible. "There," he said as he looked at Billy expectantly. "All better."

The groom, damn him, frowned. "I don't know, Rabbi. The brain doesn't look right that way."

Uh, he did not say that. I gaped in surprise.

"Oh," Seth said. "I—"

Before he could finish what I hoped wasn't going to be an apology, I shoved my way forward, yanked the brain off the cake, turned it around, and plopped it back on.

"There," I snapped at the groom. "How's that?"

He jerked, seemingly taken aback by my reaction. I stepped toward him and glared.

"Good." He threw his red-tipped hands up defensively. "It looks good."

I squinted at him and then nudged my chin toward Seth.

"Thanks, Rabbi," the groom said hurriedly.

"You're welcome," Seth replied, and then he turned to me and quietly added, "I think you just scared a zombie."

"You bet your ass I did." I crossed my arms over my chest. "Being dead doesn't give someone the right to be rude."

It took about two seconds before my words sank in, and then we both died laughing. Pun intended.

CHAPTER ELEVEN

Lord Byron said all tragedies are finished by a death and all comedies by a marriage. With joyful hearts Shannon McAllister and Damon Ridges invite you to the celebration of past, present, and future as we finish the comedy portion of our lives, join our hands in marriage, and embark on a great tragedy.

Saturday, November 17, 2007, six in the evening, the Ritz-Carlton, Los Angeles, California.

Eli Block

"HELLO."

"Hey, it's me," I said. "Were you serious the other night when you were talking about buying a house?"

"Uh-huh," Seth mumbled. I could tell he was chewing something, and then he swallowed and said, "I've been living in this tiny apartment for six years. I think I'm ready for a little more space and a yard and walls I'm allowed to paint."

"Cool. I'm having brunch with David Miller today, so I'll ask him to put together a list of places and call you to go see them. Sound good?"

I heard a door close. "David's your Realtor friend who owns a bar, right?"

Over the years, I'd taken Seth with me to the occasional dinner or movie or brunch with my friends. He was never a big talker, but everyone liked him and, most importantly, I liked having him around. Seth had met David more than once, so I found it amusing that he described my friend based on his job. Every other guy I knew would have described David based on his appearance (the man was drop-dead gorgeous) or his dick size. I'd never had the privilege of getting a firsthand view, but by all accounts, his piece was legendary.

"Yup, that's him. Noah and Clark are coming and probably some other people too. Do you want to join us? I'm sure everyone would love to see you." And by everyone, I meant me. Not that my friends wouldn't like having him around, but saying they'd *love* to see him was stretching it.

He sighed. "I wish I could, but today's the first day of Sunday school and I want to be there to greet the kids."

Of course he did. Seth truly cared about every member of our congregation; it was what made him such a great rabbi. I loved that about him.

"Don't worry about it. You'll come with us next time. What day's good for you to go see houses with David?"

"Umm," Seth said distractedly. "I'm pretty flexible.

Let's choose something around your schedule. Between your classes and your social life, it's not easy to get an appointment with you."

"Whatever. I see you almost every day." I paused the second the words left my mouth. Huh. Seth and I had always spent a good bit of time together, but since I'd moved back to Emile City, we rarely went two days in a row without hanging out. Then the other part of what he'd said registered. "You want me to go house hunting with you?"

"Of course." He sounded surprised by my question. "I'm buying a house; I have to make sure we both like it."

My heart warmed in reaction to how much he valued my opinion, and I smiled to myself. "Okay. I know your schedule, so I'll set everything up with David and let you know the date. Sound good?"

"Yes. Thanks, Eli. I'm heading over to the temple now." I heard a door and then the familiar beep-beep sound a car makes before you put on a seat belt. "I'll call you when I'm done and we can hang out, okay?"

"That's perfect."

"SURE THING. I'm happy to help Seth find a place," my friend David said. "I need to send him a card to thank him for referring Micah Trains to me."

I snorted, knowing from Seth that his friend Micah was

not an easy client.

"Seriously. He's a good guy. I like him a lot, and I know I can find the right place for him." David paused and quirked one side of his mouth up. "Eventually." He took another bite of his breakfast and asked, "Anyway, do you know what Seth wants in a house?"

"Well, he likes to be close to work, so something in EC West. And he said he wants a yard and a little more space. He's in a one-bedroom now, so I don't think he needs anything huge."

David ate the last piece of his egg-white omelet, then got his phone out and started typing up notes. He glanced at me. "Does he want it to be move-in ready or is he okay with doing some remodeling?"

"Hmm, I don't know. He's pretty busy and I don't think design's really his thing. I can help a little, but with school and work, it's not like I have a bunch of time either."

"Let me know if you need help," my decorator friend Caleb said. "I'm happy to do it."

"Thanks, Caleb."

"No problem." He furrowed his brow in thought. "I don't think I've met Seth, have I?"

I shrugged and took a bite of my pancake. "I don't know. Probably. I've brought him around a bunch of times."

Caleb turned to his roommate and said, "Drew, do we know Seth?"

"He's that guy Eli's always rattling on about," Andrew

said. "The, uh…Noah, what do you call him?"

"HCC. Hopeful childhood crush," Noah supplied easily.

I tossed a fried potato at my friend, stuck out my tongue, and said, "Screw you, Noah. And I think you mean hopeless."

He shook his head and smirked. "No, I don't."

"Show me a picture," Caleb said. "I'm sure I'd remember if I'd met this guy."

I got out my phone and scrolled through the pictures. Seth was gorgeous. That wasn't just my opinion—everyone thought so. His soft, curly hair, his kind, warm eyes, his smooth, perfect skin—it was indisputable. But the photographic evidence didn't support that fact.

"Here's one." I handed my phone to Caleb. "It's from a wedding last month, but he doesn't look anything like this. I swear, it's like he goes out of his way to find the worst lighting."

Caleb looked at the picture and frowned. "Why are the people you're with wearing dirty clothes?"

"It was a zombie theme."

He darted his gaze up from the phone and stared at me. "For a wedding?"

I nodded.

"I guess that explains the red teeth."

I leaned over and looked at the picture. "Uh, nope. The red teeth are from the food coloring in the cake. I'm pretty sure that wasn't on purpose."

Caleb arched his eyebrows.

"Hey, I didn't bake it and I didn't eat it. Don't give me

that look."

Andrew glanced at the phone, sneered, and said, "And they say letting *us* walk down the aisle would mock the sanctity of marriage." He shook his head in disgust. "What fucking sanctity?"

Caleb squeezed Andrew's shoulder and handed me back my phone. "He looks sort of familiar, but I can't place him."

"YOU GOT the door?" Caleb asked Andrew.

"Yup."

Andrew held open the door to Seth's new house, and Caleb and I shuffled in holding the huge painting I'd bought him as a housewarming gift. It was an abstract with different shades of red and some gold undertones. The second I saw it, I knew Seth would love it, so I ignored the price and plunked down my credit card.

"Where are we putting it?" Caleb asked.

"I was thinking in the living room, right over the fireplace. What do you think?"

We got the painting into the room, leaned it against the wall, and then Caleb looked around, assessing the space.

"Yeah, that's a good spot for it," he said. "You're sure Seth won't mind us hanging a picture on his most prominent wall without asking him?"

Andrew snorted.

Caleb snapped his head toward him, narrowed his eyes, and said, "What?"

"It's a painting, Cae. A, he can move it. And two, do you see what I see?" He motioned to each of the walls. "It's not like there's anything else hanging in here."

"That's because he closed on this house on Tuesday, moved in on Wednesday, and flew out to LA on Thursday so he could be there for a tux fitting and rehearsal dinner on Friday. He was a groomsman in his friend's wedding," I said. "You should have seen this place when he left. There were boxes everywhere. I think the only things he set up were his bed and the coffeemaker."

"It doesn't look bad," Caleb said. "A little empty, but not bad."

"That would be because I've spent the last three days unpacking," I explained.

Andrew arched one of his pierced eyebrows. "That was nice of you."

I shrugged. "I'm house-sitting for him, so I'm here anyway. Might as well make myself useful."

"This is a great space," Caleb said.

"I think so too. I like how you can see all the trees through the big picture window."

"Uh-huh. And the rounded ceiling's a great architectural feature too."

I looked up. "The ceiling's rounded?"

"Yeah, see how it curves down on the exterior walls?" he said as he pointed at the juncture where the ceiling met the wall.

"Oh. I hadn't noticed that. I'll have to point it out to Seth when he gets home."

"How long's he in LA?"

I sighed. "Until next Monday. His friend got married yesterday, and it didn't make sense for him to come home and then turn around and fly right back out again on Wednesday to spend Thanksgiving with his family. Plus, his uncle is getting married next Sunday, so…"

"Wow, look at you pouting," Andrew said. "Noah's nickname for this guy is spot on. He really is your HCC."

I didn't bother denying what Andrew said because he was right, but it was silly for me to be upset about going a week and a half without seeing Seth, especially because I talked to him at least twice a day. Besides, with as hard as he worked, he deserved a vacation.

My father thought so too, which was why he'd insisted Seth take the time, even though it meant my dad had to officiate—no joke—three weddings in one week. There was one that afternoon, another on Monday, and a third on the Tuesday before Thanksgiving. Apparently everyone had the same idea of getting hitched when people were already in town for the holiday. Amazingly, none of the weddings had themes. I was pretty sure Seth thought my dad had found some way to work that out.

Thinking about Seth's paranoid suspicion made me laugh, which helped me shake off my no-Seth doldrums. Forcing myself to focus on the positive, I said, "On the plus side, I get to stay here, so I have a reprieve from living under my parents' roof."

"I don't know how you do that," Andrew said with a shake of his head. "We're going to New York for Thanksgiving, which means I have to spend a meal with my parents. I'm considering self-medicating just to get through that. If I had to live with them, I'd lose my mind."

"It'll be fine, Drew," Caleb said gently. "I'll be with you the whole time."

Andrew grunted.

"My parents aren't bad," I said, feeling guilty for complaining about them when they did so much for me. "And if I live with them, I can use whatever money I make to pay for school, which means no debt when I graduate."

"That's good," Caleb said.

"It is," I agreed. "But it's still nice to get a little break, which is why I don't mind house-sitting, even if it means unpacking a million boxes."

"Speaking of unpacking," Caleb said. "Let's get this picture hung so I can poke around." He glanced at me. "That's okay, right? I love these old houses and I always like to see what people have done to them and what's still original."

"Sure," I said.

We had the picture centered over the fireplace a few

minutes later, and then Caleb was off, commenting about molding and windows.

"You want something to drink?" I asked Andrew.

"Sure. What do you have?"

I headed toward the kitchen and he followed me. "I picked up some Diet Coke, water, and—"

"Eli, I know you have a major crush on this guy," Caleb said as he walked into the kitchen waving something. "But I think framing a picture of the two of you and putting it on his nightstand is a little much." He held up a picture of me and Seth that my mother took a couple of years earlier. "And, by the way, I remember where I know him from."

"I didn't put the picture up. It was already there when I got here on Thursday. And what do you mean you know him? I thought you said you hadn't met Seth."

"I didn't think I had, but remember how I told you he looked familiar? This picture looks more like him than the zombie wedding one you showed me, so it hit me. I met him when I lived in New York. He was seeing my friend Nate Richardson."

I felt like the world fell out from my under my feet.

"What do you mean seeing?"

"Well, maybe not *seeing*." Caleb furrowed his brow in thought. "I don't remember exactly. I just know Nate brought him dancing one night. I remember because he looked really out of place there."

My heart started beating again once I heard Caleb's

explanation and realized he had misconstrued the situation. "That's because he's straight," I explained.

"Uh, no, he's not," Caleb argued.

"Trust me. Seth's been my best friend for years. I know him better than anyone. Just because he went to a club with your friend Nate doesn't mean he's gay." I scoffed. "He's been to Two of a Kind with me and—"

"How about the fact that he was making out with Nate? Is that enough to earn him a gay card?"

I somehow managed to sit down. I wasn't sure how it happened. One minute I was standing, the next minute my butt was in a kitchen chair, Andrew was grasping my arm, and Caleb was crouching in front of me.

"Eli, are you okay?" Caleb asked. "Breathe."

"Wha—" My voice wouldn't cooperate, so I cleared my throat and tried again. "What do you mean, making out?"

"I don't know." Caleb shrugged. "They were kissing and touching each other. It's not like they were fucking on the dance floor or anything, so I didn't pay much attention. Are you okay?"

"I think I'm going to be sick." I stumbled out of the chair and raced to the bathroom, making it just in time to hit the toilet with the contents of my stomach. Caleb and Andrew were right behind me.

"What the fuck?" Andrew yelled. "I know you have some kind of crush on this guy, Eli, but you can't make yourself sick every time you hear he's been with someone else. It's not like you can expect him to be a monk, right? So he made out with some guy. What's the big—"

"Thirteen years," I rasped. "That's how long I've had what you're describing as a crush." My entire body was shaking. "And he's straight!" I yelled, which pushed me into a coughing fit. "That's the big deal," I said once I could talk again. "He isn't supposed to be making out with men at all." Just saying the words made my stomach turn over and I started dry heaving.

"Shit," Caleb gasped.

"Why would he do that?" I asked myself. "Why would he be with a guy but not with me?" I stood up, barely keeping my balance. "Where's my phone?"

"I don't think you should—"

I patted my pocket. "Here it is." I yanked my phone out and started tapping on the keys.

"I think we should go," Andrew whispered to Caleb. "He needs some privacy."

"Are you going to be okay?" Caleb asked me.

I nodded, put my phone up to my ear, closed the toilet lid, and slumped down.

"Call me later, Eli," Caleb said.

I nodded again and raised my trembling hand in a wave.

When I got Seth's voice mail, it was all I could do to keep myself from smashing my phone against the wall, but instead I said, "Call me," and then I hung up.

CHAPTER TWELVE

After the fire, after all the rain, I will be
the flame. — Cheap Trick

Lisbeth and Harold Sloan request the
pleasure of your company at the marriage
of their daughter
Marie Frances to Jordan Jacob Lawson
Sunday, November 18, 2007, at eleven in
the morning.

Seth Cohen

THERE ARE some moments in life that you never, ever forget. They're turning points, little things that make a huge difference. Sometimes you don't even realize you're in the midst of one until much later. But other times you know right away. That was what it was like for me on Sunday, November 18, 2007.

It was two o'clock in the afternoon and I was sitting in my mother's kitchen in LA, catching up with my parents, my brother, and my sister-in-law, when I heard my phone ring in the family room.

"I'll be right back," I said as I got up.

"Is that Eli Block again?" my mother asked. My entire family had been teasing me about how much I talked to him.

I felt my neck heat. "Maybe."

The message he left wasn't long. Two words: "Call me." But from the way he sounded—weak and shaky—I knew something was wrong. I dialed his number as I rushed into the guest bedroom I was staying in so I could have some privacy.

When he picked up, he didn't bother with the usual greetings and instead said, "Want to tell me about Nate Richardson from New York?"

That was when I knew I was smack dab in the middle of a turning point in my life. I could tell he'd been crying, which wasn't how I'd wanted things to go. But what I'd wanted no longer mattered. We were where we were, and I needed to be very careful in how I handled the next few minutes, because it could make or break my future with Eli, which would make or break me.

In an instant, I knew what I had to do. "I can be at the airport in an hour and I'll catch the next flight home," I said as I tossed my suitcase onto the bed. Two seconds later, I had it open and started throwing my clothes inside.

"What are you talking about?" Eli said.

"I'm not doing this on the phone," I answered. "I need to see your face and—"

"Seth?" Eli whimpered.

My heart constricted in pain. "I'm coming," I assured him. I darted my gaze around the room to see if I'd forgotten anything. When nothing stood out, I zipped up my suitcase and hauled it off the bed. "I need to hang up so I can drive to the airport."

"I have to know who he is, Seth," Eli begged. "I don't think I can wait."

I hated the pain I heard in his voice. "He's just a guy," I told him.

"My friend Caleb said you made out with him." Eli gulped loudly. "Is that true?"

"Yes, it's true, but it was just an experiment." I winced at how horrible that sounded. "I'll explain everything as soon as I get home. I promise."

It took less than five minutes for me to tell my family about my unexpected change in plans, another five for me to call the airline and get booked on the next flight to Emile City, and then I was in my rental car, driving toward the airport.

It was late by the time I pulled up to my new house. All the lights were off, so if Eli's car hadn't been in the garage, I would have thought he'd gone back to his parents' place instead of waiting for me. With my suitcase in one hand, I fumbled with my keys, eventually got the door open, and stepped into my mud slash laundry room.

Being a homeowner was a new treat and the house Eli and I had picked out was amazing, but in that moment I couldn't even appreciate the luxury of having my own washer and dryer because my focus was on the man I hoped was somewhere inside.

"Eli?" I called out. It was deadly silent, and I started worrying that maybe he was gone after all. He could have gotten a ride from someone, which would explain why his car was still there. I toed off my shoes and left them with my suitcase in the laundry room, walked through the kitchen into the dining room, and called his name again. "Eli?"

There was a rustling sound followed by the click of a table lamp, and then I saw him. He was sitting on the couch, wearing pajama pants and a huge sweatshirt—one of my old ones from college. His eyes were red-rimmed and puffy, and his skin was pale.

"Oh, Eli," I rasped as I hustled over to him.

"An experiment?" he asked hoarsely.

Even though hours had passed since we'd hung up, I knew he was continuing the conversation from our phone call.

"Yes," I answered as I slowed my pace.

"What does that mean?"

I tried to figure out how to put what I'd been going through four years earlier into words. "I needed to know what it was like. For me, I mean. I needed to know what it was like to be with a guy."

"To *be* with a guy?"

"Not like that," I said emphatically. "We kissed and there was a little groping. That's all." I sighed and took a step closer to him. "He didn't mean anything to me, and I'm pretty sure I meant even less to him. We didn't even exchange numbers."

He nodded, pursed his lips, and asked, "Were there any others?"

It was time for full disclosure. "One other one. Yes."

"Well?" Eli shouted and threw his hands up. "Are you going to tell me?"

I was grateful for the show of emotion. Seeing him frustrated was much less painful than seeing him sad.

"I was in LA visiting my parents and my brother. We met at a bookstore and had dinner the next night."

He jumped up. "A date! You went on a date with a guy and you didn't think to tell me!"

"Eli, it wasn't a big deal." I held my hand out and kept my voice calm, trying to placate him. "It was dinner. A little eating. A little conversation."

He paced from one side of the room to the other. "And after?"

"After dinner?"

The dirty look he shot me made me flinch. "Yes!"

"There was no after," I explained hurriedly. "We paid the bill and said good night."

Eli's shoulders relaxed as the fight seemed to leave his body. "There was no after?"

I nodded.

"Did you see him again?"

"No." I shook my head.

"You didn't see him when you were back in LA this weekend?" he asked suspiciously.

"No. I haven't seen or spoken to him in more than two years."

I stepped closer to Eli.

"Why not?"

He moved farther away.

"I don't know." I dragged my fingers through my hair in frustration. "Because I wasn't interested in pursuing anything, I guess."

Suddenly, Eli's shoulders slumped and his eyelids drooped; he looked sad again. I didn't understand why my answer would have given him that reaction.

"So you tried going out with a guy and it didn't work?" he whispered.

Ah, that was it. "I tried going out with *that* guy and it didn't work," I clarified.

Eli raised his gaze and met mine. "Because he's a guy?"

"Because there weren't any sparks." I tried moving closer to him and was grateful when he didn't step away that time.

"Because he's a guy?" He looked at me with trepidation and chewed his lip nervously.

I shook my head and stepped even closer. "Because he wasn't the right *person*."

Eli gulped and whispered, "The right person?"

"Yes."

"And who's the right person?" His voice was shot, the words barely audible, but I was close enough to hear him by then.

"You, Eli." I reached out and did an internal victory dance when he didn't jerk away, then I wrapped my arms around his shoulders and drew him close.

When our lips were scant inches apart, he clutched my shirt, looked at me wide-eyed, and said, "Seth?"

"It's always been you," I mumbled, and then I leaned forward and kissed him.

At first his body was stiff, his lips were still, and his fingers were clenched into claws digging into my shirt and skin. I kissed him anyway, gently pressed my lips to his, opened and closed them slowly, and licked him every so often. He panted, short bursts of air leaving his nose at a rapid pace while he fisted my shirt like he was paralyzed with fear.

"Oh, Eli," I whispered as I brought one hand to his face, cupped his cheek, and caressed his smooth skin. "Don't be scared."

"I'm not."

But he was trembling and his heart was racing; I could feel it.

"Come here, baby," I said and veered us toward the couch. "Let's sit."

He followed easily, not releasing his grasp on me or moving his laser focus from my face. The couch hit the back of my knees, and I sat, tugging him with me. He glanced at my legs and then back at my face, seemingly confused by what he was supposed—or maybe it was allowed—to do. I explained it to him with actions instead of words by tugging him until he was sitting on my lap, his knees on either side of me.

"This is okay, right?" I asked as I moved my hand across his chest and down to his flat belly.

He gulped and nodded. I noticed he wasn't hard—it would have been obvious in the soft pants he was wearing—but before I fell into a bout of insecurity about whether he wanted me, I reminded myself that he was nervous and probably more than a little confused, and he wouldn't be trembling and hanging on to me for dear life if he wasn't interested.

"I like touching you," I confessed, hoping my admission would put him at ease. I moved my heated gaze over him and added, "And looking at you. Can I take off your sweatshirt?"

"I can't believe this is happening," he mumbled.

I wasn't sure if he was talking to himself or to me.

"It is," I assured him. I shoved my hand under the sweatshirt and made contact with his skin. He gasped and the muscles on his stomach flexed. Wow, was that ever sexy. I grabbed the bottom of the shirt and looked at him questioningly. "Can I?"

He nodded. I put both my hands on his belly and dragged them over his body as I pushed the shirt up, making sure to give him as much sensation as possible. When I had his shirt rucked up to his chin, I tilted my head toward his arms and said, "Up."

His hands immediately flew above his head. I smiled at his eagerness. Yeah, he wanted this. It wasn't a surprise, because he had always made his physical desire for me known. The concerns I'd had were about whether he'd want to stay around once those were sated, and whether I'd want to. I'd figured out the answer to the last question years earlier. As to the first one, well, standing on the sidelines while he bounced from one boyfriend to another had been a double-edged sword.

On the one hand, knowing he could be with someone else caused me to worry that he didn't truly want to be with me. Seeing his relationships end after what I considered a short period caused me to worry that he wasn't interested or ready for a true commitment. But as time went by, I started seeing things differently.

I noticed how hard he tried to find the positives in whoever he was dating, almost like he was talking himself into making relationships work. I noticed that he didn't go barhopping but instead focused on the long-term potential of anyone he spent time with, sharing thoughts about what his parents or I would think of his boyfriend du jour or how his career would mesh well with Eli's plans for the future. Either Eli was more mature than I'd given him credit for, or he'd grown up somewhere along the way. I didn't know which and, frankly, it didn't matter.

Because whatever the reason for the core of strength and determination I now saw underneath the handsome, bubbly exterior, I'd come to suspect something else: the reason those relationships of his didn't last wasn't because of an aversion to commitment; it was because he was with the wrong guys. And when he finally finished school—the out-of-state part, anyway—and came home to stay, I'd made a plan to slowly show him that he meant more to me than I'd previously let on. I'd figured easing him into that realization would be the right approach after years of pushing that part of him away. Clearly, that hadn't worked out like I'd planned, but with Eli in my arms, looking at me like I was everything he could ever want, I couldn't bring myself to regret the change in plans.

Eli and I were exactly the same height, so with him sitting on me, his sculpted chest was easily accessible. I pushed the shirt over his head and, at the same time, I leaned forward and swiped my tongue across his left nipple.

"Oh God," he gasped.

I circled the tip of my tongue around his areola over and over until I had the shirt shoved past his hands. I tossed it on the floor and then really got to work, gripping Eli's waist and holding him still while I sucked his flat brown nipple into my mouth. I licked and suckled one side until it was puckered and swollen and then I moved to the other, lavishing the same attention on it. Eli bucked and I was immensely pleased when I felt a hard rod bumping into my stomach.

There we go.

I tangled my fingers in the back of his hair, tugged his face down, and kissed him again. It was hungrier that time, my concern for calming his skittish nerves gone by the wayside in reaction to his arousal. Speaking of his arousal...I moved the hand that wasn't in his hair down to his lap and had my first contact with a dick that wasn't my own.

Eli arched his back, and his mouth dropped open as his eyes widened in shock. "Oh God. Oh God. Oh God," he chanted.

"Yeah?" I said when I realized what was happening. I doubled my efforts, kissing him deeply, tangling my tongue with his while I tweaked his nipple with my left hand and rubbed the heel of my right hand down his shaft and over his balls.

He tasted so good, smelled so good, felt so good. I'd never been more turned on in my life, and I wondered how I ever could have thought being with him would be anything less than amazing. Nothing had ever felt more natural and right than making Eli Block writhe and pant and whimper with desire.

"Eli," I breathed into his mouth. I gripped his erection through his pants and stroked him gently but firmly.

"I—"

I licked his lips.

"Seth, I—"

"I know," I told him. I looked straight into his eyes and said, "Do it."

"Seth!"

Wet heat soaked through his pants, and he shook so hard he almost fell off my lap.

"So sexy, Eli," I told him. "You're so unbelievably sexy."

He slumped forward, rested his head on my shoulder, and circled his hands around my neck.

"Let's get these pants off you, okay, baby?" I kissed the spot behind his ear. "You're going to start feeling sticky any second now."

I twisted sideways until I had Eli parallel to the couch and then I lowered him so he was lying on his back and I was crouched between his thighs. I hooked my fingers in his waistband and rolled his pants down, scooting backward with them until I was able to pull them off one leg and then the other. I crumbled up the fabric and used it to wipe Eli's semen off his belly. Once he was clean, I tossed the pants over my shoulder and looked at the gorgeous body spread out in front of me.

Slender legs, covered in a light smattering of hair, bony hips, and long-fingered hands cupped protectively over a package I'd felt but hadn't yet had the pleasure of examining.

"Why are you hiding from me?" I asked.

He tensed but moved his hands to his sides. His dick was still hard, but the rest of him didn't seem particularly excited. I paused and said, "Eli? Do you want this?"

"Do I want to be with you?" he asked breathlessly.

"Yes."

"Are you kidding me right now?" he said incredulously, suddenly animated. "I've been ready for more than half my life!"

I snorted and said, "There's the spirited Eli Block I know and love."

He whimpered and hoarsely said, "Seth, do you…"

"What?"

He opened his mouth, then slammed it shut and shook his head. "Never mind." He dragged his gaze over my body, landing his focus on my groin. "Quit talking and take your pants off."

"You really are quite the charmer, you know that?" I teased.

"Seth," he whined and squirmed. "I want to see your dick."

"Subtle too."

"Seth!"

I'd always admired Eli's straightforward style, even when it made me somewhat uncomfortable, but never more than in that moment.

"I'm kidding," I told him. "I love how honest you are."

"Honest? I'm horny!" He shot up to a sitting position and reached for the button fly on my jeans. "You want something done right, you might as well do it yourself," he muttered as he yanked the fabric down and to the sides, causing all the buttons to push out of the holes.

He started shoving my jeans and boxers past my hips,

and I peeled my shirt off, so within seconds, I was naked other than the denim pooled around my knees. I stood up, letting the pants land on the floor, and held my hand out to Eli.

"Come to bed with me."

All his attention was focused on my groin, so he didn't respond.

"Wow," he said, sounding awestruck. "You're even more beautiful than in my fantasies." He reached a single finger forward and ran it over my crown, down a prominent vein in my shaft, and over my balls. Then he looked up at me, licked his lips, and said, "Will you let me taste you?"

I shivered. "Definitely."

He leaned forward.

I put my hand on his shoulder, stopping him before he reached his mark and caused any restraint or logic I had to fly out the window. "In bed," I said when he glanced up at me in confusion. "The first time we do this should be in a bed."

I reached my hand out again, and this time he took it and stood. "Whatever you say, old man."

"Is this really the right time for that nickname?" I asked him with a fond shake of my head.

"Anytime is a good time for that nickname. Because it's *awesome*."

Before he knew it was coming, I reached around him and goosed him. He squeaked and I turned on my heel and ran into the bedroom.

CHAPTER THIRTEEN

We're all a little weird. And life is a
little weird. And when we find
someone whose weirdness is
compatible with ours, we join up with
them and fall into mutually satisfying
weirdness—and call it love—true love.
— Robert Fulghum, True Love

Kathy Pearson and Carl Miller invite
you to share in their union.
Monday, November 19, 2007,
five thirty p.m.

Seth Cohen

ELI WAS fast so he made up my lead quickly, and by the time
we reached the bedroom, he was close enough that a well-

timed jump had both of us tumbling onto the bed with him on my back. I flipped us over, smiled as I looked down at his no longer petrified face, and said, "Gotcha!"

He squinted, and the next thing I knew, I was flat on my back with Eli straddling my hips and holding down my arms. "Nope. I've got you!" he said triumphantly.

I relaxed all my muscles and gazed into his eyes. "Yes, you do."

Everything stopped and the moment turned serious, just like that. Eli gulped, looked at me hesitantly, and bent forward a hair. When I didn't move away, he seemed to gain confidence and kept going until he barely touched my lips with his.

I surged up, tilting my head to the side and parting my lips to take him in. He darted his tongue into my mouth and moaned, kissing me again and again. With his concentration elsewhere, he loosened his grip on my arms, so I was able to easily raise my hands to his face. I cupped his cheeks, massaged his temples, and kept him close while our lips and tongues connected time and again.

"Mmm, Seth," he said after we'd been kissing long enough that both our lips were probably swollen. He thrust his hips against mine, grinding our erections together. "You're so hard. Can't believe you're hard for me."

"It isn't the first time, baby. You turn me on so much."

Though he didn't stop or slow the delicious friction he was giving us by rolling his hips over mine, he flattened his hands on either side of my head and pushed up until he was looking into my eyes.

"Why didn't you ever say anything?" he asked.

"Because—" I sighed. "I had to be sure."

"Had to be..." He furrowed his brow. "What does that mean?" Before I could even open my mouth to answer, he shook his head and said, "You know what? Never mind. I can ask you about that later. I'm not going to blow this moment by talking." He paused and then curled up one corner of his mouth and snorted. "I said blow."

I strongly suspected that no matter how old he got, Eli would always keep his youthful spirit, which pleased me to no end.

"Yes, you did." I rubbed my hands over his shoulders and biceps and said, "What do you want to do now?"

"You'll let me?" he asked, his expression one of hesitancy warring with hopefulness.

"Yes," I said even though I didn't know what he wanted. I caressed his chest and cupped the side of his neck. "I'll let you do anything."

He trembled and whispered, "I still can't believe this is happening."

"You will," I promised as I traced his lower lip with my thumb. Then I moved my palm to his nape and tugged him back down for another kiss. His lips were soft and plush, his skin warm and silky, and the muscles underneath taut and firm. He was perfect. "I love kissing you," I said. "I could do this forever."

He cried out, nodded, and lapped at my lips desperately. It took me a moment, but then I noticed his eyes were wet and he was shaking.

"Shhh," I said, trying to bring back the calm that had inexplicably left him. "It's okay."

"I want you so much," he rasped. "You don't...you can't..." He squeezed his eyes shut. "So much."

"I'm here," I pointed out. "I'm here and I'm not going anywhere. Take whatever you want."

He hesitated for no more than a second, and then he pounced, licking and kissing and nibbling on my neck, caressing any part of me he could reach, slowly working his way down my body until my rock-hard dick nudged his chin. He took me in hand, stroked me, and said, "You're hard as a rock."

I chuckled at the consistency in our thoughts and combed my fingers through his hair.

With his gaze glued to mine, Eli parted his lips, extended his tongue, and licked my crown. I hissed and tilted my hips, trying to get closer to his amazing touch. He didn't tease or make me wait. He swirled his tongue over my sensitive skin, coating me in slick saliva, then dropped his lips over my shaft, taking me into his hot, wet mouth.

"Eli, so good," I moaned.

He cupped my balls with one hand, circled the other around the base of my erection, and sucked his way up my cock before dropping back down again. What he was doing felt amazing, but looking at the pleasure on his face while he did it made the experience feel like heaven on earth. I moved my finger over his stretched lips, and he moaned, the sound vibrating over my dick and making me gasp.

"I'm close, Eli," I warned him. He whimpered and sucked harder, gyrating against the bed. "Are you going to come again?" I asked breathlessly.

The expression on his face and the noises he couldn't hold back gave me my answer.

"C'mere." I grabbed his arm and tugged, but he didn't budge from his mission of giving me the most amazing blow job of all time. "Eli, come up here." When he still didn't move, I sat up, knocking him off his target, and then knelt between his thighs and cupped his balls. "Together," I explained.

Whether he understood or not, I didn't know, but he bucked into my touch and let me lead him up until he was kneeling in front of me and his cock was slotted next to mine.

"Like this," I whispered as I wrapped my fingers around both of us.

He nodded and then I felt him brush his hand against mine before he palmed our dicks too. I rested my forehead against his, and we both looked down at our shafts nestled together and our hands moving over them at an increasing pace.

"So hot," Eli said, sounding awed. "Oh God, so hot."

I moved my head just enough to brush my lips over

his cheek and then resumed the position, looking back down in time to see white cream shoot from his slit.

My mouth opened, my muscles tightened, and my breath stopped, all in one glorious moment, and then I groaned as rope after rope of thick cum pulsed out of my dick and onto our hands and chests.

"Oh!" Eli moaned. "Look at you." He whimpered and breathlessly said, "So beautiful."

We stayed in that position—kneeling on the bed, touching foreheads, languidly stroking our softening members—until we caught our breath.

"Mmm, too sensitive," I told him as I twined my fingers with his and moved them away from my sated cock.

He looked into my eyes, slowly raised our joined hands to his mouth, and then darted his tongue out and licked our ejaculate from our palms and fingers. I didn't interrupt, just watched and enjoyed the erotic show until he was done. Then I wrapped my arms around him and pulled us onto the bed so we were lying on our sides. I licked my way into his mouth, tasted our combined seed on his tongue, and groaned when my dick tried to fill again.

We stayed that way, lined up from toes to head, exchanging kisses. The stress of the day combined with my frantic travel, the late hour, and the mind-blowing orgasm had me feeling languid and tired. I kissed Eli one more time and then sat up and started to scoot off the comforter so I could pull it over us.

"Are you freaking out now?" he asked nervously.

I snapped my head to the side and looked at him in confusion. "Why would I be freaking out?"

He shrugged.

"Eli?"

"We had sex," he said, as if I hadn't been with him for what had been, to that point, the best experience of my life. "I mean we didn't, you know"—he arched his eyebrows meaningfully—"but that was still sex." He paused and furrowed his brow. "Right?"

"Definitely." I hunched down and kissed him. "You know what I usually like to do after I have sex with you at night?"

"Uh, this is the first time you've had sex with me at night," he pointed out. "Or anytime."

"I meant in my head." I tapped the side of my head, waggled my eyebrows, and grinned.

His mouth dropped open. "You beat off to fantasies of us together?"

"Oh, yeah." I kissed my way across his jaw to his ear. "Imagining it doesn't feel as good as doing the real thing with you, but it still wears me out." I sucked on his earlobe. "Most nights I'm so wound up thinking about you, I can't go to sleep unless I jerk off first."

He parted his lips, as if to say something, closed them, then drew in a deep breath and tried again. "I've never heard you talk like this," he said.

I would have told him that was because he'd never been in bed with me, but that wouldn't have been true. "That's because I never have."

"I seriously can't believe this is happening," he said. "It's surreal. I feel like...like..."

"Like what, baby?" I gently stroked his face. "What do you feel?"

"It feels like this is a dream, like it isn't really you."

"It's me," I assured him.

"No." He shook his head. "You don't touch me and kiss me and call me 'baby' and look at me like...like..." He was trembling again.

"This is me. It's just"—I thought about how to explain myself—"another side of me."

"Another side of you?" he asked suspiciously. "I've known you all these years and suddenly there's another side of you?"

I shrugged and smiled, trying to lighten the mood. "Hey, it's new to me too."

That suspicious look came back. "It's new to you?"

I nodded wearily.

"You mean it's an experiment, like with Caleb's friend. You're—"

"No!" I snapped. "This is nothing like what happened with that guy in New York. He was hung up on someone. I was hung up on you. We spent most of the night talking about that and, yes, we necked some, but—"

Eli started laughing.

I rolled off him and laid back down on top of the comforter, deciding warm snuggles weren't quite in reach. "Why are you laughing?" I asked tiredly.

"You said 'necked.'" He snorted. "Who says 'necked'? That's such an old-man word."

He'd gone from aroused to confused to angry to amused, all in what felt like a matter of seconds. "Your emotions are all over the place," I mumbled, not realizing that was the wrong thing to say until it was too late.

He flew out of bed, threw his hands in the air, and yelled, "All over the place? You think my emotions are all over the place?"

Not only did I think that, but he was demonstrating my point right at that moment.

"Uh," I said, not wanting to make the same mistake again. I sat up and tried to come up with a non-anger-evoking response. "I, uh—"

"The guy I've always wanted but never thought I could have is suddenly saying and doing all the things he said he'd never say or do. I'm sorry if my needing a minute to readjust my entire world order is coming across as emotional and all over the place!"

Damn, he was cute. It was the first thought that entered my mind and one I normally would have kept to myself. But not anymore.

"You're adorable, Eli, you know that?"

"Oh, so, now I'm adorable!"

"You've always been adorable." I held my hand out to him, palm side up. "Come back to bed."

"What in the hell is happening here?" He dragged his fingers through his hair and started pacing. "You're gay all of a sudden, is that it? You just decided at age thirty-three that you're going to be gay?"

"I'm pretty sure it doesn't work that way," I said reasonably.

He narrowed his eyes dangerously. "I know that! Don't you think I know that?"

Okay, so humor wasn't the right approach to soothing his feathers. I decided to go with facts.

"I'm not gay. I'm bi. It isn't something I just decided, but it did take me a while to figure it out."

"You're bi?"

I nodded.

"Seriously?"

I nodded again.

"I didn't think that was a real thing."

I sighed in frustration. "You were in an LGBT club all through college, Eli, and you never noticed the B? Come on."

"Sorry," he said sincerely.

"It's okay. It doesn't matter anymore anyway."

"What do you mean?" he asked in confusion. "Why doesn't it matter?"

"Because I'm with you now, and you're a guy, so

everyone will assume I'm gay, which is fine. It's all just labels, anyway, right? I don't care where they slot me."

"Uh, yeah, sure, I guess." He gulped. "What do you mean you're *with* me?"

"Eli?"

"Yeah?"

"We're naked in my bedroom with dried cum on our stomachs. What do you think I mean?"

He looked down at his stomach and then back at me. "So this isn't just for one night?"

"Do I strike you as a one-night stand kind of guy?"

He shook his head and stepped toward the bed. "You're not going to change your mind in the morning?"

"No."

He gulped and got closer. "So we're, uh, dating now?"

I furrowed my brow. "Dating?"

"Yeah, uh, that's what people do at first, right? They, uh, date."

I scooted to the edge of the bed and held my arms open. After a brief hesitation, Eli stepped between my knees and put his hands on my shoulders. I held on to his hips and looked up at him.

"I told you once that sex should happen when your dick, your brain, and your heart are all on the same page. I'm there, Eli. I'm on that page. I wouldn't have done this if I wasn't."

"What, ehm, what are you saying?"

"I'm saying I want you to move into this house we picked out together."

His knees buckled, so I tightened my grip to keep him from falling. I got up just long enough to push the blanket aside, then I sat back down and pulled him with me. I dragged him to the center of the bed and covered us with the blanket.

"You want me to move in here?"

I nodded.

"When?"

"Now."

He coughed. "Now?"

"Well"—I quirked my lips up—"not right this second because, like I already pointed out, we're both naked, but, yes, I want you to move in now."

"Wow. Here I thought I'd have to ease you into this with some secret dating and then maybe an appearance in public and eventually work my way up to boyfriend status but, no, you want to get straight to it."

His tone confused me. "Is that a problem?" I asked. "Do you want to move slowly?"

"No, it's not a problem. Hell, I admire your style, getting straight to the point, but no way do I think you're going to feel this way in the morning."

"I won't, huh?"

"No. Way," he said firmly. "Even if you are bi, it's not like you've ever acted on it, New York necking guy aside. Tomorrow, you're going to wake up and feel ashamed and want to pretend none of this happened. You'll be all uncomfortable around me, and we'll barely be friends. Then I'll have to tell you it was just a hand job, no biggie, straight guys do shit like that sometimes. And you'll say you agree but you won't really, so you'll still be tense, and maybe, if I'm lucky and I never, ever bring it up again, things can get back to normal."

"Huh." I had to admire how his mind worked. There I was, thinking about sex and sleep and nothing else, and he had managed to create an entire story in his head. It was a nonsense story, but that didn't make it any less impressive. "You've really thought this through, haven't you?"

"Yeah."

I moved my hand under the blanket and grazed his hip before cupping his butt and caressing it. His reaction was immediate—a hardening shaft poked my hip. I leaned forward, kissed his neck, and whispered, "Care to make this interesting?"

"Interesting, uh, how?" he asked huskily.

I wiggled my fingers in his crease. And felt wetness seep from his dick. I loved how easily I could ramp him up.

"How about a bet?"

"A bet?" he said, his voice cracking. "What kind of bet?"

"Winner's choice of anything he wants in the bedroom." I massaged his pucker with two fingers.

"Anything?"

"Uh-huh." I licked my way from the base of his throat

up his chin and into his mouth at the same time I added just a touch of pressure to his rosebud. "Do we have a deal?"

His breaths quickened and more precum dripped from his shaft.

"Eli?" I asked, wiggling my fingers and then massaging the tight opening again. "Do we have a deal?"

"Yes." He pushed back against me, rolling his hips to increase the sensation I was giving to his ass. "It's a deal."

I put the tip of one finger on his pucker, looked into his eyes, and said, "Do you want me to show you what I'll be collecting when I win?"

He hesitated, fear warring with desire on his face, and because I'd heard every detail about all of his relationships, I knew why.

Eventually, he whispered, "Yes."

I smiled at him. "Thanks for trusting me, baby." I kissed him tenderly and then moved my hand from his butt to his hip and rolled him onto his back.

"What're you doing?" he asked.

"Giving you a demonstration of my prize."

Before he could ask more questions, I wiggled under the blanket, lined my mouth up with his engorged shaft, and sucked him down.

"Ungh!" he keened and bucked. "Seth! You need to..." He tried pushing me off, but I wouldn't budge, then he flailed, his legs shook, and his dick swelled even more before he emptied himself down my throat.

When I was sure he was spent, I placed a chaste kiss at the tip of his crown, crawled up his body, and lay down beside him.

"What... Why..." He paused, swallowed, and when he caught his breath, he said, "Why'd you do that?"

"Because I wanted to show you what I want as my prize for winning the bet."

"I thought you'd want to fuck me."

"I do," I said. "And when it happens, I'm going to make it so good for you, Eli." I licked his lips. "You'll see. I'm going to make it everything you thought it would be before you tried it that first time." I kissed him. "You're going to love it."

"Oh God."

"But that's not what I want for the bet."

"It isn't?" he asked breathlessly.

"Nope." I shook my head. "When I win this bet, I want you back in my mouth, screaming my name when you come."

He was trembling again, so I pulled him close, covered us with the blanket, and wrapped my arms around him. After all the tears and the emotional ups and downs, not to mention three orgasms in one night, I knew he had to be tired.

"Go to sleep, baby. Everything will be better in the morning." I kissed his forehead and he clung to me. "I'm going to win the bet. You'll see. I'm going to take such good care of you, Eli. But right now, you need to sleep."

Amazingly, he did.

CHAPTER FOURTEEN

The parents of the bride think the groom isn't good
enough for her. The parents of the groom think he's too
young to settle down. Neither of our children listens to us
so at least we have that in common.

With sadness and frustration, Harry & Louise Schultz and
Jack & Elaine Silverman invite you to share in our joint
tragedy as our children Rachel and Adam exchange
marriage vows and begin their new life together.
Tuesday, November 20, 2007,
three in the afternoon.

Seth Cohen

BASED ON the grittiness in my eyes and the exhaustion in my
limbs, I guessed that my internal alarm clock had woken me
close to my usual six o'clock hour even though I'd gotten to
sleep well after midnight. That meant Eli should have been
sleeping for another few hours because while I'm normally
an "early to bed, early to rise" kind of person, he's more the
"stay up, sleep in" type. And yet, he wasn't curled up next to
me in bed.

Without raising my head, I patted the empty space on

the mattress and croaked, "Eli?"

"I'm right here," he said.

I blinked my bleary eyes and tried to focus in the direction of his voice. It took several seconds, but then I noticed him sitting on the floor. His hair was wet, like he'd just showered, and he was leaning against the wall with his legs bent at the knees and pulled protectively against his chest.

I twisted onto my side and said, "Why are you awake?" My voice sounded hoarse and tired to my own ears.

He shrugged and kept staring at me.

As my brain slowly reached consciousness, I started noticing more details. "Why are you on the floor?"

"Because there isn't a chair in this room."

That was true, but it didn't actually address my question. "Why aren't you in bed?"

"I'm wearing shoes and the same jeans I've had on for the past few days, and I don't want to get the bed dirty."

We were talking in circles. "When did you get dressed?"

"After my shower.

"And you decided to get up and shower because?"

"It was morning."

I considered asking him why he'd woken up so early, but that sounded very much like a repeat of the question I'd asked at the beginning of that annoying little exchange. So instead, I said, "Eli, take off your clothes and come back to bed."

"Really?" He sounded genuinely surprised.

At first, I was too tired to understand his reaction, but then some more fog cleared from my mind and I remembered our bet.

"I'm not freaking out," I pointed out. "My feelings haven't changed with the rising of the sun. Now get your cute butt back into bed so I can cuddle with you and go back to sleep."

"You're tired."

Good. He understood. "Yes."

"So you're not really awake yet?"

"I don't want to be, but you keep talking instead of snuggling." I blew out a frustrated breath. "Eli, come to bed."

He stood up and hesitantly approached me. "Should I keep my clothes on?"

"Are you cold?" I furrowed my brow. "I'll wrap myself around you and cover us with the blanket so you'll be warm."

"It's not that." He fidgeted with the bottom of his shirt. "But..."

"What?"

He chewed on his lower lip and looked at me from underneath his lashes. "I don't want you to get upset if you wake up and I'm in your bed naked."

"But I'm asking you to get naked," I huffed.

"Well, right *now* you are, but you're not really awake yet."

If my inability to follow our conversation was any

indication, he was right about that.

"You think when I wake up I'll suddenly develop an aversion to your dick?"

"Not suddenly, but—"

"Eli, dammit, I won the bet. It's morning. I still want you to move in with me and I still like your dick, which I will prove by worshipping it over and over again for the rest of our lives, but first I need more sleep. So, please, in the name of all that is good and holy, take off your clothes and get back into bed!"

"The rest of our lives?"

I was never going to sleep again. I'd just be talking all the time. "I'm a commitment kind of guy. You know this."

He gulped. "Yeah, I know."

"Good. Because I'm done with the two of us playing around the edges of this thing. The tension was killing me."

"Edges? What edges?" he asked breathlessly. "I had no idea there were edges."

I'd been working up to telling Eli I wanted to be with him ever since he broke up with his last boyfriend and I'd really upped the ante since he'd moved back home—little comments, a good bit of touching... I'd even bought the house *he'd* liked most. No way he had missed all that, even though he'd found out about my one male hookup and turned my well-orchestrated plan into a shambles before I'd gotten to the part of my plan where I said the words.

"If we're both in town, we don't go more than two

days without seeing each other," I said. "We spend practically every minute together when one of us isn't working. We talk on the phone multiple times a day. Do you do that with anybody else?"

He shook his head.

I arched my eyebrows. "Neither do I. See? Edges."

He kept playing with the shirt he had yet to remove. I would have yanked the thing off him myself, but I was too exhausted to get up.

"That's because I, uh,"—he blushed and dropped his gaze—"well, I maybe stalked you a little."

I sighed tiredly. "At the beginning, maybe, but for the past few years that hasn't been true. I call you as much as you call me." I looked into his eyes. "It's been a long time since the days when you happened to show up at my office around the time I was ready to go home."

His cheeks reddened again. "I did that because I wanted to be with you," he rasped.

"I know. I want that too, which is why I'm keeping you. Now get in bed."

"You're keeping me?"

Was I being unclear? Maybe I was using too many words and I needed to take the simple approach. "Yes."

"Okay, fine," he said, reluctantly. He peeled off his shirt and toed off his shoes. "But you don't get to be mad at me when you're fully awake."

I sighed, said, "I promise," and then I flipped the

blanket up to make a spot for him.

"I didn't make you suck me off. You did that all on your own." He shuffled from one socked foot to the other. "I didn't even ask you to."

"No, you didn't," I agreed, trying not to smile because I knew he was actually worried. It was hard, though, because he was unbelievably cute.

He unbuttoned and unzipped the tight jeans he still favored and then glanced at me and said, "You know, uh, some people would say going down on a guy is pretty gay."

"Well, *some people* are masters of stating the obvious."

"Did you—" He sniffled. "Did you used to go down on your girlfriends?"

No sleep ever again. Ever. I let go of the blanket, rolled onto my back, and stared at the ceiling. "Do you really want to talk about my exes?"

"Uh-huh."

He didn't sound sure, but he was an adult, had been for some time, and I had to take him at his word.

"Yes, I did with two of them." It had been one of my favorite things to do, actually. I rubbed my hands over my tired eyes, took a moment to mourn the fact that they wouldn't be getting more rest, and then looked at him. "I'll tell you anything you want to know, Eli. I won't keep secrets from you. But are you going to let me hold you while we talk about this or are you too anxious?"

"I'm not anxious," he said defensively.

"I know you too well for you to pretend, so don't bother." I slowly sat up. "My vote is for you to be in this bed so I can touch you while we talk." I opened my arms. "How about it?"

After another couple of seconds of hesitation, he climbed onto the mattress and into my arms. He was still wearing his socks, which I didn't point out because I thought he looked adorable bare-ass naked with white gym socks. I got us situated under the blanket with me lying on my back and Eli resting his head on my chest. His soft dick and balls were pressed against my thigh, and I found I liked how that felt. I gave him a squeeze.

"So what do you want to know?" I asked as I gently stroked his hair.

"You had sex with them?"

"My ex-girlfriends? Yes. I only had intercourse with one of them, but sex in general? Yes."

"Did you like it?"

"Yes."

"And you liked doing what we did last night too?"

I gripped his chin and tilted his head so I could look in his eyes. "I *loved* what we did last night. That was the best experience of my life."

He trembled. "Seth, if we do this, I don't think I can—" He gulped. "I don't think I can share you."

I jerked in surprise. "Who the hell said anything about sharing?"

"You've only been with women before, and you said you liked it with them—"

"So if a guy dated a few brunettes and then he falls for a redhead, does that mean he's going to cheat?"

"That's not the same thing," he said.

"For me it is." I took a few breaths to clear my anger at his assumption. Understanding myself hadn't come easily, so expecting all the pieces to quickly fall together for him wasn't fair. Plus, after a few years reading and learning about people's impressions of bisexuality, I knew he wasn't alone in thinking we couldn't be monogamous. "We're all attracted to a range of people, right?"

He didn't answer.

"You've been with other men, Eli. I'm not the first. And you were attracted to them. Right?"

"Yeah."

"But there are some men you're not attracted to. I mean, you've been asked out and turned men down because things didn't click?"

He nodded.

"It's the same deal for me. Some people turn me on and some people don't. The only difference is, with you it's men and with me it's *people*. That's all." I paused. "You with me so far?"

He nodded again.

"Okay. So if you're with me and a man you find attractive comes on to you, are you going to take him up on it just because he's your type?"

"No!" he shouted adamantly.

"See?" I said with a smirk.

He chewed on his lip, scratched his head, and burrowed closer to me. "So you really want to be with me? Just me?"

"Yes." I narrowed my eyes. "And Eli?"

"Uh-huh."

"I don't share either. Not ever."

He shivered and I felt his dick rising against my hip. "Okay," he whispered.

"Okay?" I confirmed.

He nodded.

"Good. Now can we get some sleep?"

"Yeah." He wiggled against me, his shaft seeming to harden with every pass it made against my leg.

I chuckled, suddenly feeling fine about delayed sleep. "You need some help with that, baby?"

"Help with what?"

I reached down and palmed his shaft. "Help with this."

"Ungh." He moaned, bucked, and gripped my waist. "Seth!"

"Maybe I should collect my winnings now after all," I whispered into his ear. He whimpered. "That way I can wear out that active brain of yours and help you get to sleep."

He was panting and humping into my fist.

"But that's not the only reason." I pushed him onto his back and tweaked his nipple. He groaned. I loved how sensitive they were, so I leaned down and tugged one between my teeth. "Want to know the other reason?" I stroked his shaft and suckled on his nipple, eventually letting it go as I settled between his legs. "Eli? Do you want to know?"

"Yeah," he said breathlessly.

I sat back on my heels, held his dick so it was sticking straight up, and kept my gaze locked with his as I bent forward and licked him like a Popsicle.

"Seth." He fisted the sheets. "Oh God."

"The other reason is because I like how you taste," I said while gripping his thighs and pushing them out and to the sides. That left his gorgeous butt on display, and I took full advantage, dropped my face forward, buried it between his muscular cheeks, and puffed my hot breath over his pucker.

He screamed. Honest to goodness screamed. I'd never considered myself an egotistical man, but I must have had some of that in me because seeing the pleasure I gave Eli made me feel like I was something special.

"Hold your legs, baby," I told him.

He looked down at me, wide-eyed and red-cheeked, but didn't move. I chuckled, reached for his hand, uncurled his fingers from the sheet, and placed it on his leg. Then I did the same thing with his other hand.

"Anyone ever done this for you?" I asked even though I suspected the answer.

Over the years, I'd learned that Eli's bed partners hadn't met all his needs. He was shockingly open and honest about all things sexual, so I knew he masturbated a lot and that he liked to finger himself while he did it. But when he had tried to take that act to the next level by being the receptive partner during sex, he'd felt no pleasure, only discomfort.

I'd given that issue a lot of thought—a *lot* of thought—and after some online research, I was pretty sure I knew how to relax him enough for him to enjoy the feeling of taking me inside. But that would come later. I wasn't in a rush, and, frankly, I was looking forward to all the other things I'd get to do with him along the way.

"No," he answered. "And you don't have to."

"Have to?" I cupped his cheeks and spread them apart. "Oh, Eli," I said, my voice gone husky. "I *want* to."

I bent forward and licked my way from the end of his crease up to his balls and back down again. I knew he was moaning, I could hear him, but my own sounds of pleasure were just as loud. Touching him like that, licking and tasting, could become an addiction. When I had him slick and trembling, I pressed my mouth against his pucker and pushed my tongue inside.

"Seth!" he shouted as he arched his back.

I didn't let go of my prize. I just held on to his butt and kept laving, sucking, and tongue-fucking his opening.

"Please," he whimpered. "Please, I...please."

He was trembling and breathing so hard I was worried he'd pass out, so I gave his insides one last wiggle of my tongue and then I pulled out. "Damn," I said and bit his butt cheek. "I could do that forever." I squeezed and massaged the firm globes. "But right now, I think I'd better give you what you asked for." I licked his balls and then sucked them into my mouth for a moment before saying, "Because you asked so nicely."

I released his hands from his legs, thinking his muscles were probably sore, and then I lowered them to the bed and massaged him from calf to thigh and back. He trembled and kept those pretty green eyes focused right on me. I liked that.

"Is that better?" I asked, referring to his muscles. "Still tight?"

"It's good."

I kissed his calf and smiled. "Good." I crawled up, grasped his dick, and swallowed as much of it as I could without choking.

"Seth!" He thrust his hips, and I let him, enjoying the feeling of him taking control of my mouth. As worked up as he was, he couldn't last long, so after only a few sucks up and down his shaft, he emptied himself into my mouth. "You're amazing," he said, sounding awed. He shivered. "Amazing."

I knee-walked a couple of steps until I was straddling his hips, then I took myself in hand and started tugging. "You make me so hard, Eli." I looked at his gorgeous body and handsome face. "Make me want so much."

"In my mouth," he said desperately as he shot up and grabbed my hips. "Please." He pulled me forward. "Come in my mouth."

I nodded. He lay back down and I moved over his body, planted my knees on either side of his chest, and rubbed my prick over his lips. He whimpered and opened for me, letting me move my glans on his waiting tongue.

"You ready?" I asked as I fisted myself quickly, my orgasm just within reach.

With his mouth hanging open, he couldn't answer verbally, so he nodded instead.

"Good." I braced my free hand on the headboard. "Here it comes, baby." I swallowed hard and arched my neck. "Here. It. Comes." I erupted, white heat pulsing out of me and into Eli's waiting mouth. "Yessss," I hissed, reveling in the pleasure and the eroticism of spending myself into him that way. "God," I said shakily once I was done. I wiped my glans across his lips—top then bottom—and moaned when he licked them, then me, and swallowed. "What you do to me, Eli." I lowered myself on top of him, slanted my mouth over his, and kissed him ferociously. "What you do to me."

MIRACLE OF miracles, we got some sleep. Both of us. A lot of it. The next time I woke up, Eli was exactly where I wanted him—nude and plastered to me. He was lying on his side, one leg thrown over my hip, one arm curled over my chest, and his head buried in the spot where my neck and shoulder meet. I took a few minutes to relish that, to enjoy finally having the man I'd longed for and lusted after in my arms.

I hoped the rest would ease his fraying nerves. It wasn't that his frenetic ups and downs bothered me; truth be told, I found them pretty charming. But I didn't want him to be upset and I saw how drained he'd been the previous night and that morning. That thought gave me the idea to make him breakfast. With his sleep and his fuel replenished, he was bound to feel much better.

Creating as little motion as possible, I slid out from under Eli and climbed out of bed. He made a small sound, like a whimper and a sigh, and then curled into a ball and buried his face in my pillow. My breath caught at the sight of him, safe and comfortable, in my bed. It was hard to look away.

What had started out as a complete lack of awareness when he was a kid and then morphed into nervous and amused interest when he was a young man had grown and flourished over the years, and now Eli Block was my confidant, my friend, the person who made me laugh with joy and relax in safety. It had been a slow, gradual process taking him from a boy I didn't notice to a man who, to me, took over the room until I could see nothing else. Eli was my everything and my heart hurt looking at him.

When I reluctantly tore my gaze away from the beauty in my bed, I noticed the boxes I'd left stacked along the perimeter of the room were gone. I poked my head in the closet and found my clothes neatly organized. After grabbing a pair of sweats and stepping into them, I left the room.

The living room and dining room were in the same condition as the bedroom—no boxes. The knickknacks and pictures I'd collected were artfully displayed on furniture, which had been haphazardly placed when I left but was now perfectly arranged. A gorgeous painting hung above the fireplace. I loved abstracts and red was my favorite color, so the art truly called to me. After admiring it and enjoying the layered distinctions in what at first glance seemed like a simple piece, I walked into the kitchen where I found the same situation—boxes gone and cabinets neatly organized.

"Aww, Eli," I said to myself, smiling at his kindness. I should have known he'd unpack and put the house together for me. He was that kind of person: thoughtful and generous. And I was lucky, so lucky, to call him mine.

I hadn't had a chance to stock the house with food before I left for LA, but I'd gotten the staples so I had what I needed to make pancakes. I found fruit in the refrigerator and bananas in a bowl on the counter, which I assumed Eli had bought. I sliced the bananas and arranged them on top of the sizzling pancakes, sprinkled them with brown sugar, and then flipped them over. In between cooking batches of pancakes, I chopped the rest of the fruit and tossed it together to make a salad.

It wasn't long before I had breakfast plated and was on my way into the bedroom. My dilemma about whether to wake Eli up or let the food wait until he was done sleeping on his own was resolved when I found him sitting in bed,

rubbing his hands over his eyes, the blanket pooled at his waist, exposing his lean chest. He looked adorably sleep-rumpled and sexy at the same time.

"Good morning, beautiful," I said, because he was.

He dropped his hands and blinked those mesmerizing green eyes at me. "I thought maybe it was a dream."

I grinned and winked. "I feel the same way." I set the plates on the nightstand and then crawled into bed, straddled Eli's lap, and threaded my fingers through his hair. "Hey, you." I kissed him gently. "Do you feel any better after getting some decent sleep?"

He nodded, threw his arms around my chest, and hugged me tightly.

"I bet you're hungry. I made banana pancakes."

"I love banana pancakes," he said against my skin, the words muffled but still understandable.

"I know. I put brown sugar on top like you like." I tilted my chin toward the nightstand, causing Eli to raise his head and follow my gaze.

"You made me breakfast in bed?" He sounded odd.

"Sure I did." I kissed his cheek, then his chin, then his neck. "I want to take care of you. Feeding you is a part of that." I licked his neck and nibbled on his earlobe. "Speaking of which, thank you for taking care of everything here while I was gone. The house looks great, and that painting you got is perfect."

"You like it?" He smiled excitedly. "It's a housewarming

present."

"It's amazing. I think I'll see some new aspect to it every time I look." I traced his spine with my fingers and kissed his cheek. Not touching and kissing him was impossible. "So what should I get you as a housewarming present?"

"What do you mean?"

"Well, you're moving in here, right?" I lapped at his lower lip, tugged it between my teeth, and then let go. "I should get you a present. Do you want a painting from that same artist or something else?"

"I'm sorry." He gulped. "I'm still stuck on the part of that where you said I'm moving in." He searched my eyes. "You're sure?"

"We've been over this. I want you, Eli, in my life, in my house, and in my bed." I brushed his hair off his forehead. "What do you say?"

"Yes. I say yes." He shivered. "Yes."

"Good." I smiled. "Let me feed you and then we can get dressed and head over to your parents' house."

"My parents?" he asked in confusion.

I reached over to the nightstand, got a plate, forked some fruit, and held it up to Eli. He opened to me right away, closed his mouth over the fork, and pulled the fruit off. It was the most erotic act of eating I'd ever seen. My throat suddenly felt thick, and I had to clear it before I could answer his question.

"Sure. We need to tell them you're going to be moving

in and you won't be here for Thanksgiving." I winced. "Hopefully they won't be too mad. With as many people as they have over, maybe they'll be grateful for the extra seating space."

He swallowed down the food in his mouth and gaped at me. "Why won't I be there for Thanksgiving?"

"Oh." I realized we hadn't talked about the logistics of what we were about to do. "My uncle is getting married on Sunday, so it'll be a good chance for you to meet my whole extended family, but I figured we'd go to LA tomorrow or Wednesday so we can spend Thanksgiving with just my immediate family. I think it'll be easier for you to get to know them in a smaller setting."

"You want me to meet your family?"

I cut off a piece of pancake and fed it to him. "Of course I do. We're going to be living together. My mother will show up unannounced and camp out on our front porch if I don't bring you to meet her."

He gulped. "Okay, so we're going to my parents' house and we're going to tell them that we're together now and I'm moving in here."

"Yes."

"And then you want to take me to LA to meet your family and introduce me as the man you're living with in a non-roommate kind of way?"

There was a time, years earlier, when I'd been worried that if I acted on my feelings for Eli, I'd find out I wasn't actually comfortable being with a man, that it wouldn't feel right. Sitting there in that moment, with Eli in my bed, my body still singing from what we'd shared earlier that morning and my heart warm from the knowledge of how much he cared about me and how deeply my own feelings for him ran, I knew unequivocally that I'd been wrong. There was nothing more natural than being with Eli and walking through life with him by my side.

"Yes," I said firmly.

He looked into my eyes, seemingly searching them again, and then he took a deep breath and grinned. "Well, all righty, then. Let's tell the parents." He stuffed a piece of pancake into his mouth and said, "This should be interesting."

CHAPTER FIFTEEN

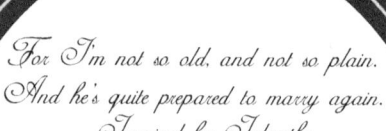

For I'm not so old, and not so plain.
And he's quite prepared to marry again.
— Inspired by Iolanthe

Dorothy Sutton and Scott Cohen
invite you to join us to witness our
commitment to each other as we are
married.

Sunday, November 25, 2007, two in
the afternoon, Temple Jerusalem, Los
Angeles, California.

Eli Block

"YOUR DAD said he'll be done with the wedding in time for us to go there for dinner tonight," Seth said as he walked into his—according to him, soon to be our—living room. "We can get a flight to LA tomorrow morning so we don't have to fly Thanksgiving Day."

The original plan had been to go talk to my parents on Monday, but between the sex and the sleep, the day had gotten away from us. Monday night wasn't an option because my dad had been officiating a wedding, so we'd had to push things to Tuesday. There was yet another wedding that day, but it was in the afternoon, so Seth had called to confirm what time my dad would be home and let him know we'd be coming over.

"I'm amazed he didn't tell you to do the wedding instead of him the second he found out you were in town."

Seth sat down next to me, and I mean *right* next to me. My breath caught and my heart raced. We'd sat together countless times on countless sofas, but it hadn't been like that. Never before had he pressed his body to mine, caressed my knee and thigh, and nuzzled my neck. It wasn't that he was trying to start another round of "Oh, God, yes, please" but more like he wanted to be close.

"He did," Seth said. "But I told him we had a bad connection and I couldn't hear him."

"Oh," I said breathlessly, his proximity alone enough to

make me a little light-headed. I shivered, moaned, and spread my legs to give him better access to anything he wanted. "You called his cell?"

"Nope." Seth smirked and kissed my chin. "He was on his landline."

I furrowed my brow. "But you were calling from your houseline. Why would you have a bad connection?"

"We didn't." He rolled his hand over my knee and inner thigh.

Over the past couple of days, Seth had been all over me, touching me all the time, gazing at me with this heart-melting expression on his face, kissing me over and over again. I loved every moment of it, soaked up his attention and felt like I was glowing, like I'd never stop smiling, like I truly knew what it meant to be happy. But I was still hesitant to let myself believe it was real.

When I moved home to Emile City, I knew my life would change. I'd be starting my career in what I hoped would be a part-time way while I got my doctorate in music. I'd have a chance to spend more time with friends I'd missed. I'd leave the life of a transient student and start my real life.

Those were my expectations, anyway. As it turned out, the biggest change wasn't one I'd expected or even let myself fantasize about: Seth Cohen, the man I'd wanted since I knew what it was to want, suddenly wanted me back. Or at least it felt sudden to me. I was still wrapping my brain around all of it, still wondering if at any moment I'd wake up from the most amazing dream ever, but Seth was forging full steam ahead, which was why he had called my father.

Forcing myself to remain focused on the conversation at hand, despite his arousing touches, I said, "You're saying Mister Play-by-the-Book lied to his boss?" I was trying to sound shocked but instead came off as amused, because I was.

"He knew what number I called from," Seth said. He dragged his hand up my belly to my chest and played with my nipple through my shirt. I was sensitive there, really sensitive, which I assumed he had noticed because he paid them a lot of attention. "It wasn't a lie. I was making a point. It's his turn to suffer through some weddings." He lapped at the skin on the base of my neck and sucked up a mark right under my shirt line. "Besides, I already had plans to spend the day with you."

"I cannot believe I'm hard again," I rasped. "With as much action as I've been getting the past couple of days, I'd be worried my dick was going to fall off if it wasn't for that challenge."

The hand that had been on my knee and thigh was heading toward my groin when Seth straightened, stopping the forward progression, and said, "What challenge?"

"Oh, uh." I cleared my throat and tried to focus through the seemingly constant haze of lust. "That jack-off challenge I did."

He looked confused.

"Didn't I tell you about that?"

He shook his head.

"Oh." I smiled. "So when I was, uh"—I thought back—"about seventeen, almost eighteen, I thought it'd be fun to see how many times I could get off in one day."

Seth snorted in amusement, wrapped his arms around me, and pulled me onto his lap.

"What?" I asked.

"Nothing." He shook his head and smiled. "That sounds just like you, is all. I met you not long after that, remember? You were a ball of hormones."

I bit his chin, because I could, and said, "Quit teasing me, old man, or you won't get the benefit of those hormones."

"Oh, is that right?" He arched one eyebrow. "You're going to cut me off?"

I thought about it and furrowed my brow. "No. That'd be stupid because I'd be punishing myself." I wiggled and rubbed my butt over his semihard shaft. "But I'm sure I can figure out some way to punish you without impacting my orgasms."

"Speaking of orgasms..." Seth said expectantly and let the sentence trail off.

"What...oh! Right. So anyway, my parents went out of town for the weekend, and I was old enough to stay home alone. I got a bottle of lotion, some snacks and sodas, and pretty much holed up in my bedroom the entire time."

"How'd you do?" He caressed my backside.

"Ten times," I said. "It was a personal best, for sure,

but by the end it wasn't as much fun because my dick was sore and a little chafed."

Seth's eyes widened. "You jacked off ten times in one day?"

"Yeah." I shrugged. "I mean, I only got a couple of drops out in the last few, but I was aiming for a record and I'm not a quitter."

He stared at me for a few seconds, then threw back his head and laughed deeply.

"What?" I asked.

He tugged me close, tucked my head under his chin, and held on tightly. "Nothing." He shook his head and squeezed me. "I just love you," he said in amusement and then laughed again.

The world stopped spinning and I froze, not blinking, not breathing. It was possible my heart even stopped beating.

"Eli?" Seth cupped my chin and tilted my head up so he could look at my face. "What's wrong?"

"You love me?" I croaked.

He looked genuinely confused. "Of course I love you." He paused and then paled. "I forgot to tell you, didn't I?"

I nodded and gulped.

"Damn. It was part of my plan, but everything got thrown off when you heard about Nate Richardson and—"

"Uh-huh, whatever." I looked into his eyes. "You love me?"

He smiled then, a warm ray of sunshine, and his eyes

softened as he gazed at me. "I love you so much, Eli." He drew in a shaky breath. "So very much."

My hesitation about whether he'd change his mind about being with me, about moving me into his house, and about building a life with a man—instead of a woman—by his side melted away in the wake of those words.

"It's your turn." Seth's eyes twinkled in amusement, and he smiled wryly.

"Huh?" I asked, feeling overwhelmed by having everything I'd ever wanted suddenly land in my lap.

"I told you I love you," Seth explained as he combed his fingers through my hair. "The traditional response to that is 'I love you too.'"

"Oh." I blinked for what might have been the first time in minutes.

"Let's try this again." Seth brushed his lips over mine, cleared his throat, and said, "Eli Block, I love you."

When he looked at me and arched his eyebrows expectantly, I snapped into the moment and whispered, "I love you too, Seth." I cuddled against him and held back tears of joy. "I love you too."

YOU KNOW what's the only thing weirder than the guy you've been obsessing over forever telling you he loves you and essentially wants to spend his remaining days boinking your brains out? Finding out your parents already knew about it.

"I'm glad you two finally got things sorted out," my father said between bites of my mother's famous vegetable medley. "The tension was killing me."

I dropped my jaw and my fork.

"See?" Seth calmly said as he tipped my mouth shut, picked up my fork, and handed it to me. "I'm not the only one who felt that way."

"Eli, honey, you're picking at your food. Don't you like it?"

"No."

She gasped.

"Uh, I mean, yeah, I like it."

She moved her gaze from my face to my plate and back up again. I stabbed my fork at whatever was underneath it, raised it to my mouth, and chewed something; I had no idea what because my senses were failing me, starting with my sense of touch and including my sense of taste.

My mother beamed when she saw me eating, took a sip of her water, and then excitedly said, "Oh! I have a wonderful idea. I can pack up your room and move your things into Seth's house while you're visiting the Cohens."

"No!" I shouted, visions of my mother going through my porn and folding my cum rag bouncing in my head. When she narrowed her eyes and pursed her lips, I cleared my throat, lowered my voice, and said, "I, uh, appreciate the offer, Mom, but I'll take care of packing my stuff."

My father shook his head, made a tsk sound, and then said, "Well, he's your problem now, Seth." He flicked his gaze to my mother. "Do we have any more of that pie Gladys Leroy brought over?"

"His problem now...what the hell, Dad? I'm not some damn Victorian maiden being given away to her betrothed!"

"Not with that language, you're not," my father responded.

"Really, Eli," my mother added. "We're at the dinner table." She turned to my father. "I think there's one piece of pie left and I have some brownies if the boys want dessert too."

"I'd like a brownie," Seth said, completely nonflummoxed by the exchange. He pushed back his chair, stood up, and started gathering plates. "I'll take these into the kitchen and bring out the pie, Avi. Is it in the fridge?"

My father nodded. "Yes. The brownies are on the counter. Go ahead and bring me one of those too."

"I'll get the milk," my mother said as she helped Seth gather plates, then she strolled into the kitchen.

"What about you, baby? Do you want a brownie?" Seth asked. He hunched down and nuzzled my cheek. "You didn't eat much. Are you feeling okay?"

I jerked my gaze toward my father to see his reaction to Seth calling me "baby" and being so affectionate. He was leaning over one of the serving bowls and nibbling on the remnants of whatever had been in there, completely unaffected by our exchange.

"Don't you think it's weird?" I whispered to Seth.

He sat down and leaned close to me. "What?"

"The way my parents are acting."

He darted his gaze around the room. There was nothing to see other than my father getting ready to lick a bowl clean.

"What do you mean?" he asked.

"You know. They're all, 'Oh you and Seth are a couple now. Great. Pass the peas.'"

"There were peas?" my father said, making me realize he could hear us. He furrowed his brow and looked around the table. "Where?"

I ignored him and focused on Seth. "See?"

"You weren't exactly discreet about your feelings for me, Eli," Seth pointed out. "Why would they be surprised?"

"Because," I hissed. "You always said you weren't interested!"

"Oh, that." Up until that point, Seth had been holding the dirty plates, but he set them down and took my hands between both of his. "Like I told you, that changed a long time ago."

"Well, yeah, but how did *they* know?"

"Because we have eyes," my father said helpfully.

"And ears," my mother added as she walked into the room.

I gaped.

Seth cupped my cheek and gazed at me fondly. "And because I told them."

"You did?" I probably sounded awestruck. I certainly felt that way.

"Yes. I had a plan, remember? I was going to court you and—"

"Court?" I snickered. "Who says court?"

"Eli!" my mother snapped. "Don't be rude. Seth was being very romantic."

"Sorry, old man." I smirked at him. "Please, do continue," I said in my impression of a formal old-world dialect.

"Are you sure you want him, Seth?" my father asked. "He can be a sarcastic little pain in the butt."

Seth looked at me, his eyes glowing with happiness and a smile stretched across his handsome face. "Yes, but he's *my* sarcastic little pain in the butt, and I'm keeping him."

I considered making a dirty joke about his butt and working in a snip about my dick not being little, but I refrained. I figured that showed some serious emotional maturity on my part.

REMEMBER HOW I said the only thing weirder than finding out Seth wanted to be with me was finding out my parents already knew about it? I was wrong. That wasn't the only thing.

"Eli, honey, it's so great to finally meet you!" Seth's mother Dee Dee said the second we walked into her house. She kissed my cheek, hugged me, and said, "Are you hungry? I bet you are after that flight."

"Hi, uh, Mrs. Co—"

"It's Dee Dee or Mom. Do you want some chicken? How about soup?"

No way was I calling her "Mom." I was already freaking the fuck out and I didn't need another Jewish mother. One was plenty.

"Oh, thanks, Dee Dee, but I'm not really hungr—"

"How about a little snack?" She circled her hand around my elbow and started leading me away from the entryway. "You're too thin." She frowned. "I'm going to talk to your mother about that."

Right. Because my mom would totally appreciate that kind of advice. Dee Dee might as well tell her she's an unfit mother guilty of extreme neglect.

I flicked my panicked gaze to Seth, who not so helpfully liberated me from the suitcase I was holding and wandered away in the opposite direction, saying, "We're in the same guest room I always stay in, right, Mom?"

"Yes, Seth. I made up the bed and left clean towels for you and Eli."

"Thanks, Mom." Seth, the traitor, left me there. "Is Dad at work?"

"Yes, but he'll be back any minute." Dee Dee didn't stop walking until were in the kitchen. "I made mandelbrodt. Your mom said it's your favorite."

"My mom?"

"Yes. I called her this morning to find out what you like to eat." She led me to a chair and stared at me until I sat down. Then she humphed in satisfaction and went over to the counter. "That's how I knew to add in chocolate chips." She placed a plate overflowing with the biscotti-like cookies in front of me. "You can eat those until your stomach settles."

Who said anything about my stomach?

"Then we'll have dinner."

After I ate the entire pan of mandelbrodt?

"Do you want milk?" She didn't wait for my answer, just went to fridge, got the milk, and poured me a forty-four ounce cup of it. Then she hovered there until I picked up a piece of mandelbrodt and bit into it.

Oh my God. I *did* have two Jewish mothers. Where was Seth? How long could it take to put suitcases down?

"Mom!" I heard Seth yell. "I'm going to go pick up Dad. His battery's dead. Eli, do you want to come with me?"

"No, dear, he's eating."

No way would Seth just take her word for that without asking me or coming in to see how I was doing.

"Okay. I'll be back in half an hour."

I was going to kill Seth. Kill him. Assuming I was still conscious when he came back. If I had to eat that entire plate of food, my stomach was sure to burst.

"So." Dee Dee cleared her throat. "Eli."

I snapped to attention and focused on Seth's mother. Something in her tone made my stomach drop. The piercing gaze didn't help. Neither did the raised eyebrow.

"Seth gave up a lot to be with you."

Oh God.

"You understand that, right?"

"I, uh…" What the fuck was I supposed to say? I gulped. "I'm going to take good care of him."

She narrowed her eyes. "I'm not referring to sex, young man."

Neither was I! Oh. My. God. Neither was I!

"He could have had a wife. Someone to manage things at home so he can focus on work, make sure he's eating well." She paused. "Make sure he calls me regularly."

"I'll do that," I rushed out.

She didn't look convinced, and I didn't blame her. I took a deep breath.

"You're right," I said, noticing her eyes widen in surprise and then narrow in suspicion. Chances were better than not that I'd throw up. "Seth could have found a woman to be with. But he chose me." I looked down at the table and fiddled with my food nervously. "And I will never take that for granted." I gathered my strength and raised my gaze. "I love him, Dee Dee. I always have. Did he tell you that?" I didn't wait for her answer before dropping my gaze and continuing.

"When I was a kid, I was sure we'd end up together, and then when I thought that wasn't going to happen—" I swallowed down the thickness in my throat. "Well, that sucked, but he was willing to be my friend and I figured if that's what he wanted then I'd be the best friend he'd ever had. Whatever role Seth wants me to play in his life, that's what I'll do and I'll do it better than anyone else because all I've ever wanted is to be with him." I looked at her and willed her to understand. "I know he's older and smarter and nicer and, well, better than me, but he's the most important person in my life, and nobody can take care of him like I will. Nobody."

The silence stretched out for what felt like a lifetime but was probably only a few seconds, and then she said, "Well, you're right about one thing."

I racked my brain to remember what I'd said.

"He is older than you." She stood up. "But the rest of it's baloney." She gazed down at me. "Seth has talked about little else but you for years now, Eli, so I know what kind of man you are, and I know my son is just as fortunate to have you as you are to have him."

What just happened? I thought she was against Seth being with me. Realization struck and my jaw dropped. That was a test. She'd been testing me. With years of training being raised by my mother, how had I not seen that coming?

"Eat your mandelbrodt," she said as she started walking out of the kitchen.

I reached my shaky hand for a piece, bit into it, and

brushed the resulting crumbs off my shirt.

"Oh, and Eli?" She stopped at the doorway, her back to me.

"Yes?" I desperately tried to catch the crumbs so I could put them on my plate before they hit the shiny wood floor.

"A wife would be able to give me grandchildren. I assume you'll make sure that happens."

I was pretty sure I was going to pass out. Deep breaths. Deep breaths.

"Yes," I squeaked.

She dipped her head in a sharp nod and left.

I briefly worried about how Seth would react to what I'd just agreed to and then decided it was his own fault for leaving me vulnerable and unprotected in his mother's clutches. Once she was gone, I stuffed another cookie into my mouth and mumbled, "Serves him right" under my breath.

"What'd you say?" Dee Dee called from somewhere else in the house.

Fabulous. On top of her military-grade interrogation techniques, she had bat hearing.

"The mandelbrodt is dynamite!" I answered. "Even better than my mom's."

See? Dee Dee Cohen wasn't the only one with emotional sabotage skills. My mother would have been proud.

CHAPTER SIXTEEN

Modern love gets me to the church on time.
— David Bowie

Lori Samms and Scott Angles together with their parents Judith and Robert
Samms and James and Loretta Angles invite you to share their joy when
they exchange marriage vows and begin their new life together.
At Sevenish on April 10, 2010.
Preston Manor, Preston, Idaho.

Eli Block

"AND HERE you say I never take you anywhere," Seth joked as we drove our rental car into the tiny town of Preston, situated in Idaho close to the Utah border.

I turned away from the nonexistent scenery and smiled at my boyfriend. "I didn't say that, but if I did, this trip would be proving my point." It took no more than three minutes to drive through the whole of the downtown, and then we were passing by farm fields and quaint midcentury houses. "Are you sure people like us are allowed here?"

He glanced at me. "People like us meaning Jewish

people, people like us meaning gay people, or people like us meaning extraordinarily adorable people." He refocused on the road. "Wait, the last one is just you, so you must mean the other two."

I smiled, reached for his free hand, and raised it to my lips for a kiss before setting it on my lap. "You're not sick of looking at my mug day after day yet?"

The previous three years had flown by in a blur of afternoons snuggling on the couch, evenings laughing while we cooked dinner, and nights burning up the sheets. Reality isn't supposed to be as great as fantasies and daydreams, but mine was even better.

"Never going to happen." He squeezed my hand. "In answer to your question, I think their Jewish population is hovering right around zero percent, which is why Loretta Angles begged me to come here and officiate her son's wedding."

"And the gay census?" I asked, feeling a little worried about being shoved into a closet, both literally and figuratively.

"I don't know." Seth shrugged. "But I told the owner of the bed-and-breakfast where they're having the wedding that we only use one bedroom at home so there's no reason for her to set aside two rooms for us here, and she told me she has a lesbian daughter who lives in St. Louis." He paused. "Do you know Ren Moroni?"

"No." I furrowed my brow in thought. "Am I supposed to?"

"Only if you're supposed to know the entirety of the lesbian population of St. Louis," he said deadpan. "The bed-and-breakfast owner seemed to think sharing a bed with you meant I should know her daughter."

"Oh!" I looked at him excitedly. "*That* Ren Moroni. Short hair? Drives a pickup truck? Plays in the rec softball league?"

Seth shot me a dirty look.

I cracked up. "Kidding!"

"Stereotyping isn't funny."

"Relax, old man."

He grunted.

I got out my phone and started typing.

"Who're you texting?" he asked.

"Kelsey."

"Noah's friend Kelsey?"

"Uh-huh."

"Why?"

"Because she's a lesbian." I sent my text and then looked at him, trying to keep my expression innocent. "I'm asking her permission to deviate from the PC rules when I don't mean any harm and nobody else is listening." I paused. "She has authority to do that, right? It's, like, part of their code?"

"You're not funny."

My phone dinged, indicating a text had come in. I glanced down and then held the phone up triumphantly.

"See! Kelsey thinks my joke was fucking hilarious." I pointed at the phone. "Her words, not mine."

He flicked his gaze toward the phone, looking wholly unimpressed. "This is the same woman who thinks it's funny to give you phallic-shaped food and then loudly warn you not to put it in the wrong hole. Her opinion of humor isn't to be trusted."

I rolled my eyes. "She does not."

He pulled his hand away and raised one finger. "The cucumber at Jonathan and David's house."

I snickered. "I forgot about that. Anyway, it was one—"

A second finger joined the first. "The hot dog at Noah and Clark's barbeque."

"Okay, fine two tim—"

"The carrot at Caleb and Andrew's fancy dinner thing."

"That was ridiculous," I scoffed. "Who would put one of those tiny baby carrots up their butt?"

"Well, Caleb said it was organic."

"If I cared about the all-natural qualities of everything that went up my ass, I'd have a lot less fun in bed," I pointed out.

One of the things I hadn't expected when I'd longed for a relationship with Seth was how uninhibited he'd be in bed. In his day-to-day life, Seth was a model of restraint and professionalism, but I'd learned that when it came to sex, he had no problem getting down and dirty. Because of our long-standing friendship, he had known how much I liked pleasuring my own hole and how little I'd enjoyed butt action with other people. It hadn't taken long for him to remedy that with patience, a killer tongue, and liberal use of anal toys that got me relaxed and stimulated enough to take his thick cock with no discomfort.

"Speaking of your gorgeous butt," he said. "I saw on the bed-and-breakfast's website that each room has its own Jacuzzi tub, so I picked up a new toy."

That was enough to get my dick interested. "What kind of toy?" I asked huskily.

"You'll see." He smirked.

"Is it in your suitcase?" I unbuckled my seat belt, kneeled on the seat, and twisted around, reaching for the suitcase.

"Eli!" Seth shouted. "That's not safe. Buckle up."

I rolled my eyes. "Where is it?"

"Seriously." He grabbed my shirt and tugged.

"Both hands on the wheel," I goaded him. "Safety first, remember?"

He growled.

"Is it in the main compartment or one of the zippered pouches?" I started opening the suitcase.

"If I get in an accident, you'll fly through the windshield."

I dug through his clothes. "Well, then, don't get in an accident. Seems like an easy solution to that problem."

"I can't control the other drivers on the road."

"There aren't any other drivers on this road." I heard a crinkling sound, looked under Seth's shirts, and found a brown paper bag. "Aha!" I said victoriously. "Is this it?"

He glanced at me, nodded, and said, "Yes. Now sit down and put on your seat belt."

I sat down, ran my hand down the inside of his thigh, and said, "Are you sure?" while giving him my best sultry look.

It was hard not to laugh when he looked at me incredulously and said, "What do you think you're doing?"

"Seducing you." I licked my lips exaggeratedly.

"Eli Block, quit screwing around!"

I cracked up, scooted back to my seat, and pulled on my seat belt.

"You think you're pretty funny, don't you?" he said.

"Yeah, I do, old man."

"Keep that up and I won't play with our new toy."

Playing with the new toy meant playing with me, which was something I knew Seth loved to do, so I doubted he'd stick to that threat. He got off big-time on playing with my hole—fingering me, rimming me, and putting all sorts of toys inside my channel and rubbing them against my gland. Sometimes it was a prelude to fucking, but other times he got off just by driving me to the brink over and over again and watching me finally fall over the edge in a puddle of sweat, tears of passion, and sticky ejaculate. During those times, he loved to look at my hole while he beat off and then shot on my sensitive skin. Like I said, prim and proper Rabbi Seth Cohen turned out to be really down and dirty.

"It's waterproof?" I asked as I pulled out the silicone vibrating plug.

"Uh-huh."

I wiggled in my seat, clenched and released my butt, and rubbed the heel of my hand over my nuts. "Drive faster."

"THIS IS our room," Seth said as he unlocked the door to the room we'd be staying in for the weekend. He herded me inside quickly, flipped the lock, and put down the suitcase. "There's an exterior wall on one side and the room on the other side had a plumbing leak, so she can't put any guests in it."

"How'd you manage that?" I left my suitcase next to his and toed off my shoes.

Seth unbuttoned his shirt and shrugged it off. "I said I'm a really light sleeper and any noise makes it hard for me to rest, so she said we can stay in here."

"You lied?" I asked, pretending to be appalled but not doing a great job of it because I was bouncing from foot to foot taking off my socks.

"It was for the greater good." He kicked off his shoes, unbuckled his belt, and shoved his chinos down over his hips.

"And what greater good is that?" I pulled my shirt over my head.

"Well." He stalked toward me and I froze with my hands on my jeans button and my gaze riveted on the hard, thick flesh swinging between his legs. "With what I have planned for you, I'm pretty sure you'll be making lots of those sexy noises I love."

"Sexy noises?" I asked distractedly, my focus still on his rising flesh. I licked my lips.

"You want to suck me, baby?" He took himself in hand and stroked his big palm over his shaft.

I was on my knees in a flash, a whimper the sound of my agreement.

"Only a little, okay? I want to be inside you tonight."

"Ungh," I moaned, just the thought of Seth stretching my hole and sliding into my passage almost enough to have me creaming my pants. I lapped at his slit, closing my eyes in pleasure at the flavor of his early seed. "Mmm, Seth."

"You like that, baby?" He rubbed his glans over my lips and tongue. "Want more?" I parted my lips, tipped my head back, and locked my gaze with his. "That's it." He traced my lips with his finger. "Love how eager you are." He placed his crown on my lower lip and slowly pushed inside. "It's so hot." He cupped my cheek and looked at me lovingly. "You're so beautiful."

After a few strokes, he tangled his fingers in my hair and rocked his hips back and forth. I let him do all the moving at first but then the urge to suck became too strong to resist. I clasped his hips, digging the tips of my fingers into his butt, and tugged him in and out as I tightened my lips around him. The unmistakable sounds of wet sliding and aroused moaning filled the room in an erotic symphony.

"We need to stop," Seth gasped, not slowing down one bit. "You're so good at that, but..." Though he looked pained, he stepped back, removing his cock from my mouth.

I whimpered at the loss and looked up at him in confusion, my mind a haze of lust and need.

"I want to make love to you, baby." He hunched down and lifted me to my feet. "And I want to play with your tight little hole." Those words made me whimper. "Let's get in the bath, okay?" He unzipped my jeans and shoved them down along with my briefs. "I want to test out our new toy."

I nodded, gulped, and rasped, "Please."

He led me to the bathroom, caressing me while we walked and taking little breaks to kiss my neck, my chin, my nose, and my cheek. "I'll get the water ready," he said when we were standing in front of the large bathtub. "You wait right here." He caressed my cheek, kissed my forehead tenderly, and then turned around and started working on the bath.

I waited, enjoying the view of his tight backside as he bent over and the play of muscles as he stretched.

"Ready, baby?" He helped me into the tub, and once I was sitting said, "I'll be right back. Need anything?"

"No." I shook my head. "I'm good."

He kissed the back of my hand and walked out of the room. I sank into the tub and closed my eyes, letting the silky heat of the water and bubbles relax me.

"I can't decide if that's sexy or funny."

I blinked my eyes open to see Seth leaning over me, a couple of bottles of water in one hand and the paper bag containing the toy in the other.

"What?" I asked.

He tilted his chin toward my groin, and when I followed his gaze, I saw my dick bobbing above the bubbles.

"Oh my God, that's huge! What is it?" I asked in mock fear. "It's a snake! It's a bat! It's"—I looked at him wide-eyed—"Superdick!"

He shook his head, opened a bottle of water, and handed it to me. "Here you go, Superdick. You're probably thirsty."

"Thank you." I took the water and gulped it all down.

He put his half-finished bottle on the ground next to where he'd set the paper bag and then he climbed into the tub, settling himself behind me and wrapping his arms around my chest.

"I love you, Eli," he whispered in my ear and nuzzled my neck.

I draped my arms over his and leaned back against him. "I love you too."

I was deeply relaxed, feeling loose, my breathing slow, when I shot up in a panic, splashing water over the edge of the tub, and said, "Did you call your mother? You forgot on Monday and then she called on Wednesday and you promised you'd—"

"Yes." He chuckled. "I called her yesterday."

"Oh, good." I slumped in relief.

He stretched his leg and turned off the tap with his foot. "I think it's cute how you're always so worried about me calling her."

"Cute?" I asked incredulously. "You think it's cute? I'm afraid for my life here."

"Oh, come on. You're being silly. You know my mother would never hurt you."

"Not physically, maybe. But mentally's a whole other story. It'd only take her a few seconds to have me standing in a corner, rocking back and forth and mumbling nonsense."

"You've been watching *Blair Witch* again, haven't you?"

"No, I haven't," I said in a rush.

He arched an eyebrow.

"Okay, fine, I have. What're you going to do about it? Make me watch twenty hours of musicals as penance?"

Quick as lightning, he was kneeling in the tub and pinching my butt.

"Seth!" I squeaked and laughed. "Stop!"

He didn't stop.

"That tickles!"

"It does?"

He totally knew it tickled.

"Cut it out!" I shrieked.

I kept wiggling, but I didn't move away, so he kept

pinching until eventually I collapsed on him, rested my arms on his shoulders, and kissed his neck. "Stop," I said softly.

He did, immediately replacing the pinches with a wonderful caress.

"Mmm, I like that." I licked my way to his ear and suckled on his earlobe.

"I love touching you." He slid his fingers into my crease and kept his palms on my cheeks, massaging my muscles as he stroked my sensitive channel.

I rocked my hips, rubbing my erection against his belly and pushing back into his touch. "'S good," I mumbled.

"Yes, it is." He kept one hand on my ass, cupped the back of my head with the other, and tugged until our lips met.

On the list of things I'd learned about Seth was that he adored kissing. He'd hold me and ghost his hands over my butt or my back or my face and never stop moving his mouth over mine. It was amazing. Sometimes when I had a hard day with something at work or school or whatever, he'd order a pizza so we didn't have to cook and then spend the night on the couch with me, making out.

"Eli, baby." He kissed his way down my neck. "Turn around." He tipped me slightly back and nibbled on my nipples before sucking on them. "I want to play with you."

I nodded but didn't move. My nipples were sensitive, and when he pulled his mouth away, he replaced it with his fingers, tweaking and twisting.

"Seth," I moaned and gazed into his eyes, needing

to see his expression. I loved the way he looked at me. No matter how many years passed, I felt a little surprised and a lot awed by the adoration in his face and the knowledge that it was aimed at me.

"I'm right here, baby." He caressed my cheek. "Let me make you feel good."

I gulped, nodded, and scooted off his lap. "Where do you want me?"

"Let's rinse the soap off first." He used his toe to flick the lever on the tub so it would drain and then he reached around me, turned on the tap, and directed the water into the handheld showerhead. "Turn around and I'll get you clean."

Doing what he said, I faced the opposite direction and immediately felt the warm water trickle over my head and shoulders. He poured water over me slowly and when my hair was wet, he set the showerhead down, squeezed shampoo on my hair, and massaged it into my scalp. By the time he had the shampoo rinsed out, the rest of the water had drained out of the tub.

"Kneel," he whispered into my ear.

I did and he rotated the showerhead all around my body—shoulders, chest, back, belly, and ass.

"Bend over." He kissed the back of my neck. "Hands on the bottom of the tub, shoulders down, butt up."

I trembled with arousal. Seth was confident and aggressive in bed, which was a huge turn-on. But he was also tender and affectionate, which made me feel safe letting him take the lead.

"Like this?" I asked when I was in position, my forehead resting on the bottom of the now empty tub and my ass in the air.

"Yes, baby, just like that." He ghosted his palm over my backside. "So beautiful." He gripped one side of my ass and spread me open, then he drizzled warm water on me, washing off any remaining soap. "There you go." He kissed my butt and set the showerhead down. "All clean."

I knew what was coming next, but knowing isn't the same as experiencing, so I cried out when Seth made contact with my rosebud, licking and sucking and driving me mad with lust. When he pressed his tongue into my body, I shouted out some strangled version of a prayer or his name or both and scrambled for my dick, taking myself in hand and stroking as I rocked back against Seth's talented mouth.

I felt amazing, so aroused and needy that I couldn't stop shaking. Which was why I was surprised when Seth pulled his mouth back and said, "Are you cold, baby? You're shivering."

I tried to tell him that every one of my nerves was focused on the pleasure he was giving me so temperature wasn't registering at all, but my tongue felt thick and my mouth felt dry. Besides, he was already solving the perceived problem by reaching around me and turning on the water.

"Let's fill the tub again." He gently straightened me until I was kneeling in the tub with my back pressed to his front. Then he rubbed his palm over my chest, caressing and massaging my pecs as he kissed my neck and shoulder. "Plant your hands on the wall, Eli."

I did immediately, bending over and pressing both palms to the cool tile.

"Now spread your knees." He rubbed his hands down my inner thighs, and I scooted them apart as far as I could within the confines of the tub. "That's perfect." One last kiss to my back and then Seth's heat moved away.

I heard the rustling of the paper bag followed by the popping of a cap, and I tilted my butt up in invitation. Almost immediately, he rubbed slick fingers against my opening, circling the sensitized skin.

"I like how you touch me," I mumbled.

Seth kissed my shoulder. "I like it too," he said as he pushed a lubed finger past my tight entrance and into my hole.

"Ungh," I moaned and grunted, enjoying the feeling of penetration.

"You're so hot inside." He was leaning over me, pressing his finger in and out and his face close enough that I could feel his hot breath on my neck. "So tight." He licked my back and fucked me with his finger while I moaned and writhed and felt myself relax and open to his touch. "There you are." He gave me a gentle bite. "I think you're ready for more now."

He pulled his digit out and then I felt the slick silicone

slowly entering my body. Seth knew me well, both who I was and how my body worked. He knew I needed patience to stretch and accommodate something inside and he always gave it to me. Inch by inch, he pressed the toy forward, all the while caressing my flank, whispering soothing words, and kissing my back.

"How do you feel?" he asked once it was all the way in my passage.

I clenched and released, enjoying the feeling of being spread and filled with no discomfort. "Good." I wiggled from side to side and hissed at the movement against my prostate. "Really good."

"I'm glad." He kissed my nape, turned off the tap, and said, "Let's sit."

I nodded. "Okay."

Seth sat down, leaned against the end of the tub, and pulled me between his spread thighs—my back to his chest. "Put your legs on top of mine."

I draped my legs over his and hunched down, the position leaving my hips tilted so my plugged hole was accessible. Seth reached around my belly and slid his hand between my thighs, taking hold of the base of the toy and tapping it. The movement was slight, but the impact inside me was intense.

"Seth," I cried out when I felt my gland being stimulated over and over again.

"God." He wrapped his free arm around me and

started pinching my nipples. "I love making you feel good."
He nipped at my neck. "Love hearing you scream my name."

With his all-over sensual assault, I was pretty sure I
was babbling incomprehensibly.

After an interminable amount of pleasure, I gathered
the mental power to say, "I want you inside me."

"I want that too."

I rose to my knees, and Seth came with me, keeping
his arm around my chest and lending me support. He kissed
my left shoulder and then kept going, moving his lips across
the entire span of my back and ending at my other shoulder.
While he gentled me with his mouth, he slowly removed the
toy from my sensitive channel, giving me the same pleasure
and sensation on the way out as he had on the way in. Between
the warmth of the room, the silkiness of the water lapping at
my thighs, and the intense desire scrambling my brain, I felt
like I was in a dream, relaxed and hazy.

"Are you ready for me?" Seth said into my ear. We
were both kneeling, and I felt his heated flesh touching my
puckered opening.

"Always."

He gripped my hip, anchoring me, as he slowly
penetrated me with his rigid dick.

"Oh, Seth." I trembled and put my hand over his,
needing to connect with yet another part of him. "Feels so
good."

"For me too, baby." He bottomed out and then held

me tightly, caressing me with his hands while he made small circular movements with his hips.

I twisted my head back and looked at him, begging a kiss with my eyes. He met me right away, lapping at my lips before pressing his tongue between them, making the kiss passionate from the start.

"Mmm," I moaned and started rocking my hips, causing more friction inside my channel.

"Eli!" he shouted, his cracking voice telling me he was close to the edge.

"You can go harder," I assured him. "I want you to."

He shook, his whole body trembling against mine, then he squeezed me tightly for a moment before taking a deep breath and moving back, slowly dragging his cock out of me until just the crown was pressed inside.

"Please," I rasped.

He clasped my hips and in an instant, I was impaled again, a hard shove making me gasp and cry out in pleasure.

"Ungh," he grunted and plundered my hole, sliding in and then yanking out before slamming back inside again. "Bring yourself off, baby." He moved faster, harder, his grip on my hips tightening. "I can't. I need to—" He moaned loudly, his aroused noises melding with my cries and the sound of skin slapping against skin.

I reached one arm over my shoulder and circled it around his neck and wrapped my free hand around my dick, tugging in time with his strokes.

"Seth," I said when I felt the crest approaching. I looked over my shoulder, my gaze locking with his. He was moving frantically, chasing his orgasm. His expression was focused and so aroused it looked almost pained, but mostly it was adoring, deeply adoring. "Seth!" I shouted as the first shot of ejaculate left my dick.

"Yeah?" he asked desperately. When he flicked his gaze down and saw the creamy seed pulsing over my hand, his eyes widened, and he roared, shoving in one last time and staying deep inside me as he stiffened and came hard.

Once my balls were completely drained, I slumped, my bones feeling like rubber. Seth held on and slid back to a sitting position, taking me with him and staying inside my quivering body. I raised my hand to his mouth in invitation, and he took it, licking my seed off my fingers.

"Love you," he whispered.

I looked back at him, kissed his chin, and said, "Love you too."

CHAPTER SEVENTEEN

> With this hand, I will lift your sorrows. Your cup will never empty, for I will be your wine. With this candle, I will light your way in darkness. With this ring, I ask you to be mine. — The Corpse Bride, Tim Burton
>
> Join Jennifer Dalton and Donald North along with their families as they join as one. Wednesday, July 3, 2013, 5:00 p.m.

Eli Block

ONE OF the advantages and disadvantages of working with Seth was that I was regularly invited to join him at weddings. I say "invited" because that was how it was always phrased.

"Oh, Eli, of course we'll make sure to have room for you too. Please feel free to come with Rabbi Cohen. As long as you're there, can you sing for a few minutes or can you play the piano during the bride's march or blah blah blah." You get the idea.

I could have said no if it actually bothered me,

especially because in addition to working as a cantorial soloist, I had gotten a job teaching music at the university, so my time was very limited. But the truth was, I was happy to help members of our congregation on their big day, and I liked being able to spend time with my boyfriend. So my complaints were mostly for show.

Of course, every once in a while, the Seth wedding curse would rear its staple-gunned head, and then every whine was heartfelt. That actually happened, by the way. A wedding decorator honest to goodness staple-gunned her assistant's forehead. She claimed it was an accident. I wasn't so sure. There was a lot of blood, but the wound wasn't very deep, so bygones and all that.

Anyway, I was becoming a regular on the wedding circuit. Which was why I was at yet another hotel, being escorted to yet another ballroom so I could see the piano where I'd be sitting—and playing—during the ceremony. Seth had gotten cornered in the lobby by a gaggle of people needing him to solve the crisis of the day, but he promised to catch up with me.

"Do you want me to play something to keep people entertained while they're taking their seats or do you just want me to play the march when Jennifer walks down the aisle?" I asked the groom.

"Oh, you don't have to...well, would you mind? Because that would be great. I know Jennifer would love it."

"It's not a problem." I shrugged. "I'll be sitting there

anyway, right? Might as well make myself useful."

"Thanks, Eli. I can't tell you how much we appreciate it. Jennifer really wanted this to be nice, but you wouldn't believe how expensive weddings are. I mean, we did as much as we could ourselves, but even with that, there wasn't room in the budget to hire musicians."

I patted his back. "I'm happy to help."

The room where the wedding was being held adjoined the reception area, which would make it easy for guests to move from one space to the next.

"We can cut through here," Donny said as we turned a corner. "It's a staff entrance, but we've been using it all day to decorate the room."

He opened a small door at the end of the reception ballroom and I followed him inside. Donny had had a long, busy day, and he was on a mission to show me the piano. I assumed those were the reasons he didn't recognize what I immediately saw when I walked into the room.

"Uh, Donny." I stopped in my tracks and leaned over one of the large, round tables, trying to get a closer look at the centerpiece.

"Yeah."

He hadn't noticed me stopping, so he was surprised when he turned around and found himself several feet ahead of me.

I glanced at him and pointed at the glass bowl. The bottom was lined with rocks and three stalks of bamboo grew out of it. "This centerpiece—"

"Oh." He rolled his eyes. "We got engaged in Hawaii, and they're really big on bamboo there, so Jennifer thought it'd be meaningful to use it at the wedding. Plus, like I said, we were doing as much as we could ourselves. She worked on these with her sisters."

I flicked my gaze to bowl and then back to him. "She made these centerpieces?"

"Yeah. She bought the bowls and the shiny rocks at a craft store and found the bamboo at the Asian market. She was up half the night, but"—he smiled proudly—"it looks good, right? You can't even tell they're homemade."

"Well, uh—"

"We need to hurry. People will be getting here soon." He started walking.

"Sure, but, Donny?"

"Come on, Eli, I need to show you the piano." He was almost at the door.

"Donny!"

"What?" He flipped around, looking annoyed.

"Your fish are, ehm, they're—"

He furrowed his brow. "What are you talking about?"

I pointed at the bowl. "The, uh—" I squinted. "Are those goldfish?"

He came toward me. "Yes. Well, no. I mean, they were supposed to be. Jennifer said to buy goldfish but I was crazy busy all week, and by the time I went out yesterday to get

them, the pet store didn't have any so I got those instead."
He gestured toward the bowl nearest to him. "They're called
Mollies, I think, but they look just like goldfish, so…" He halted
and peered at the bowl. "Why is the fish floating?"

There could only be one answer to that question, and
anyone over the age of six should know it, so I didn't respond.

"Is the fish dead?"

Yup. That was the answer.

He rushed to the table, snatched the centerpiece, and
held it up. "Holy shit. It's dead." He jerked his head toward
me. "The fish is dead."

I bit my bottom lip, considered my options, and then
realized I didn't have any. "Not *it*," I said. "*They*."

"What do you—" Realization must have struck
because he dropped the bowl, splashing water onto the white
tablecloth, and frantically darted his gaze around the room.
"Oh holy fucking shit."

Yeah, that sounded about right when you realized
your wedding reception had turned into a pet cemetery.

"They're all dead." He stared at me. "Why are they all
dead?"

"Well, I'm not an expert, but my best guess is that
these fish need to be aerated."

"What does that mean?"

"It means they need oxygen and there isn't any in a
bowl of sitting water."

"But…" He walked over to another table and then

another one. Death was there to greet him at every turn. "That's not possible. We saw this in Hawaii. They had them everywhere. Restaurants. The hotel. This party where—"

"They probably had different fish."

He looked at me wide-eyed. "That matters?"

"The kind of fish?"

He nodded.

"Yup. Goldfish you could have done, but Mollies." I shook my head. "Not so much."

"Oh my God. Jennifer is going to kill me."

"No, she won't," I said, even though I thought she very well might.

I mean, he said she'd been up all night making the damn centerpieces and she gave him one job, which he failed dismally. Death was a possibility. I looked at the bowl. Strike that. Death was a reality.

Donny was in full-on freak-out mode, dashing from table to table, tugging at his hair, and saying ridiculous things like, "I deadfished our wedding."

I wanted to point out how that sounded and that there were worse versions of deadfishing, but I sensed the time wasn't right for humor. So, instead, I rolled up my figurative and literal sleeves and said, "It'll be okay. We can fix this."

"How?" he shrieked. "I deadfished the wedding!"

Okay. He really needed to stop saying that. My self-control was only so strong.

"We'll get rid of the fish."

"We can't get rid of the fish! They're the centerpiece. We need a centerpiece."

Yes. They needed a centerpiece. Rain or shine. Living or dead. Something had to grace the middle of the table.

"You'll still have a centerpiece."

That stopped his mad dash from one place to the next with no discernible purpose. "We will?"

I nodded.

"How?"

I dipped my hand into the bowl, fished out the dead fish, and said, "Voila! Death-free centerpiece."

"But Jennifer wanted fish."

Oh, for fuck's sake. Weddings stripped everyone of their common sense.

"Donny! Your wife doesn't want to be deadfished." I couldn't help it. The opportunity was right there. Besides, he was too stressed to notice. "The centerpiece looks good with just the rocks and bamboo."

He stared at the tables, presumably considering his options, of which he had none, and then he dipped his chin and said, "You're right." He squared his shoulders and started rolling up his sleeves. "Okay. Let's get these fish out of there."

It was going to be a big wedding, so there were around thirty tables and each bowl had at least one fish in it, some had two.

As soon as Donny gave me the go-ahead, we jumped into action, rushing around the ballroom, yanking fish out of bowls. I'm not going to say it was fun, but it was sort of fun.

"What are you doing?"

I flipped around to see Seth standing just inside the doorway with Sheila, the mother of the bride.

"The fish are dead!" Donny shouted, not slowing in his mission. I said a silent prayer that he'd refrain from saying deadfish again. Or at least until his soon-to-be mother-in-law was out of the room. "We need to get them out!"

Seth and the bride's mother looked confused. "They're Mollies," I explained. Based on their expressions, I didn't think they understood. "These fish need oxygen. There wasn't any, so they suffocated. Now they're dead and floating fish are not romantic."

I liberated another corpse from a centerpiece and added it to the growing pile in my hands.

"Seth, come help."

He walked over to me, but I could tell that he wasn't quite caught up yet.

"Here." I held my palms out to him. "Take these."

"What am I going to do with dead fish?"

"I don't know. Burial at sea?" I jiggled my hands in annoyance. "Find a toilet. Find a trash can. Just come grab the fish. My hands are full and I need to get more out."

He cupped his hands together and I poured the fish into them. His hands were bigger than mine, plus, because he wasn't on the seek-and-retrieve portion of the mission, he could keep them in that position.

"Wait," I said when he started to walk away. "Come with me and hold them until they're all gone."

Donny must have liked that idea because he said, "Sheila! Come help me like that." The bride's mother rushed to his side without complaint.

"If we hurry," I whispered to Seth, "we can get more fish than them."

His jaw dropped, which looked sort of like a gaping fish impression. Kind of ironic.

"It isn't a contest, Eli."

"Well, it can be," I pointed out.

I'd reached for the next bowl, ready to retrieve a fish, when Seth said, "It's alive! That fish is alive. Don't get it out."

I looked at the bowl. Although the fish wasn't floating like its comrades, it was swimming very sluggishly.

"He'll be dead soon, Seth," I said, dropping my hand in the bowl. "We need to get him out."

"You'll kill it!"

I looked at my boyfriend incredulously. "The lack of oxygen will kill it. What do you want us to do? The fish won't make it long enough for us to get an oxygen tank and a little itty-bitty fish mask in here. This is the only way we can save it."

"Save it? How will taking it out of the bowl save it?"

"I'm saving it and this entire wedding from pain and horror and screaming. It's merciful. Like euthanasia for fish." I caught the fish and started pulling my hand out. "Think of it like fishanasia."

I dropped the fish into his hands. "How many is that? Do we have more than fifteen?"

"Eli!" Seth hissed. "Dr. Kevorkian didn't count his kills."

"That's only because he didn't have any competition."

Seth opened his mouth to respond but was interrupted by Donny's shout from across the room. "Done! How many did you get?"

I arched my eyebrows at Seth in a "see?" look and said, "Let me count. I think we won."

"No way," Sheila snapped. "Donny. How many do we have?"

I adored her.

Seth snapped his mouth shut, slumped in defeat, and held his hands out for my inspection.

OUR FAST thinking saved the day as far as fish drama went, but the wedding hadn't even started yet, so there was plenty of room for fiascoes to unfold. And unfold they did.

"Do you hear yelling?" Seth asked.

We were in a small sitting area next to the ballroom. The guests had started to arrive, so I'd have to go start playing soon.

"I think it's all the people talking at the same time."

He tilted his head to the side and furrowed his brow. "No. I'm pretty sure that's someone screaming."

I was about to disagree when I heard, "Mom! Fix it! You have to fix it!"

Seth shot up off the chair in a flash. "That's Jennifer."

I was on my feet right after him. "And do you hear how she's talking to her mom? That's terrible. I love Sheila!"

He slowly panned over to me and shook his head. "Come on. I think they're in there." He pointed to a small suite down the hall and then hustled over.

We heard muffled shouts and what sounded like furniture bumping. Seth knocked on the door. "Jennifer? Sheila? Is everything okay?"

"No!" Jennifer yelled through the door.

"It's going to be fine," Sheila said, but she sounded strained.

"Is there anything we can do to help?" Seth asked.

I elbowed him.

"What?" he whispered.

"This is why you have wedding issues. There's hysteria behind this door, and you're offering to run in." I grabbed his arm. "Let's go sit. I'm sure they'll figure it out."

He looked truly shocked at the suggestion. "I can't do that. They might need help."

Which was one of the many reasons I loved him. I leaned closer and kissed his cheek. "You're a good man, Seth Cohen." I wrapped my arms around him and squeezed tightly.

"I'm thankful every day that I get to live my life with you."

He beamed at me. "You know, I've been meaning to talk to you about that. I was thinking—"

The door swung open. "Rabbi Cohen, can you hold the dress together while I zip it?"

Seth looked as surprised as I felt. "Sure, I, uh, what?"

Sheila grabbed his arm and yanked him into the room. I stayed right on his tail, partly because I was curious and partly because I was concerned about his well-being. Jennifer was still shouting, but it sounded like it was intermixed with sobs.

When we got into the room, I saw the bride's back. Literally, her back. She was wearing a dress—white, beaded, layered—but the zipper was hanging open.

"We can't get the dress to close," Sheila said.

"I'm fat!" Jennifer choked out between tears. "I'm a fat bride!"

"You're beautiful, honey. I think it's the dress. The zipper is a little—"

"It's not the dress! It's the cupcakes. I shouldn't have eaten the cupcakes."

Sheila picked up a box of Kleenex and walked over to her daughter. "You can eat a cupcake, it's—"

"Twelve!"

"What?" Sheila started dabbing at Jennifer's face.

"You know I bake when I'm nervous."

Her mother nodded.

"Well, this morning I decided to make some cupcakes for my bridesmaids, just to be nice and help settle me down, you know?"

Sheila nodded.

"But then I ate them."

I winced.

Sheila, bless her, looked unfazed. She just got a fresh Kleenex, gently wiped at the edges of Jennifer's eyes, and said, "No more tears, honey. You're a beautiful bride and Donny loves you."

"Twelve, Mom! I ate twelve cupcakes."

"Were they good?" Seth asked, stepping smack-dab into the conversation. He was a brave man.

"What?" Jennifer asked, seemingly taken off guard at the question. I knew I was.

"The cupcakes." Seth slowly moved closer, like he was approaching a wild animal on one of those nature shows. "Were they good? I assume they were if you ate them."

"Yes." She sniffled. "They were good."

Another step closer. "That must mean you're a great cook."

She shrugged.

Seth got within arm's reach of her. "I bet Donny loves your cupcakes."

"He does." She nodded. "He says they're even better than those six-dollar cupcakes at the fancy bakeries."

He closed the distance between them, patted her back,

and said, "I'd love to taste those cupcakes sometime. Do you think Donny would mind sharing the next batch with me?"

Good rearing took over and distracted Jennifer from the dress calamity. "Of course he wouldn't mind, Rabbi Cohen. I'd be happy to bring some over to the temple just as soon as we get back from our honeymoon."

"That'd be wonderful." He smiled at her. "I can't wait to taste them." He took a breath and looked at the back of the dress. "Now, what can we do to help with this dress?"

"It looks like the zipper might be a little damaged," Sheila said. "Jennifer was having some trouble zipping it when I was helping Donny with the—" She paused, cleared her throat, and then continued. "She was having trouble when I was out of the room, so her maid of honor tried to help but I think she might have pulled a little too hard and bent the teeth."

Seth squatted down and examined the zipper. Then he glanced up at Sheila. "I don't think this—"

"Maybe if I hold the two sides together, you can find a way to get it up," Sheila said.

That sounded vaguely dirty, but try as I might, I couldn't figure out how to spin it into a joke.

"Okay," Seth answered.

Sheila got next to him, grasped both side of the dress, and tugged, bringing them together. "Okay, go ahead."

Seth fiddled with the zipper and, after a few false starts, he was able to get it sliding. He moved slowly with

Sheila just ahead of him, bringing each portion of the dress together inch by inch. By the time they reached the top of the dress, Seth was standing and Sheila was smiling.

"We did it!" Sheila said triumphantly.

"Oh my gosh, Rabbi, thank you so much!" Jennifer said. "I can't tell you how much I—" She turned around midsentence so she could face Seth, but the twist was more than the already strained zipper could handle and the dress popped open, this time with a distinct tearing sound.

"Shit!" I yelled.

"Oh no," Seth said.

"Mom?" Jennifer gasped, her breaths immediately coming faster.

The dress was hanging open again, but this time the issue was a separation of the fabric from one side of the zipper. I was sure all was lost when the door flew open and the maid of honor came running in, a shopping bag in hand.

"I got the Spanx!" she said, kicking the door closed behind her. She reached into the bag and yanked out something tan and small. "Put this on." Then she paused, seeming to notice we were in the room, and said, "Uh, hi, Rabbi. Hi, Eli. I brought Jennifer some Spanx."

"Spanx?" I mouthed to Seth.

He shrugged.

"What's Spanx?" I asked.

She held up what looked like an exceptionally low-cut, nude-colored bathing suit. "It's a bodysuit," she explained.

"It'll smooth and slim, uh, everything, so we can get the dress zipped."

"The dress ripped," Jennifer said, falling into a chair. "There's nothing we can do."

"Maybe we can sew it," Sheila said.

"Mom, how are we going to sew it? We don't have time or the right thread or—"

"What about glue?" the maid of honor suggested.

For whatever reason, I thought someone would listen to logic. "We can't just glue a—"

"I have nail glue!" the maid of honor said. "It's really strong!"

Jennifer looked up hopefully. "Do you think it'll work?"

I absolutely did not think it would work.

"We don't have anything to lose," Sheila said.

"Except a layer of skin when you glue a dress to it," I mumbled.

"I'll try it." Jennifer bounced out of the chair. "I'll put the Spanx on first so it fits better." She started shrugging out of her dress.

Slightly runny makeup and hysteria aside, Jennifer was a pretty woman and I didn't relish the thought of Seth seeing her naked. Not that I was the jealous type, but I was an eensy bit of the jealous type.

"Well, it sounds like you have it all under control," I said, grabbing Seth's elbow. "We'll see you in there."

"Okay." Jennifer didn't slow in her disrobing. I said a

mental thank-you for bras.

"Are you sure you'll be okay?" Seth asked. Thankfully he was looking at Sheila rather than the now half-undressed Jennifer.

Sheila, bless her, stepped in front of her daughter and waved us off. "We're good, Rabbi. Thank you for your help."

When Jennifer walked down the aisle thirty minutes later, she looked gorgeous. Her hair and makeup were perfect and her dress was stunning. Apparently Spanx and nail glue were a magic combination. Not magic enough to keep the bride from passing out during the middle of the reception due to oxygen deprivation from having her lungs constricted, but, thankfully, it was after the cutting of the cake and the first dance, so the pictures were mostly done. And I heard the chemical burns from the glue wouldn't leave lasting scars, which was a happy bonus.

BY THE time we got home from what I decided I'd forever call the Dead Fish Wedding, my stomach felt like it was eating itself.

"I can't believe they didn't serve dinner." I grumbled as I ripped open the refrigerator and looked for whatever I could eat fastest. "They had all those pretty tables with the china and the silverware and the not dead centerpieces but no food! What was the point of all the dishes if there wasn't going to be food?"

"Sit down, baby." Seth strolled into the kitchen and took my spot in front of the fridge. "I'll make you something to eat."

I was breaking out in a cold sweat and shaking, so I did what he said and collapsed on a kitchen chair. "How is it you're not starving? We got there at four and it's after nine. We totally skipped dinner."

"They served some food." He put the frying pan on the stove and lit the burner.

"Tiny little puff pastries filled with mushrooms or olives or whatever are not dinner. They're an appetizer, maybe."

"They were good, though, right?" He cracked eggs into the pan and whisked them with a fork.

"Yes. The two I was allotted were good."

He sprinkled shredded cheese into the pan. "And the cake was good," he said.

"Yes. But again, I only got one slice."

"I think they were trying to keep costs down." He put two pieces of bread in the toaster.

"Then they should have invited fewer than three hundred of their dearest friends." I looked him over. He seemed fine. A little distracted, maybe, but fine. "Seriously, how are you not hungry?"

"I'm hungry but I ate a sandwich before we left, remember?" He got the butter out of the fridge. "I offered to make you one."

"Well, I wasn't hungry then and I thought we'd get dinner."

Seth spooned the eggs onto two plates and started buttering the toast. "If there's one thing I've learned by going to all these weddings year after year, it's that you can't count on anything, least of all edible food." He slid one plate in front of me, along with a fork, knife, and napkin. "What do you want to drink?"

"Water's good." I picked up my fork and dug into my meal. Seth set my water down and then got his own plate and drink and joined me at the table. "Thank you," I said once I'd swallowed enough egg to ease the sharp hunger pains.

"You're welcome, baby." He reached over and combed his fingers through my hair. "Let me know if you want more."

His sweetness and caring never failed to make my heart swell. "I feel better already." I raised my free hand up, grasped his, and squeezed it. "Thanks for taking care of me."

"You do the same for me." He drew in a deep breath. "Which brings me back to what I started telling you at the wedding today. I've been thinking. You lift me up. You support me. You never rub me the wrong way and—"

"Sounds like you're describing a bra," I pointed out and took a bite of toast. "Speaking of bras, did you check out Jennifer's rack?"

He rolled his eyes. "Are you being stupidly jealous again?"

"No." I swallowed and lowered my gaze. "Maybe." I looked up at him from underneath my lashes. "But I don't do it much anymore."

His warm brown eyes twinkled. "I know you don't. And you know I love you and don't want to be with anybody else—rack or not."

"I know." And I did. He showed me by the way he touched me tenderly and gazed at me lovingly. He showed me when he put up with my bad days and laughed at all my jokes. He showed me by holding me in his arms every night and kissing me goodbye when he went to work in the morning. "I'm not really jealous. I just forget sometimes because you're gorgeous and people look at you"—I winked—"and I want to put a sign around your neck that says you're taken."

"Well, I don't know about a sign, but maybe a ring." Seth slid out of his chair and dropped to one knee.

"What are you doing?" My fork clattered against the plate and my heart started racing.

He pulled my hand onto his raised knee and gazed up at me. "Eli Block, will you marry me?"

Of course I said yes. Well, first I flew out of my chair, tackled him to the ground, and shoved my tongue into his mouth. But later, when we were wiping cum off the kitchen floor, I said yes.

CHAPTER EIGHTEEN

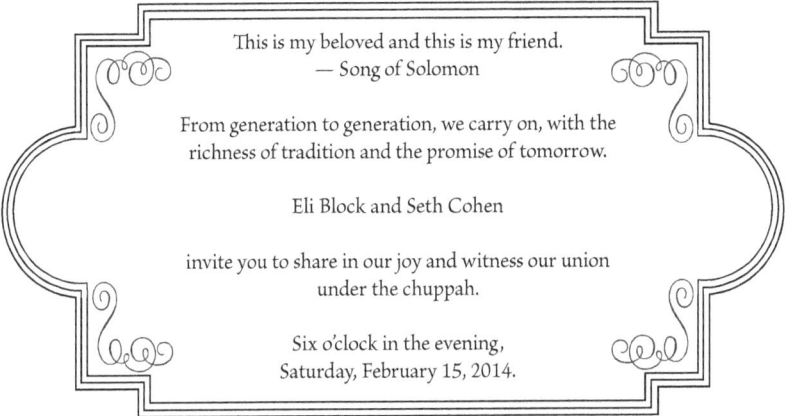

This is my beloved and this is my friend.
— Song of Solomon

From generation to generation, we carry on, with the
richness of tradition and the promise of tomorrow.

Eli Block and Seth Cohen

invite you to share in our joy and witness our union
under the chuppah.

Six o'clock in the evening,
Saturday, February 15, 2014.

Seth Cohen

WHEN I made the decision to follow my heart and pursue a life walking beside Eli, I assumed that meant I might never walk down the proverbial aisle because, at the time, there wasn't legal recognition of marriage between two men. But six years later, that had changed. Marriage equality was the law of the land in quite a few states, including my home state of California, and the US Supreme Court had overturned a key provision of the Defense of Marriage act, giving federal recognition to marriages conducted in those states. The ability to marry brought with it legal rights and responsibilities, emotional relief and joy, and the potential to start an interfamily battle so profound the destruction of the Temple would seem small in comparison.

Okay, so that was a little dramatic, but here's the thing: Avi Block—Eli's father and the man who had been my mentor and my boss before he retired—was a rabbi. Robert Cohen—my father, the man who had raised me, loved me, paid for my education, and helped me grow into the person I was—was a rabbi. Even my brother was a rabbi. There were a lot of rabbis in our lives and in our families, so, needless to say, from almost the instant Eli and I got engaged, a battle began to brew about which rabbi would officiate our ceremony.

Anybody who wasn't a blood relative was immediately dismissed as a nonoption lest blood be shed by our sure-to-be enraged families. My brother Jed wasn't an issue. He kindly told me he wouldn't do the job even if I begged because he wanted his children to have a relationship with their grandfather, and being disowned wouldn't be conducive to that. So that left my dad and Eli's dad vying for the position.

Not surprisingly, our mothers solved the problem by pointing out that there was nothing preventing our fathers from officiating the ceremony together. Neither of them was thrilled at the prospect of sharing the honor, but admitting that when the other man was pretending to be fine with it wasn't an option. Basically, they were in a game of chicken, each one waiting for the other to throw a fit and be the bad guy. That didn't happen and their attempts at passive-aggressive guilt tactics were a joke compared to what both Eli and I were used to from our mothers, so ultimately, the issue was resolved with the joint-officiating compromise.

The decision of where to hold the wedding was a less controversial topic. Though Eli and I would have loved to get married in EC West at Temple Beth Shalom, our marriage wouldn't have been legal that way. So we agreed to get married in the congregation where I grew up and where my father was the rabbi emeritus and my brother was the head rabbi.

Which brought me to why we were in LA for our last Valentine's Day as an unmarried couple: our wedding was the following evening. As far as why we were spending Valentine's babysitting my niece and nephew, well, we figured we had a honeymoon coming up where we'd have each other to ourselves and get to be mushy and romantic. My brother and sister-in-law, on the other hand, rarely had the chance to be alone as a couple. Plus, Eli and I didn't get to see my—soon to be *our*—niece and nephew often, so we wanted to spend as much time with Stephen and Sarah as we could.

"Seth!" Eli called to me from somewhere down the hall.

I set down the book I'd been reading to the kids and walked in his direction. "Yes?"

He poked his head out of the bathroom and said, "There's something weird in the toilet."

"Weird how?"

"I don't know. Come look."

I stepped into the bathroom and followed him to the toilet. "Oh. Those are mini marshmallows," I explained.

He arched his eyebrows in question.

"Jed said they were using them to help Stephen learn how to pee in the toilet."

"Huh." Eli looked at the marshmallows and then nodded. "Like target practice? Smart."

"Yup. But if you need to go, maybe you should use the powder room next to the kitchen. I'm not sure how we're supposed to deal with flushing or where to find new ones if these swirl down the drain."

"No problem. And based on the color of the water, I'm pretty sure they're not *dealing* with flushing at all."

"Uncle Seth!" Stephen's little voice rang out along with his footsteps. "You didn't finish the book." He turned the corner and ran into the bathroom, his sister hot on his trail.

"Sorry, buddy." I hunkered down. "I was just showing Uncle Eli your marshmallows."

"Oh!" He beamed. "I can make 'em move." He put his hands on his waistband in a flash and then he was pushing down his pants.

"Cool!" Eli said, stepping next to him. "Let's see." He sounded just as excited as Stephen about the prospect.

I wondered whether I'd be walking into our bathroom sometime in the near future and finding it strewn with white balls of fluff.

"I'm hungry!" Sarah cried. At least I think that was what she said. She was just over eighteen months old, so her words weren't always easy to understand.

"Let's go make you a snack." I reached for her hand, but she jumped away and shook her head furiously.

"No. I stay."

I cupped Eli's nape and gave him a light massage. "You okay with both of them for a minute while I rinse off strawberries?"

"Sure. We'll be out as soon as we're done drowning the marshmallows, right, Stephen?"

"Yes!"

When I walked out of the room, Stephen was climbing up on the stool next to the toilet and Sarah was digging through a plastic bin holding bath toys. It was a nice little domestic scene. A few minutes later, I had the strawberries rinsed, sliced, and scooped into little plastic bowls, so I went back to the bathroom to see if Eli needed help.

"Why is Stephen's underwear on his head?" I asked when I saw my nephew wearing his pants and shirt in the normal locations but seemingly confusing his briefs with a hat. Sarah was still occupied by her bath toys, which she was lining up on the edge of the tub.

Eli shrugged and propped Stephen up on yet another stool, this one in front of the sink. "Because he wanted to."

"That's your reason?"

He grinned at me and said, "It's the *best* reason, old man."

I froze. He was right. And he was amazing. And the next day he was going to stand up in front of our family and friends and say he'd always be mine. My throat suddenly felt thick. "I love that about you."

"What's that?" He was helping Stephen rub his sudsy hands together. "My super-duper reasoning skills?"

"Those are pretty great. But I was thinking about the way you always find the joy in life." I smiled at him and ran my hand down his back. "I love how you never get constrained by how things are supposed to be."

He put Stephen's hands under the water and rinsed off the soap. "If I'd let myself worry about how things are supposed to be, I might not have gotten you." He turned off the tap, toweled off Stephen's little hands, and glanced up at me. "And how much would that suck?"

I gulped. "A lot."

"Oh, cool. Was that an offer?"

He lost me. "Huh?"

He picked Stephen up and gave him an airplane ride back to the ground, "vroom" noises and all.

"The sucking a lot." He waggled his eyebrows. "I assumed that was an offer for later tonight when we're back in the ho—" He frowned and looked at something off to my side. "What's Sarah chewing?"

I flipped around. "She was playing with her bath toys.

I don't think any of them are small enough to go in her mouth, though."

I squatted down, scooped my niece into my lap, and said, "What's in your mouth, honey? Show Uncle Seth."

She squeezed her mouth shut and shook her heard.

"Sarah," Eli said, kneeling next to us. "I need to see what you're eating."

"No!" she shouted, giving Eli a front row view of her open mouth.

He paled, fell back on his butt, and made a retching sound. "Don't swallow tha—"

Sarah gulped down whatever was in her mouth.

"What?" I asked in a panic.

"She"—another retching sound—"she"—he pointed at the toilet—"ate the marshmallows."

I winced and tried to hold my own gag reflex in check.

"No fair!" Stephen yelled. "I want 'arsh 'ellows!"

He made a dash for the toilet, but thankfully, Eli stopped him. "Kitchen," Eli rasped, his throat probably sore from the almost vomiting. "We eat food in the kitchen."

"When did Jed say they'd be back?" I asked as we led the two kids out of the bathroom slash snack center and into the kitchen.

"Not a minute too soon," Eli responded.

I lifted Sarah into her high chair and strapped her in. "You said you wanted kids," I said, reminding him of something he'd mentioned once or twice over the years.

"That means we'd have this fun every day."

"*Your mother* said we had to have kids." He walked into the kitchen and started filling sippy cups with water.

I had been joking around, but suddenly, the conversation no longer struck me as funny. I looked up from the high chair and met his gaze. "Does that mean you don't actually want them?"

He paused in his task, a lid in one hand and a filled cup in the other. "Do you?" he asked hoarsely. That time I was pretty sure emotion was the cause, not imminent vomiting.

I thought about it, really thought about it. I loved having Eli to myself, but seeing a little version of him running around our home, watching him laugh and play with our child, raising a person together...those ideas made my heart soar.

"Yes, I think I do," I said.

His nostrils flared as he sucked in a quick breath. "Me too."

"HAPPY VALENTINE'S Day, baby," I whispered in Eli's ear.

We were in our hotel room after our adventures in babysitting—freshly showered, stark naked, and dancing.

"You're pretty good at this," he said as he laid his head on my shoulder.

"Not as good as you, but I'm learning." I rubbed his

back and pressed my nose to his hair, feeling equal parts calm and aroused from his scent.

"Well, if dancing means your naked parts pressed against me, I promise to teach you anytime," he said saucily.

I lowered my hand and gave his backside a squeeze. "Tomorrow we'll have to dance in our tuxes, too many eyes, but after that, it's a deal. Naked dancing anytime you want."

He leaned back and gazed into my eyes. "We're getting married tomorrow."

I smiled and kissed the tip of his nose. "I know."

"I think we should have a little advance"—he ground his groin against mine—"celebration."

I chuckled. "What do you have in mind, Mister Cheesy?"

He dipped his head and licked a path from the base of my neck to my lips. "I want to fuck you."

I trembled, gulped, and nodded. Eli liked to bottom more than he liked to top, which worked out well because I liked topping more often. But both of us enjoyed switching things around, too, and based on the rapid hardening of my dick in reaction to his words, my body was all in favor of feeling Eli pounding inside hard and deep.

"C'mere." I gripped the back of his head and tugged him forward, mashing my lips against his.

He whimpered and melted against me, moving his mouth over mine, licking my tongue and nibbling on my lips.

I led us to the bed and lay down, pulling Eli on top of me. Then I spread my legs and he settled into the spot between them, his dick slotting next to mine and giving us delicious friction as we writhed together.

"Eli," I gasped against his mouth, tilting my hips and wrapping my legs around his thighs. "You feel so good." I ghosted my hands over his shoulders and back, enjoying the feeling of his hot skin and sinewy muscles.

"Mmm," he moaned and thrust against me. "You're so hot." He arched his neck and humped faster. "I'm close already."

I managed to stretch my arm far enough to reach the nightstand, and after a couple of fumbles, I got hold of the lube. "Let's get you inside, baby." I flipped the cap, slid my free hand over Eli's back, and poured some slick onto my palm. Then I tossed the bottle and wedged my hand between our bodies, taking hold of his rigid dick and stroking him. "Ready?" I asked when I felt him shaking.

He nodded, seemingly too aroused for words, and sat back on his heels. I reached between my legs and rubbed the remaining lube against my pucker.

"Now?" Eli asked when I gripped his waist and tugged him close.

I gazed at him and smiled. "Always."

He pressed his cock to my entrance and lowered his body onto mine. "And you call me cheesy?"

I flung my legs around his waist and pulled him down, forcing his crown past my tight ring of muscles and into my passage.

"I guess we're both a little cheesy," I said breathlessly.

"How about"—he pumped his dick all the way in—"we think of it as sweet."

We stopped talking after that, the feeling of joining together too intense. Eli gazed into my eyes as he thrust in and out of my body. I cupped his ass and encouraged him, digging my fingertips into his firm globes and pulling him into me over and over again. When my hands slipped and I dipped my fingers into his channel, he hissed, the need clear on his face. I wiggled one finger down and pressed the tip into his hole as he pushed his rigid cock into me.

"Seth," he groaned.

"Yes, baby. What do you need?"

He stilled above me and panted. "More."

I removed my hand, fumbled for the discarded lube, and drizzled it into his cleft, making him shudder. Then I circled my finger around his entrance at the same pace he was circling his hips against mine.

"You want me inside?"

"Yes."

I pushed my pointer finger into his hole past the second knuckle, and he practically vibrated with excitement. I rocked my hips up, reminding him that his dick was still inside me, and he moaned, dragging his cock out of my channel and simultaneously fucking himself on my finger. We set up a rhythm, not too slow and not too fast, both of us enjoying the feeling of being filled and filling each other.

All the while, our mouths met in soft kisses, our gazes never strayed, and our hearts beat in sync—faster and faster with every pump.

"Don't want to come like this," Eli said suddenly. He pushed his dick in all the way, circled his hips in a sensual motion that rubbed his balls against me, and then slowly pulled out.

"You want me inside?" I pushed in a second finger as I asked the question, already knowing the answer.

He nodded rapidly. "Yeah."

"Gladly."

I wiggled my fingers, and he slammed his lips against mine, taking a hard hungry kiss and not stopping until I gripped his dick and squeezed.

"Climb on," I said roughly.

We found the lube again and slicked me up. I held my dick out, and Eli straddled me and lowered himself onto it, inch by delicious inch.

"Love that feeling," he whispered huskily and shivered as I stretched his passage. "Nothing better."

I placed my palms on his knees and rubbed them up his thighs to his groin. Then I cupped his balls and caressed them. He dropped the rest of the way down, taking me completely inside.

"Oh God." He arched his back, reached back, and held on to my knees with both hands.

I thrust my hips up, and he immediately started

bouncing up and down, taking me inside and then moving his tight passage up my cock before slamming back down again.

"Seth!" he shouted. "Seth, Seth, Seth."

I dug my heels into the bed and bucked up, shoving myself up into him over and over again. When his shouts turned into desperate wails and his face looked tortured with pleasure, I grasped his dick and tugged. Within seconds, Eli was shooting off in my hand, coating me with his hot ejaculate. I came right away, shooting deep inside his welcoming body.

Once he was spent, he collapsed on top of me and held on tightly. I kissed his sweaty brow and hugged him. We stayed that way for a long time, enjoying the warmth of being together, but then the sticky fluid started getting uncomfortable.

"Can you reach the tissues?" I asked.

He tried to stretch but couldn't, so he had to climb off me to get the box from the nightstand. We wiped off the bulk of the mess and decided to deal with the rest later, both of us feeling too sated to move.

We lay on our sides and snuggled—touching, kissing, and breathing each other in.

"Did I ever tell you about my wish?" Eli asked after a long while.

"I don't think so." I tried to remember but couldn't. "What wish?"

He wedged his leg between both of mine. "That first day I saw you at camp, when I was eleven, I couldn't stop thinking about you. Later that night, we were walking back to our cabins from the evening campfire and I looked up and saw all these stars. There were way more there than at home, or at least I could see more of them." He smiled at the memory. "I saw one of the stars shoot across the sky, and I thought I'd better make a wish. Falling star and all, right?" He grinned at me and I nodded. "Well, I wished for you." He petted my chest. "I looked up and then said the words quietly, so the other guys wouldn't hear me."

I wrapped my arm around his waist and pulled him flush against me. "What'd you say?" I whispered.

"I asked for you to be mine forever and ever." He bussed his lips over mine, combed his fingers through my hair, and gazed into my eyes. "And after tomorrow, you will be."

"I've been yours for a long time, Eli. But I'm glad we can finally make it official."

AFTER ALL the dramatic weddings I'd seen in my career, my own wedding was surprisingly stress-free. The weather was mild. Everyone arrived on time. Animals, and their fluids, were blessedly absent. And the most adorable, kind, smart, wonderful person I'd ever met walked with me down the aisle.

Eli and I reached the front and stood under a chuppah

canopy made of the tallitot prayer shawls Eli and I had worn in our bar mitzvahs. We listened to our fathers take turns reciting words that were mindless in their familiarity and yet sounded brand new when they were applied to us. And then it was our turn to share our vows. We turned away from our fathers and faced each other, gripping each other's hands.

"Eli." I gazed into beautiful green eyes, shimmering with emotion and shining with love and affection. "I promise to be honest and open with you; to cherish, enrich, and support all that is special in your personality; to trust in you throughout our lives during times of happiness and times of sorrow; to be your partner and your friend; and to dedicate myself to helping you realize your potential to be the best version of who you are."

I took his hand in mine, slipped a gold band around his ring finger, and said, "With this ring, I am wed in the religion of Moses and Israel. I will be loyal to you, nourish you, and respect you."

He trembled, took in a few deep breaths, and blinked rapidly to hold in the tears threatening to slip from his eyes. I squeezed his hands, and when he looked into my eyes, I mouthed, "I love you, baby."

He nodded, squared his shoulders, and started talking.

"Seth, I promise to work side by side with you to build a home where holidays are observed; a home dedicated to charity and kindness; a home where candles, blessings, and wine decorate the table; a home that is a link to all of Israel; a home ringing with song, music, and children; a home we can call our own."

I placed my palm on his and lost my breath when I felt the metal slide onto my finger.

Eli gazed into my eyes, his cheeks wet but his smile bright. "With this ring, I am wed in the religion of Moses and Israel. I will be loyal to you, nourish you, and respect you."

Everything was silent for several long seconds. All I could see was the man standing in front of me, the man who would always be standing in front of me.

"Eli," Avi said. "Do you take this man to be your lawfully wedded husband, to honor and respect, to cherish and adore, in good times and in bad, for as long as you both shall live?"

"I do."

"Seth," my father said. "Do you take this man to be your lawfully wedded husband, to honor and respect, to cherish and adore, in good times and in bad, for as long as you both shall live?"

"I do."

We were already kissing by the time our fathers, in unison, pronounced us husbands.

THE ~~END~~ BEGINNING

ABOUT THE AUTHOR

Cardeno C.—CC to friends—is a hopeless romantic who wants to add a lot of happiness and a few *awwws* into a reader's day. Writing is a nice break from real life as a corporate type and volunteer work with gay rights organizations. Cardeno's stories range from sweet to intense, contemporary to paranormal, long to short, but they always include strong relationships and walks into the happily-ever-after sunset.

Email: cardenoc@gmail.com

Website: www.cardenoc.com

Twitter: https://twitter.com/cardenoc

Facebook: http://www.facebook.com/CardenoC

Pinterest: http://www.pinterest.com/cardenoC

Blog: http://caferisque.blogspot.com

OTHER BOOKS BY CARDENO C.

SIPHON
Johnnie

HOPE
McFarland's Farm
Jesse's Diner

PACK
Blue Mountain
Red River

HOME
He Completes Me
Home Again
Just What the Truth Is
Love at First Sight
The One Who Saves Me
Where He Ends and I Begin
Walk With Me

FAMILY
The Half of Us
Something in the Way He Needs
Strong Enough
More Than Everything

MATES
In Your Eyes
Until Forever Comes
Wake Me Up Inside

FRIENDS
Not a Game

NOVELS
Strange Bedfellows
Perfect Imperfections
Control *(with Mary Calmes)*

NOVELLAS
A Shot at Forgiveness
All of Me
Places in Time
In Another Life & Eight Days
Jumping In

AVAILABLE NOW

He Completes Me
(2nd Edition)

Not even his mother's funeral can convince self-proclaimed party boy Zach Johnson to tone down his snark or think about settling down. He is who he is, and he refuses to change for anyone. When straight-laced, compassionate Aaron Paulson claims he's falling for him, Zach is certain Aaron sees him as another project, one more lost soul for the idealistic Aaron to save. But Zach doesn't need to be fixed and he refuses to be with someone who sees him as broken.

Patience is one of Aaron's many virtues. He has waited years for a man who can share his heart and complete his life and he insists Zach is the one. Pride, fear, and old hurts wither in the wake of Aaron's adoring loyalty and as Zach reevaluates his perceptions of love and family, he finds himself tempted to believe in the impossible: a happily-ever-after.

Home Again
(2nd Edition)

Imposing, temperamental Noah Forman wakes up in a hospital and can't remember how he got there. He holds it together, taking comfort in the fact that the man he has loved since childhood is on the way. But when his one and only finally arrives, Noah is horrified to discover that he doesn't remember anything from the past three years.

Loyal, serious Clark Lehman built a life around the person who insisted from their first meeting that they were meant to be together. Now, years later, two men whose love has never faltered must relive their most treasured and most painful moments in order to recover lost memories and secure their future.

Love at First Sight
(2nd Edition)

The moment naïve, optimistic Jonathan Doyle glimpses a gorgeous blue-eyed stranger from afar, he believes in love at first sight. Unfortunately, he loses sight of the man before they meet and then spends years desperately trying to find him. Just as he is about to give up, Jonathan gets a break and finally encounters David Miller face to face.

Successful, confident David turns Jonathan's previously lonely life into a fairy tale, giving him more than he ever imagined. But the years spent searching were hard on Jonathan, and he's terrified his young son and scandalous past will destroy his blossoming relationship. For David and Jonathan to build a future together, they'll both have to dig deep: David for the courage to share himself in a way he's never considered and Jonathan for the strength to tell the truth.

The One Who Saves Me
(2nd Edition)

At fourteen, Andrew Thompson and Caleb Lakes become best friends. As the years pass, they stand by each other through family trauma, school, and the start of their careers. They share their first sexual experiences, learning and experimenting, and they talk each other through countless dates and breakups.

Decades of trust and loyalty build a deep and abiding friendship, one that surpasses any relationship in their lives. But when the parameters of their unique friendship change, neither man knows how to break out of their established roles to build something new. After all, boyfriends come and go, but best friends are forever.

Just What the Truth Is
(2nd Edition)

People-pleaser Ben Forman has been in the closet so long he has almost convinced himself he is straight, but his denial train gets derailed when hotshot lawyer Micah Trains walks into his life. Micah is brilliant, funny, driven...and he assumes Ben is gay and starts dating him. Finding himself truly happy for the first time, Ben doesn't have the willpower to resist Micah's affection.

When his relationship with Micah heats up, Ben realizes has a problem: his parents won't tolerate a gay son and self-confident Micah isn't the type to hide. If Ben wants to maintain his hold on his happiness, he'll have to decide what's important and own up to the truth of who he is. The trouble is figuring out just what that truth is.

Where He Ends and I Begin
(2nd Edition)

Aggressive, physical, and brave, Jake Owens is a small town football hero turned big city cop who passes his time with meaningless encounters believing he can't have who he really wants: Nate Richardson, his best friend since before forever. Thoughtful, quiet, and kind, Nate is a brilliant doctor who has always known who he is and has never been able to shake his crush on loyal, courageous, *straight* Jake.

After a passionate night together, Nate realizes Jake isn't as straight as he assumed, but he worries that what they shared was a fluke, a result of too much closeness for too long. For Jake, the question isn't how they ended up in bed together because he has always known that Nate holds his heart, it's how he'll convince Nate that he wants and needs to stay there.

www.ingramcontent.com/pod-product-compliance
Lightning Source LLC
Chambersburg PA
CBHW070652180626
46817CB00006B/2336